SILVER FLAME

Karpov Kinrade

DARING BOOKS

KarpovKinrade.com
Copyright © 2016 Karpov Kinrade
Cover Art Copyright © 2016 Karpov Kinrade
~~~~~
Published by Daring Books
~~~~~
First Edition
~~~~~
ISBN-10: 1939559464
ISBN-13: 9781939559463
~~~~~
Hardback
~~~~~
ISBN-10: 1939559472
ISBN-13: 9781939559470

License Notes

Disclaimer

This is a work of fiction. Names, characters, places and incidents are products of the author's imagination, or the author has used them fictitiously.

For Tiffany and Brynne...
amazing assistants who sacrifice sleep to help these
books launch and who are just incredible to work with.
Thank you!
We appreciate you both deeply

TABLE OF CONTENTS

1   Imprisoned 1

2   Passages 32

3   The Black Lotus.. 45

4   Tavian Gray.. 76

5   Sly Devil 96

6   You Know So Little.. 125

7   The Pleasure Palace 140

8   The Primal One...170

9   Unchained.. 191

10 Shadow And Flame 219

11 Silver Flame 239

12 Darkness And Moonlight 254

13 Reforged 260

14 The Bargain 273

15 Vengeance 278

Epilogue..292

Court of Nightfall 301

About The Authors 323

NOTE FROM THE AUTHOR

This is *Silver Flame*, book 3 in the *Vampire Girl* series. For your enjoyment, we highly recommend you read the books in order. Book 1, *Vampire Girl*, and book 2, *Midnight Star*, can be found wherever books are sold. Happy reading!

1

IMPRISONED

"Let's just say there's pain involved. Lots of pain."

—Asher

I've been imprisoned before, but those prisons were cloaked with finery to give the illusion of freedom. The Fae still treated me like a Princess, even while locking me up.

Now there is no finery, no illusion. The bars are steel. The hard-packed dirt beneath my feet reeks of urine and blood. The straw-filled mat that serves as my bed is covered in mold and insects. It's rough like sandpaper and worse than the floor. There's a pot for relieving myself in—the only "comfort" I'm afforded. My hands and face are coated with mud. My eyes ache from crying. I see no other cells past the bars. I hear no one but my guards—who do not speak to me. Even

Yami has abandoned me. He has disappeared, and I no longer feel his presence.

I will spend the last of what remains of my life in this cell. Alone.

My mother will perish in hell forever.

And Fen.

Fen is gone.

Memories flash through my mind. The stone hallway. Ace and Levi on either side of me. Ace stepped back, protecting me with his frail body. "I believe I will be claiming my month with the princess, brother. From now on, she is under my protection. If you wish to kill her..." Ace paused, staring straight into his brother's eyes, "...you must kill me first."

Levi's ice-blue eyes softened, but only for a moment. He pointed his silver sword at me. "She is the enemy, brother. You must see this. You must step aside."

"No," Ace said with a power to his voice I'd never heard before. He ran a hand through his dark, messy hair, his eyes intent on the Prince of Envy. "The Princess deserves to face trial before sentenced to death." It was sometimes easy to forget the dreamy-eyed inventor was actually a powerful vampire-demon in his own right. Not someone to trifle with.

"I don't want to hurt you," said Levi, staring at his brother, his jaw clenched hard, a lock of white-blond hair failing across his forehead.

I've seen how he is with Ace. Of all his brothers, Levi has a soft spot for the Prince of Sloth.

He shook with rage, but he did not attack. Not yet. Ace's presence was enough. Enough to give pause.

Ace limped forward, keeping his body between Levi and me. He stifled a moan from the pain the movement caused, and I could tell he was still badly wounded. If it came to a fight, we were screwed.

I held Spero, my sword. It was broken in battle but had been reborn from the magic of Midnight Star, half black metal, half steel.

Yami was invisible to all but me, curled around my neck shivering. I wanted to slap the silly dragon. If he'd just embrace his powers we'd stand a chance. A giant dragon with the magic Yami wields could fight all the princes of hell if necessary.

But Yami still didn't know how to control his power anymore than I did. One minute it was there, the next, just a shadow of a memory. And there is nothing more infuriating than knowing you have power but not knowing how to channel it. Especially when your fate is sealed, and your days are numbered.

The thump of boots against stone flooring reverberated through the hall, and Zeb, Niam and Dean turned a corner running. They froze, frowning at the scene before them. Levi faced his brothers, about to say something, but I had to speak first. I needed them to side with me. "Fen is dying!" I yelled. "I must get back to him."

Only Zeb and Dean twitched at the mention of Fen. The others didn't even seem to hear. Their cold gazes were fixed on me. On my ears.

"How is this possible?" whispered Zeb. The Prince of Gluttony normally maintained a polished look, with his dark hair perfectly coiffed and his clothes pristine. But now he was bloodied with battle, disheveled, adrenaline running high, like us all.

"She is the last of the High Fae," Levi said. "That is why the Druids awakened shortly after she returned here."

Niam and Zeb raised their swords higher.

Ace moved closer to me. "She is no threat, brothers. She saved me, remember. She's trying to save Fen now."

This time, the princes softened at the mention of their brother. "Where is Fen?" asked Zeb. "Show me to him!"

Levi scoffed. "Fen can wait. Don't you see, brothers? This is another scheme. Another tale woven to distract us from what truly matters. Her. She is the High Fae. If we kill her, the Druids will return to slumber. Peace will return to our lands. We must end her now. Before it's too late."

Niam nodded, moving forward with arm raised as if in battle. His dark skin was splashed with blood, his shaved head dusted with dirt and sweat, a savage glint in his ebony eyes. "Step aside, Ace. I do not want to hurt you, but if what Levi says is true, the Princess is an enemy."

Ace gripped his staff, his knuckles turning white. "You will not kill her."

"No," said Niam.

The others glanced at him, their faces puzzled.

The Prince of Greed lowered his sword in a peaceful gesture. "We must do this properly. We must hold court. We must have a trial. This is neither the time nor place to dispense justice."

Levi sighed. He shared a look with each of his brothers. "We are the justice of this land. Is it not our duty to protect our people? To end this war? Is it not better to sacrifice one life to save thousands more?"

He was swaying them. I could see it in the way they raised their swords, in the way their eyes filled with rage.

"Please," I said. "Hold a trial if you must, but let me go to Fen. He needs medicine." I held up what little I had been able to find as evidence.

Zeb ran a hand through his short brown hair. He turned to the princes at his side. "You can deliberate all you wish. I go to find Fen."

"So do I," said Ace. He glared at Levi. "If you choose to fight us, if you choose to kill the future Queen, then you put yourself above the law, above all other princes, as if you are King already…"

Dean and Niam seemed to ponder the words. For the first time, I thought the princes might actually let me go.

Then Levi laughed. "Don't be fools. You dare leave this to trial? With Asher and Fen present? You know they care for her more than they do our kingdom. Oh, Asher plays the slave master, but he is soft at heart. And Fen…Fen does not see clearly anymore."

The princes said nothing. They knew his words to be true. Even I could not argue.

Whatever urge Zeb had to find his brother seemed to fade.

Levi turned to me, raising his sword. "You will not fool me again, Fae. I will take your life, and then I will find my brother."

He took a step forward, but Dean surprised us all by moving in front of him and laying a hand on his chest. "And what of the contract? We are all bound to it. She must choose the next king."

"Why do we need another king?" asked Levi. "We have ruled our own realms these past few months. Why put one of us above all? We shall be the Seven Lords.

Seven Kings for Seven Realms. And with her gone, we will rule in peace."

This gave them all pause, even Ace, and the hall was silent for a moment, before Levi spoke again, his voice calmer, more collected...more persuasive. "The Princess has deceived us. I will never have her as my Queen. Will you, brothers? Will you be ruled by the High Fae? A liar and a traitor? Will you surrender our world, our people, over to the Fae by making one of them our ruler?"

Ace spoke softly. "The Fae used her as a pawn in this game. She's not responsible for this war."

Zeb clutched his dagger, thinking. "That may be true, but without her, the Druids would still slumber. Without her, my people—the ones who died today— would yet live."

My heart broke a little at that. I thought the Prince of Gluttony was on our side. He'd always been kind to me, and liked by Fen. But could I blame him, really? He'd watched friends die today, all because I woke the Druids and brought war to them. If it were my friends, my family, the people I loved in danger, would I feel any differently?

I could see that all but Ace had turned against me. Niam wanted a trial. Zeb wished to avenge his people. Dean wanted to be his own ruler. And Levi...Levi wanted me dead.

I tried to think of something else I could say. Something else I could do to sway them. "Please, I am not your enemy. I fought the Fae to save Fen. I fought the Fire Druid."

No one moved. Even in this, they did not believe me.

Ace spoke one final argument. "Brothers, do you not remember who brought her here?" he asked. "It wasn't the Fae. It was our father who arranged for Arianna to enter this world. Who arranged for her to be Queen. He must have had a reason."

"Our father is dead," Levi said.

"And have you learned who killed him?" A new voice filled the stone halls. A familiar voice. A voice that nearly destroyed my composure.

We all turned to see Fen standing there, shirtless, his heavy boots almost shaking the castle, the white globe lights faltering in the power of his presence. Asher stood beside him, a worried frown on his face. Fen held his sword, a large blade of thick grey steel etched with runes.

And then I noticed the tree tattoo covering his body…and I saw his ears. Fae ears. How could this be? An illusion spell? Some kind of trick?

The hall remained silent, all eyes on Fen as he spoke. "Perhaps you thought the Fae conceived his death? Perhaps you thought Arianna orchestrated it?

No. I killed him." His voice thundered through the halls, ripping the air apart and pulling it back together.

The other princes were stone cold, frozen in place by his words.

Fen stepped forward. "Your father told me of his plans for peace...he spoke of weakness. So I poisoned him."

I could feel the anger brewing around me. All but Asher were struck by his words. Even Ace dropped his sword a fraction, doubt clouding his face.

Why was Fen saying these things now? Here? Why was he pitting himself against his brothers? Saying 'your father' instead of 'our father?' Making himself the other.

But then I looked around and I saw. I saw what he was doing. And why. All eyes had shifted to him. The brothers edged forward, alert, focused.

He did this for me.

To give me a chance to run.

But I couldn't leave him there, with them. I couldn't let him destroy himself to save me. I moved to go to him, to stop him, to save him before he started a war with his brothers.

Before I could reach Fen, Ace's arm reached out to stop me. His grip was tight, unbreakable. Even in his weakness he was strong. My heart raced and bile rose in my throat. I turned to him, to challenge him, to explain that we had to help Fen, but Ace's face had grown cold and distant. Hard.

Tears filled my eyes, and I brushed them away with my free hand and tried to get Fen's attention, but he was deliberately not looking at me.

He was still speaking. Still confessing. Still riling them up, and Ace wasn't immune to his words. He had helped Fen and me search for their father's killer. The whole time, Fen lied to him. Even if there was good reason behind it, I could see Ace did not understand. His eyes flicked back to the Prince of War, now an outsider, a Fae, an other. The Prince of Sloth was on an edge. And the way he fell would be dictated by Fen's next words.

"And then, you chose me to find the murderer," Fen said. "Oh how I laughed at you all behind your backs. How I gloated to myself, brothers. But then again, we were never kin, were we?"

Dean drew his sword and roared. "You bastard! We should have never treated you as one of our own!"

Fen's eyes fell, a quizzical expression on his face, as if he had just learned something new. But he quickly returned to his cold, hard, disregarding performance. And that's what it was, a performance. "I understand now why I've always been better than you. Stronger than you." He stepped forward, toward his brothers. "I have the power of the Fae and vampire. I have the Earth Spirit at my side."

Eyes flashed to the white wolf baring his teeth to the right of Fen. Baron was the Earth Spirit? Tauren? But how?

By their faces, it was clear the brothers didn't know this part. Fen was saying he wasn't just Fae but a Druid as well. The Earth Druid.

But it couldn't be true, could it?

Ace spoke first, his voice soft in the echoing stone hall. "Our mother...our mother said she found a Fae babe on the battlefield that she turned to save its life. She said nothing of Spirits."

His words sent a chill down my spine. Fen wasn't lying. But then...Did he just find out? Or had he kept his true heritage secret from me?

Me. After all we shared.

"It's true," Asher said, speaking for the first time. "I was there, remember? I saw the wolf enter the infant. It took physical form many years later."

Niam turned his eyes to Asher, his jaw hard. "All this time, Asher...you knew? You knew he was the Earth Druid and you said nothing?"

"Our mother knew," Asher said. "She swore me to secrecy. Swore me just as she did you, to never speak of Fen's heritage. Would you have broken your oath to her?"

At that the princes said nothing. The rage and passion that passed between them was fading into resignation. Old relationships were breaking, making way for something new.

Asher's words gave me a brief comfort. Asher lied to his brother, but Fen never lied to me. Not about this. He didn't know.

But...

Oh god. I did this to him. I made him the enemy.

Fen and I needed to get out of here. Now. Before this shifted into something deadlier.

After all, I was the reason Druids had any power at all. And now that included the Prince of War.

Fen caught my eyes and held them. I could tell he wanted me to leave him. To save myself. But how could he think I would do that? How could I leave him here to face the wrath of his brothers alone? Stupid, foolish man. I shook my head, but he ignored me, continuing.

"Will none of you avenge your father?" he roared. "Is your fear of me too great? Do you piss your pants at the sight of me? Come!" He beat his chest with his fists. "Come at me, *brothers.*" His last word dripped with mockery.

That was all it took for Levi to charge him. Fen jumped into the air and their swords clashed.

I pulled at Ace's hold on me again, but his grip tightened. He looked angry. His jaw clenched as he watched his brothers fight.

"What are you doing?" I hissed at him. "Fen needs our help. Let me go."

Ace turned his hard glare toward me. "I think you've done enough to help, Princess." His words bit, and I recoiled in shock. This wasn't the Ace I'd come to know.

Fen fought hard, but Dean, Levi, Niam and even Zeb surrounded him, and it quickly became apparent that Fen hadn't yet recovered fully from his near death, despite his posturing. Even with Baron fighting at his side, he was weak. And he was losing.

Asher stood to the side, and I could see in his eyes he wished to help. Yet he did nothing.

I nudged Yami, pleading him to do something. "Use your powers. I know you can!"

Yami recoiled, shaking with fear.

"Please," I cried.

And then he threw himself into the fight, spitting blue fire into the fray. His flames crackled with lightning, setting a wall tapestry ablaze. I felt myself fill with rage as Yami grew bigger in size. But Levi thrashed a sword through the air, slicing into my dragon's shoulder before he could take his full form.

The blade cut deep. Yami screamed and dissolved into dust as I bent over in pain, feeling the blow in my own body as my dragon left. I fell to my knees, and Ace lost his grip on me. I groaned in pain, spit flying from my mouth.

Fen turned at the sound. His face filled with sorrow. Then rage. He ran to me, and that was the only mistake Levi needed.

He grabbed Fen from behind and swung his blade at his throat. "For our father—"

I jumped up, moving faster than I ever had, and blocked Levi's blade with my own. "Leave him be!" I screamed.

Levi turned his ire against me, and we exchanged blows, our swords ringing in the stone halls. Baron growled and tried to leap to my side, but Dean and Niam kept him restrained, looking none too pleased at having to keep an angry wolf stilled against his will.

I struck at Levi.

He parried.

He lunged.

And a third blade entered the fray, knocking both of us back.

"Stop!" Dean yelled, standing between us. He was the last person I expected to intervene. Perhaps the others felt the same, because the hall fell silent, all eyes turned to the Prince of Lust. "I love fighting and killing as much as the next demon, but this is not our way. Not against our own. We are more civilized than this. Fenris deserves a trial."

Levi scowled. "You heard him. He admitted his crimes."

Dean shook his head. "Be that as it may, we do not know the whole of it yet. A trial is the way. Our father's way. Our way."

The other brothers nodded in agreement. The anger was leaving them. They didn't want Fen dead. Not just yet. Not like this.

"And what of the princess?" Zeb asked, his voice laced with some compassion.

"She shall be tried as well," Dean said, looking over to me with an unreadable expression in his eyes.

Ace stayed quiet, his sword limp at his side, as if he didn't know what he felt anymore.

Levi didn't look happy, but everyone else agreed this was the way of it. Niam took my sword, while Dean and Zeb kept Fen under control. He struggled, but weakly, drained by the fighting. Together, we marched deeper into the castle. Levi fell to my side and squeezed my arm until it bruised, his face close to mine. "Enjoy your time in the dungeons, Princess. It's the last view of this world you'll get before you're hanged."

. . .

His words proved prophetic. For here I sit, awaiting a hanging at sunrise. Even as I think these thoughts, it feels surreal, like I am living someone else's life. This is just a movie, or book—a story made up to scare naughty children. 'Don't make deals with devils or you'll end up dead!' sounds like an excellent morality tale.

Too bad I didn't listen.

I made the deal with the devil. I thought I could outthink them. I thought I could come out of this unscathed, saving my mom and myself and all of the Fae and living a happily ever after with the man I love. I was such a fool. I still am a fool, if I'm being honest, because even now I don't entirely believe this is the end.

I can't allow myself to believe that, at sunrise, Fen and I will both be hanged. Not because of something we did. But because of what we are.

The trial, if it can even be called that, was such a farce. If I thought there was corruption in my world's justice system, it's downright perfection compared to what they do here. There was no 'jury of my peers', no evidence, no real testimony, just Levi expounding his own hateful rhetoric and convincing the princes they didn't have to worry about the contract, because with me dead, there was no contract. They'd be free to rule their own realms. As long as none of them made a claim for High Castle, no one would suffer.

No one but me and Fen, of course. We were kept separated the whole time, and Fen was given no voice as part of the council. They treated me more as animal than human. I cannot even imagine how they treated Fen.

Then they voted behind closed doors. I never found out who voted which way, but I can only assume Asher was on our side. I pray Ace was as well, but perhaps the lies he endured sealed our fate. In the end, both Fen and I were sentenced to death.

Asher brought me the news.

"I'm sorry," he said, standing outside my cell. "I brought this upon you."

I clasped the bars, still possessing some energy. "Asher, no. You fought for me in the trial—"

"No. Before that. I am the reason your Fae blood was revealed." He paused. "I dropped the contract."

The contract. That one that prevented me from revealing my true heritage. The one only Asher and his father could cancel. When my Fae powers emerged during the battle, I thought perhaps my magic had broken the oath. In truth, I was fighting for my life, I was fighting for Fen, and I barely gave it much thought.

"When the fighting started," Asher continued, "I wanted you to be able to defend yourself. So I dropped the contract, hoping your magic would aid you. I…I couldn't forgive myself if you had died because of some oath I made you swear to uphold."

"It was my choice to sign."

"But I arranged it. It is my foolish mistakes that brought you here." He started to turn away, but I grabbed his hand through the bars and pulled him back.

"My magic saved me," I said. "If you hadn't stopped the oath, I'd be dead. At least now there's a chance."

He smiled. "As hopeful as ever, Princess." His smile dropped as he held my gaze. "But this time, I am not so sure you're right."

I let go of his hand and clutched the bars tight. "There must be something more we can do. Can't you break us out? You have soldiers you could send. They can—"

"Shh," he whispered, raising a finger to his lips. He glanced at the two guards behind him, then kept his voice low. "I am doing all in my power, princess, but my brothers are watching me closely. They know I am on your side. It took calling in favors just to allow this meeting."

My shoulders slumped. "There must be something."

"Perhaps another contract," he said. I could see him thinking, thoughts and emotions spiraling over his face. "Maybe if you and Fen swore to obey the other princes."

"Then we would have to fight the Fae," I said.

"Perhaps." He smirked. "But all contracts have loopholes. You taught me that."

I stepped back, sighing. "I can't fight the Fae. And you wouldn't want me to."

His eyes fell. "No. I wouldn't."

We were silent for a moment, searching for ideas and finding none. "Did Fen know?" I asked.

Asher looked to the distance, to the light from the window. "No. He never knew he was Fae. No one ever told him."

For a moment, the cell became less cold, less dark. Knowing Fen had been honest with me made all the difference. "But...he would never have known the land you came from. The land before here. Didn't he ever wonder why he couldn't remember?"

"He thought he was forgetting, just as I have been forgetting. The pieces he could recall, yes, they were fictions told by our mother, but told so often they had become memory."

"So what changed?" I asked.

"You," he said. "You awoke his powers. But I suspect his injuries are what finally forced his body to use his natural abilities."

I nodded. It made a sort of sense, though I would have to discuss it later with Fen. How did he feel about this? Did he despise me for revealing him as Fae? For changing his life forever?

"So, what next?" asked Asher.

The only thing left.

"We hope," I said. "We hope." *Dum spiro spero. While I breathe, I hope.* I could practically hear my mother's voice in my mind, saying those words to me so many times over the course of my childhood. What I would give to have her with me now, to seek out her wisdom, to find comfort in her arms.

Asher, however, did not look hopeful, and with a resigned look, he walked away. It was the last time I saw him. Two weeks ago.

Now, I slouch against a cold wall, wrapping my arms around my knees for warmth. There are no clocks down here. No natural lighting sources. I have no way of tracking time other than the once a day slop a guard brings in for me to eat, if I can stomach it. I wonder if I'll be granted a last meal, like I would on my world. But it seems unlikely. I'll die with the taste of this rot in my mouth.

My greatest fear, my deepest sadness, is that others have to suffer with me. My mother, whose soul still lays trapped in a hell dungeon waiting for me to fulfill my contract. The man I love, who will die by my side, his only crime that of loving me back. Es and Pete, who will never know what happened to their friend.

The Fae. They will continue to be enslaved, and those who resist will be killed until there are no free Fae remaining.

And the magic on this world will die.

Do the vampires even know what they're doing? What they're condemning themselves and everyone around them to? I tried to explain, but they accused me of lying to save my own skin.

It's not my skin I'm trying to save.

Well, not just my skin.

But it doesn't matter now.

All I can do is wait.

Wait for death. Wait for the end.

Maybe this world is better off without the magic of the Fae. Maybe it is better off without me.

Minutes pass. Hours. Days. Time loses meaning in this dank, damp pit of despair. I have no idea how long I have to live. It is an odd thing, to know you're about to die, and to be powerless to choose how you will spend your last moments. There are so many things I have left undone in my life. So many words left unsaid to those I love. And now it is forever too late.

A commotion outside my cell alerts me to the guards changing shifts. They always have one or two watching over me. It started with two, but lately they've reduced the watch to one. Maybe they figure I have nothing left to fight for. Maybe the war rages on with the Fae and they need more soldiers than guards. I tried asking once, but no one would speak to me. So I just watch and think. But today, I am surprised to see a familiar face.

"Marco?"

His dark eyes flick to me, and he frowns, but doesn't answer. He stands in the spot of the guard, just out of reach of my cell, but close enough to see me, his broad shoulders filling the space and blocking out the little light from the orb.

I scramble to the bars, clutching them in my hands. "Marco! Did Fen or Asher send you? Are you here to help me?" There's a desperate pleading in my voice that makes me cringe, but I don't care. This is the first hope I've had since my fate was decided. But then Marco turns away, and my hope plummets.

"Marco? Why won't you talk to me? Please let me out. We must save Fen. We must get out of here. You were my personal guard. You swore to protect me!" I'm nearly frantic now, tears clogging my throat as I speak too loudly in the cavernous space.

He turns to me finally, his eyes cold. "The Fae killed my family when they attacked Stonehill in this last battle," he says quietly. "My parents, who were farmers. My little brother, who loved horseback riding and wanted to be a soldier when he grew up. My little sister, who wanted to be a guard when she grew older. Just like me." He shakes his head, a lock of brown hair falling into his eye and making him look boyish in his sadness. "I can't let you out, Princess. I'm sorry."

SILVER FLAME

I don't know what to say. How can I defend myself? How can I defend what I've done by releasing this magic into his life? Into the lives of the innocent people who live here. Why can't the right choice be easier to see? Why must it all be shrouded in gray?

Marco and I share no more words, and my thoughts turn to the afterlife. Does dying in this world change what happens in the next? Or would I experience the same fate regardless of the world my life ended on?

After a time, my existential crisis is put on hold by more pressing concerns of the flesh. Namely, my growing need to relieve myself. I've been loath to use the pot they provided, with guards watching my every move, but eventually the urgency of my need trumps my modesty. So I pull the pan as far away from Marco as I can and do my best not to make a mess of myself. It's not a pleasant experience, made worse so by the clearing of a throat.

I'm just finishing up when I hear something tap the bars, and I nearly kick the pot over. A man stands at my cell door.

Only the light of flickering orbs illuminates this corner of hell soaked in darkness, but even without seeing his face I know who stands there. Will he really be the last person I see before I die? Lovely. "Hello, Levi."

The Prince of Envy smirks. "Princess Arianna, how low the mighty fall. Fancied yourself queen of everything, did you? But here you are, no better than sewer vermin, and smelling much the same." He wrinkles his nose.

I glare at him. "I seem to have misplaced my perfumes."

He chuckles. "I must admit I respect your spirit. You have a way about you that attracts admirers from all walks of life. You might have even made a great queen, had fates turned out differently."

"What do you want, Levi? I'm busy."

He scowls. "Of course, I mustn't take up too much of the lady's precious time. After all, you have only a few hours remaining of your life. How does it feel, knowing you're about to die? Your tiny mortal life snuffed out in just a few short years? And no mum here to trade her soul for yours."

I'd forgotten that this all started when I died once before. How odd that I'm about to face for a second time something most only ever face once.

When I don't respond to Levi, he frowns, then leans against the bars and plasters a smile across his face that doesn't reach his eyes. "Come to the door and place your hands together. You are needed elsewhere."

"Needed? For what?" My heart is racing. Is he going to have me killed early? Will he steal the last few hours I have left just out of spite? Does he really hate me that much?

I consider refusing. Fighting. But honestly, any chance to get out of this cell is welcome, even if it is for my execution. I walk to the cell door and put my hands together, slipping them through the slit in the steel.

Marco clasps chains around them and I pull my hands back in as he unlocks my cell. Levi steps away, letting the guard do his job of securing me.

"Where are we going?" I ask, when Levi refuses to speak more about what's going on.

"You'll see soon enough. Let's just say you never had the proper Presenting, and now everyone is dying to see the true face of their admired princess."

I shiver as I think about the Presenting Levi arranged for me when I first got here. I look down at my dirt-caked body. My hair is a tangle of straw, mud and who knows what else. I smell like an animal carcass left to bake in the sun. Is this really how I will be presented to the world?

And then I remember my ears. My signs of Faeness. I used illusion magic to make myself look human the first few days of my capture, then I stopped after the guards beat me. It wasn't worth the pain. Now I'm too weak to cast the spell even if I tried.

I can guess at Levi's plan. He wants the world to hate me before I'm killed. He wants to turn all those who loved or respected me against me, so that they are more loyal to him.

And it just might work, if Marco's disdain for me is any indication. Everyone is turning against me. Ace. Zeb. People I thought cared for me, for Fen. There is no loyalty here. I was a fool to believe otherwise.

I'm dragged through the tunnels and up stairs. When we reach the main castle, my heart clenches. This is Stonehill. This is what home feels like. Or used to. Everything has changed now. It was a twist of cruel irony that Levi had both Fen and I locked away in Fen's own home. In his own realm. With his own people guarding us. A twist of the blade into his gut. And mine too.

We reach a door and suddenly I am thrust into sunlight. My eyes go blind from the brightness, so long have I been stuck in darkness. I'm reminded of Plato's Allegory of the Cave. When we live our lives in darkness, the shadows seem like the only reality, and the truth is too blinding to accept. I wonder if this is what the princes' lives are like. They are cursed in their sins, stuck in their lack of growth. Perhaps their evil is not their fault, but the fault of the curse and the darkness in which their souls are fated to live. The light hurts them, and thus makes the shadows their only source of truth.

But that does not make their deeds any less evil to those they are perpetrated on.

It takes time for my eyes to stop hurting, for my vision to return. I stumble through the training yard, the sound of swords clashing cuing me to my surroundings. But the closer I come to any group, the quieter it becomes. A natural hush falls around us, as people gawk and stare. Then the whispering begins as they join with the throngs of people following us. I am surrounded by guards now, not just Marco, and Levi leads the way as if he has already been crowned King of all the lands. He relishes this power, and covets it as he does all things not his by right.

We approach a wooden stage and my legs stumble on the steps, still weak from my time in the cell. My muscles have atrophied. Marco grabs my arms to keep me from falling on my face, and he is gentle as he helps me stand. A small kindness in the face of what's to come—one I appreciate.

"Here she is!" Levi yells to the growing crowd. I've never seen so many people in Stonehill. It's clear from the diversity of dress and style that Levi planned this ahead of time. All the realms are represented here, not just Fen's.

The crowd quiets enough to hear what Levi will say next.

The Prince grabs my arm and shoves me to the edge of the stage. The same platform used for the slave auction. The same platform used to torture the Fae they captured in battle. I wasn't here for that, but I heard the stories of what happened while I was in Avakiri. I can see the stains of blood worn into the wood under my bare feet.

The blood of my people.

We are all monsters. The Fae. The vampires. All of us, for the war we have wrought. If I somehow survive this, I will make sure this platform is destroyed. It is soaked in evil.

"Take a good look at her," Levi says. He pulls back my hair and the crowds gasp, seeing my ears for the first time. "She is one of them. She always was. She is Fae. And not just Fae. No!"

He then tugs at my dress...if you can call it that. It's a shapeless canvas thing that used to be white but is now so stained you can hardly tell. It has long sleeves and falls to my ankles, covering most of my body. Covering the tattoos that formed when I became the Midnight Star.

I know what's about to happen, and I close my eyes, the tears stuck in my throat. I take a breath and steel myself for what he's about to do as hate and anger grow in me.

I feel the prick of a knife against the skin of my back as he cuts into the cloth. I hear someone—Marco, I think—suck in his breath in shock, but no one does anything to stop Levi.

And then I am naked, the dress a crumble of rags at my feet. Levi shoves me forward again, parading me before the crowd as he shows them the tattoos that definitively prove I am of Royal Fae blood.

"She is the reason we are at war," Levi shouts to the crowd. "Look at her. She is the reason your loved ones are dead or injured. She is the reason the Druids are back. She betrayed you. Us. Our world. She used your love for her to destroy you. She is no Queen. She is no friend to our people. And at sunrise, she will pay for her sins with her life."

His hands are still on me, taking liberty to touch me anywhere he wants, to move me around like a puppet master. I have to open my eyes because he forces me to walk through the crowds as the people reach out to hit and scratch and grope my naked body. I want to hide, to cover my face, but instead I force myself to look into the eyes of as many of them as possible. Each person who touches me. Each person who cheers at my abuse. I stare at them. I challenge them the only way I can. They spit on me and throw rotten fruit at me, and still I look. Still I hold their gaze and make them see me.

Many turn their eyes at that. Many still have some conscience left. Some do not. Some laugh and gloat and my challenge goads them on further. They are lost to their hate.

There are hundreds, maybe thousands of people, and Levi seems determined that every single one of them will have a chance to defile my body. My bare feet are bruised and bleeding from the rocks I'm forced to walk over. My body hasn't fared much better.

When one man tries to put his hands where they don't belong, I knee him in the crotch. Levi backhands me, and I fall to the ground. "See how she does not submit to her punishment? How she thinks she is better than you?"

He leans down and grips my arm, then speaks to me quietly, so that only I can hear. "This can go on as long as I want. This can get worse too. I could let the men do what they clearly want to do. Throw you into a room with the worst of them until they are done."

I shudder, and he laughs.

"Or...there is another way. I can end it all. I can save your life, and the life of Fen—even the life of your pathetic human mother. I can make you Queen and give you back all your luxuries and dignity. Which is it, Princess?"

I look up at him, wondering what game he's playing at, and he smiles.

"Marry me. Choose me as the next King, and I will drop all the charges against you. I will make this whole thing go away. Like it never happened. You'll get to be my obedient queen, and Fen will live to see another day."

So this has been his plan all along. I can't say I'm surprised. But he played his cards well, putting me in this hell and then making me choose. "What if I pick a different prince? Maybe one of the others would like this same deal."

His face hardens. "I control the people now. I control your fate. I am the only one with enough power to offer you freedom."

I need to buy time, but I can't outright say no. I believe his threats. The crowds have changed in the hours we've been out here. As the sun dies down, the women and children have begun to disperse. Now it is the hardest of men who have stayed. They want what Levi is promising. I can't let that happen. I'm not sure I'd live through it.

"Give me time to think. I can't think out here like this."

He pauses, considering my words. "Very well, Princess. I'll give you time. But if you haven't made up your mind by midnight, these men will enjoy a few hours with you before sunrise." He licks his lips and stares at me with a lascivious look in his eyes. "And I'll be taking the first turn."

2

PASSAGES

"Her blood pumps through my veins, like fire and ice. I am not a man accustomed to fear, but I feel it now, filling me with its poison of doubt. What have they done with her? What will they do? What if I never see her again?"

—Fenris Vane

Levi sticks a stone into my hand and commands Marco to take me back to my cell. "You have my mark, Princess. Use it before it's too late."

I look down at the stone and see his demon mark painted onto it in black. Marco places a hand on my back and draws his sword, keeping the crowds at a distance as he guides me to the castle. When we've walked far enough to avoid detection from Levi and the crowds, Marco takes off his red cloak and drapes it around my shoulders. "I'm sorry, Princess. You didn't deserve that."

His voice is cracked and full of emotion. I can only imagine what he's going through right now. How torn he must feel. I thank him for the cloak and pull it more tightly around me, covering my nakedness and bruises and cuts as he leads me back to my cell.

My eyes adjust to the darkness again, and I stand leaning against the bars of my cage staring at the stone in my hand. If I accept Levi's offer, I will live. Fen will live. He won't be free, but he'll live. And my mother... my mother will live. I'd have fulfilled my contract, and her soul would be free, her body healed.

How can I refuse?

But...

But...

Levi would make a horrible ruler. He's a misogynistic racist blowhard who thinks he knows what he's doing, but he doesn't. He would destroy the Fae, ruin this world, corrupt everything and everyone. He's a poison that would seep into the very soul of this place.

If I refuse his offer, I am damning Fen to death, and my mother to imprisonment for eternity. If I accept, I am damning everyone else to slavery and a tyrannical ruler for who knows how long. Can I really condemn thousands to save the lives of a few? Would my mother even want me to sacrifice the safety of my people for her? Would Fen want to stay alive only to see me wed Levi while he remains imprisoned?

And what of me? Can I face my own death? I am the last of the High Fae. If my blood dies, it takes the last of this world's magic with it.

I glance at the window, the light almost faded. I must choose. And I am running out of time.

I sink onto my straw mat in exhausted defeat, my body so sore from the abuse I took on the streets that I can't point to a single spot that doesn't hurt. Through the pain, I barely feel the pouch pocking into my back. The pouch of expensive fabric tucked into the straw.

I open it and find an old steel skeleton key inside. It's rusted and ancient. With it is a small bit of parchment. I unroll it to find a note. *This key unlocks all doors within Stonehill. Free Fen. Meet me at the docks on the north-west river. There will be a boat. Come quickly.*

It is not signed, and I don't recognize the writing. Is this a trap? Some twisted game Levi is playing? Or is someone really trying to help me?

Marco still guards my door, but he is alone. I can't leave if he doesn't let me.

I stare at the key in one hand, the stone in the other. If I try to escape and rescue Fen, I could fail, ensuring our deaths. If I call for Levi, we could live. *Dum spiro spero.* While I breathe, I hope. There is no hope left if I'm dead. Agreeing to Levi's terms would buy us time to find a better solution. But what if I don't find one?

I weigh the choices in my hands. There are grave risks in both.

I drop the contents of one hand to the dirt-packed floor, and stare at my other hand.

I have made my choice. Now, I just hope I can live with the consequences.

It doesn't take long to put my plan into place, but my hand still shakes as I cut my wrist with the sharp edge of the stone and draw Levi's mark into the ground with my blood.

Only the last line is left unfinished. I look up at Marco, who frowns. "Are you sure?" he asks.

I nod. "It's the only way. You've seen what he's capable of."

Marco drops his eyes in resignation. "I'm sorry I was a part of it. Fen would never forgive me."

"If this works, Fen will know you helped me today. He will know you did your best. I'll make sure of it."

Marco nods, still frowning. "Just be careful. I have a bad feeling about this."

"Are you sure he's with Fen?" I ask.

"Yes. It's not pretty. You shouldn't have to see that."

My stomach clenches. "Fen shouldn't have to endure that," I say through a thick throat. "How long will it take Levi to get here once he feels his mark?"

"He has to cross the castle. You're in different wings of the dungeon. But still, not long."

I nod. "And you're sure about this?" I know what he's risking.

He nods. "I'm sure. I should have done this long ago."

I hold up a tin cup to him and clear my throat. "Is there any way you could get me more water? I'm parched."

He looks at the cup for a longer beat than necessary, and then takes it from my hands, through the bars. "Yes, Princess."

Once he is gone, I leave the rock with my blood dripping from it on the ground next to the unfinished demon mark, and I grip the key still in my hand.

It's time to save Fen.

...

I've lived in this castle long enough, explored the secret passages and tunnels enough to know how to get around without being seen. That knowledge comes in handy now, as I escape the dungeons and duck behind a tap-estry on the wall and into one of the many hidden pas-sages within the walls. Fen was amused when he dis-covered how much I'd learned about his castle. Now my snooping just might save both our lives, if I get lucky.

I use a small light globe I stole from the dungeon to travel through the passages, feeling my way through dust and cobwebs. My feet are still wrecked and I need clothing, but those concerns will have to wait. I'm on a tight timeline.

The sound of leather slapping against flesh and bone is all I need to know I'm in the right place. I swallow back the vomit forming in my throat and steel myself for what I know I'll see.

But there's no way to prepare yourself for seeing the love of your life tortured while you can do nothing to stop it.

And that's exactly what I have to do.

Fen hangs upright, looking as if he'd collapse if he could, if chains didn't shackle his writs to stone columns. His lips are stained dark red. Crimson streaks cover his back.

Snap.

A leather whip lashes through the air, tearing another line of flesh open across Fen's back. He doesn't cry out. He says nothing.

Levi steps into view, whispering something to his brother.

I watch through a crack in the wall, too far away to hear what Levi whispers to Fen, but close enough to see what he does next.

It makes me sick, and angry. Someday I will kill that bastard. But I am naked, unarmed and injured. Exposing myself now will only get me caught. I must wait and hope Marco does what he promised.

After what happened in the streets of Stonehill, Marco's anger at me transformed into guilt. He explained he'd spent the last few weeks spiraling out of control in his grief over his family. That Levi promised him vengeance against those who caused the battle. Against me and Fen.

But seeing the kind of king Levi would be, the kind of ruler he is, Marco couldn't support him. He knew I wasn't the enemy, that I had no control over what I was born as. So when I found the key to my cell, I took a risk. I asked Marco to help me.

He wouldn't help me escape, per se. That would be too risky, even for him. But he could get me water. And tell me where Levi was. And he could finish Levi's mark in the dirt with my blood, after I left. To give me more time to free Fen and escape.

So now I must wait for Levi to feel the pull of the mark. To come to my cell.

It takes so long I fear the plan failed, that Marco chickened out, or I hadn't left enough blood. But then Levi stops talking and looks down at his wrist.

He says something that makes Fen scream louder than any of the torture had, and then leaves the dungeon laughing.

I grit my teeth and wait until I can no longer hear his footsteps, then I push out the loose stones I know are there and climb out.

When Fen sees me, his mouth falls open.

"You know, you really have to stop getting yourself captured and beaten," I say, trying to lighten the mood.

I rush over to him and shove the key into the lock, hoping it works. It truly is a master key, because his chains fall off, and I support his body as he steps away from the beams. "How did you get here?" he asks, his voice hoarse and low. Even in this broken state, it soothes me to hear it.

"Remember, I know this castle's secrets," I say. Then something whines behind me, and I turn to see Baron chained in the corner. "Oh my god, what has that monster done to you?"

I quickly free the white wolf and check him for injuries. There are none, and Baron rubs his head against both me and Fen. I still can't believe this wolf is the Earth Spirit, but I will have to think on that later.

Fen pulls me closer to him, and I take comfort in the warmth of his body, in the hardness of his muscles and the feel of him so close. And beneath the layers of stench we both have brought with us, I can smell him. The wildness that clings to him always. The pine and woodsy scent. I breathe him in and dig my nails into his arms to hold him tighter.

I sob into his chest, all the fear and tension of the last few weeks flowing out of me, releasing in one great swell, like a wave I can no longer control or hold back.

The beat of his heart is steady and strong and I sigh into his embrace, so happy to be with him again. I haven't seen him since the trial, and I feared I would never see him again. After a moment, I pull away just enough to look up at him. He's still Fen, with his ruggedly gorgeous features, his piercing blue eyes and sandy brown hair with copper flecks always a little disheveled. But he's also more. I reach up to touch the points of his ears, now so much like mine. "This is my fault," I say softly.

He reaches for my hand and pulls it against his chest. "No. You didn't even know what you were until we brought you here. This isn't your fault. Never blame yourself."

I nod, wiping the tears from my eyes. "We don't have long. We must leave. Levi will know we've escaped as soon as he gets to my cell."

That's when Fen looks down at me and notices I'm wearing only a cloak. "What happened to you? What did he do to you?" A growl forms deep in his throat, and the new tattoo on his stomach glows a slight pale blue, radiating his magic.

"I'll explain later. Right now we have to go."

Fen presses his lips together but nods, reaching for my hand as we climb back into the secret passage. He returns the stones to their proper place and we make haste through the dark, hidden halls as quickly and quietly as we can. I know he has many questions, as do I. They will have to wait.

As we pass one door, Fen stops and holds up a hand. "We need our gear. Our weapons. Normally they'd be in the armory, but ours are a special case, so they should be kept here." He looks down at my feet. "And you won't get far without some clothes and shoes."

I can't argue with that. I'm limping along as it is.

He pushes through the door and peeks out, then ushers me in. It's Fen's quarters, though it's clear Fen's not the one who's been sleeping here. "Levi has taken my place," Fen says with venom in his voice.

I look at the disheveled bed and unfamiliar clothing that litters the floor and I seethe with rage. "That bastard."

Fen opens a few trunks until he finds what he's looking for. He hands me Spero—my sword—and the dagger Daison made for me before he died. Then he hands me clothes. "They will be too big, but they're better than nothing."

I shrug them on over tender skin as he also undresses out of his rags and into his leather armor. Light but still offering some protection. I try to look away when he's naked, but don't quite succeed. He catches me staring and smiles for the first time since the dungeon. "There will be plenty of time for that later, Princess."

I'm flustered but don't turn my eyes away. "I hope so."

And I mean it. I'm tired of waiting. Tired of second guessing. We aren't guaranteed any kind of future. I want to live my life now. Which means being with Fen. Loving him. Regardless of what the future holds. I spent so much time worrying about who would make the best king, I failed to consider that fate might conspire to take the choice from me altogether. I almost lost him once in the battle, and again at the hands of Levi. I won't lose him to my own foolishness now.

He raises an eyebrow at me as he pulls on his clothes. He says nothing with his mouth, but so much with his eyes. For a moment it's almost easy to forget everything that's happened. Everything we are running from. We are in his room. We are safe. We are together. But we can't let our guard down. He takes three long steps and is standing in front of me. He raises his finger to my cheek and runs it down my jaw. "This face, these eyes, this mouth, filled my thoughts every moment I was imprisoned. I feared I would never see you again."

I reach for his hand and hold it against my face. "I'm not so easy to get rid of."

He leans in and his lips find mine. It is a moment I have dreamt of every night. The feel of him. The taste of him. I don't want it to end. I want to lose myself in his embrace. But we are nearly out of time. We could still be caught. We could still be killed.

We pull away from each other with great reluctance and grab our swords. It's time.

It doesn't take us long to make our way out of the castle. Fen knows even more secret passages than I; this has been his home for longer than I can even imagine.

I show him the note, and he nods and leads us to the barge. I can see the questions in his eyes, but we both know this isn't the time. First, we must escape and get somewhere safe.

I have no idea where that somewhere is, but I know it's not here.

The moons are high in the sky by the time we make it to our meeting place: the docks, which I have only visited a handful of times. Usually, they're bustling with people unloading delivered goods or freshly caught fish. There is laughter and the smell of wine and the river. Now, it is quiet, dark, but for a few torches in the distance. Black waters shimmer under the pale light, and a small boat sways on the waves. From a distance I see a man cloaked in black, standing on shore with his back to us. It isn't until we get closer that I realize who it is.

Fen grabs my hand and stops me. We both hold our ground, drawing our blades. Baron leaps in front of us growling, as the man turns to face us.

He grins and holds out his hand. "Brother, you don't look nearly happy enough to see me."

Fen growls. "What are you doing here, Dean?"

3

THE BLACK LOTUS

"I know where you're going. And I know why. But consider this,
before you act rashly. Your people have fallen. They need their
prince. What will you choose, Prince of War? Who will you save?"

—Ace

We are both dumbfounded. Why is Dean here? I was
expecting Asher. Maybe Ace, though the way he was
behaving during the confrontation with Levi makes me
question his loyalty now.

Fen strides up to him. "What's going on, Dean?"

The Prince of Lust smirks. "Good to see you too,
brother. You know, we should probably table the questions until we find a place where you're not in danger of
being hanged, don't you think?"

Fen turns to me, and I walk toward the boat. "He's
right," I say. "We have to go. We can sort it out later." I

place a hand on Fen's shoulder and whisper in his ear. "There's no reason for a trap. I was already under Levi's power."

Fen mumbles something about "Levi's power" and "other dangers."

As I'm about to step onto the boat, something flies through the air.

And impales my shoulder.

I look down in shock, the pain not yet reaching my mind. A feathered arrow sticks out of my body.

There is a moment of pause, as if time has stopped, and I hear nothing. Then it all comes rushing back: noise, screaming, a frenzy. I reach for my sword but my shoulder spasms in pain, and I cannot grasp the hilt with my right hand.

I grow lightheaded and fall to the ground, my knees hitting the rocky earth with a thud.

Movies make getting shot by guns and arrows seem so easy. Guy gets shot, guy looks down, shrugs, keeps going.

What a crock.

This hurts like hell.

My vision grows dim. Fen and Dean fight soldiers dressed in black. No colors to identify their realm, but it doesn't take much to figure out. I know he's coming. He walks out of the mist and into the light of the moons.

Levi.

His red cape and white hair flick about in the cold wind. He doesn't join in the battle. Instead, he targets me with a hateful smile. And before I can blink, he is at my side, lifting me easily off the ground and pulling me away from Fen and Dean.

"You should have taken me up on my offer when you had the chance, Princess."

"I would never choose you," I say, spitting in his face. "You are selfish, childish, petty and cruel. You're not fit to rule your realm, let alone an entire kingdom. I'm better off dead than by your side."

His face contorts in rage. He honestly was not expecting me to reject him. And like so many entitled men who think women owe them something they don't, his rage turns outward, toward me. He grabs me and pulls me closer to him, squeezing my chest so tight I can barely breathe as the arrow digs deeper into my flesh. "You bitch. You think you can treat me like that and get away with it?"

My heart pounds so hard in my chest I feel like I'm going to vomit, but I don't back off. I have nothing left to lose, and maybe if I'm clever enough I can buy some time. "What are you going to do, Levi? Kill me? And deny everyone the pleasure of seeing me hanged? How will your brothers feel if you take justice into your own hands at the last hour? You think they will forgive that so easily?"

His teeth elongate and he leans in toward my neck. I brace myself. I can feel his breath on my skin, smell the sweat seeping from his body. He's nervous, worried, aroused. I have never hated someone so much as I do right now.

And as his teeth sink into me, I seethe with rage. It hurts, more than it did with Ace. Levi wants it to hurt.

He feeds on me, and it is a kind of rape, a kind of violation. I have pushed him too far. Whatever way out Fen and Dean might have accomplished will be undone by my stupidity.

I feel myself fading. He is drinking too much of my blood. Draining me too thoroughly. And gaining more power in the process.

But then something shifts. Voices. Footsteps. Heavy boots. Men arguing. Levi releases me and I slump to the ground, as a wolf howls and men scream.

...

I'm plagued by nightmares of fire and death. Of Daison dying in my arms. Of Oren torturing me. Of Fen cut down in battle. Of being paraded naked as people I tried to help abuse me in the most vile of ways. I startle out of sleep drenched in sweat and shaking.

Strong arms wrap around me. "You are safe. Calm yourself, love."

I cling to Fen, still shaking. Still plagued by images of his nearly dead body lying on the scorched battle- field. "Where are we? What's happened?" I remember trying to escape. Him. Dean. Then Levi. Then nothing. I look around to situate myself. I'm in a cave, laying on thick furs with a fire burning near me. Outside, a storm rages in the night sky, throwing snow into our shelter. We are alone save Baron, who is curled at my feet, his large head resting on my legs as he stares at me with worry—if a wolf can look worried.

"We're in hiding," he says gruffly. "You lost a lot of blood and passed out. We had to wait for you to awaken before we could leave."

I touch my neck, where Levi took a chunk out of me during his feeding. It's healing quickly, but still pain- ful. I examine my shoulder with my left hand. There are bandages where the arrow once was. "How long have we been here?"

"A few hours. You should rest more, but we can't afford to stay on this world longer than necessary. How do you feel?"

"Tired. Sore. But well enough to walk." I'm not totally sure that's the truth, though. My legs feel like jelly. But I can sense the urgency in Fen, and I know he's right.

Everyone will be looking for us. Hunting us. We've escaped execution, but for how long?

"What happened?" I ask. I don't remember anything after Levi fed on me.

"Baron saved you by taking a chunk out of Levi. While the bastard fled, Dean and I took down his soldiers. We got away just in time. If he'd had more of your blood…"

Fen lets the thought trail off, and I shudder. I came close to dying. Again.

Dean joins us through the cave's opening, a wobble to his step, carrying a flask that he's clearly been imbibing generously from. "It's good to see you awake, Princess."

"Why did you send me the key?" I ask without preamble.

He shakes his head, his dark blond hair shifting gracefully with the movement. He truly is a beautiful man, at least on the outside. "What? No thank you to the man who saved your life? I thought surely that would win me some points. Save the damsel in distress, win her hand?"

"My hand isn't for winning," I say. "And you didn't answer my question."

"Why did I save you?" he repeats, sitting down across from me. "It seemed my only chance of getting my month with you, since my brothers keep stealing my turn." He shoots a look at Fen, then returns his attention to me. "I'm convinced that with a little one-on-one time, you'll finally see how charming and irresistible I truly am."

I roll my eyes at that. "Not likely. But thanks, I guess. Now what do we do? Where do we go?"

Dean's smile grows bigger, if that's even possible. Does this man take nothing seriously? "There's only one place I can think of off the top of my head that would offer us protection."

Fen groans. "There has to be somewhere else. That's no place for Arianna."

I flash Fen a look. "Excuse me? What's that supposed to mean? I'm not a child in need of shielding. If we'll be safe there, we must go. Where is this place?"

Dean chuckles. "You'll see shortly. Let's be off then, shall we?" He takes a swig of his flask and offers it to both Fen and me. Fen refuses, but as I try to walk, pain shoots through me and I reluctantly accept.

The drink burns my throat going down, but then a pleasant tingling alleviates some of the pain, and walking isn't as hard. I hand it back to him. "Thank you, that helped."

We follow Dean through the cave. He turns to make sure we're keeping up. "It's the perfect place," he tells Fen. "We can relax, indulge in some fun, maybe even get some help with what to do next."

"This isn't a holiday," Fen says. "We'll get Ari a healer and then return to reclaim Stonehill. Besides, I will not be indebted to that demon ever again."

Dean laughs but doesn't argue.

"Where are we going?" I ask to break the awkward silence that has developed. And because I'd really like to know.

"We must meet with Sly," Dean says. "There's a place called The Black Lotus. Sly Devil runs it. It's a no-kill zone for beings from all realms and worlds. A safe space, more or less. Sly knows everything that happens everywhere, and everyone who's doing it. If anyone can help us, it's him."

"For a steep price," Fen mutters.

Dean laughs. "Ignore him. He's just still pissed about his last favor being called in. It involved a mermaid and a hit man. I'll tell you the whole story sometime when Fen isn't around to ruin it."

"Where is this place located?" I ask.

"Portland," Fen says. "So that part of your contract will be fulfilled."

"And my mom will be safe…"

He nods and I squeeze his hand and smile.

"So, The Black Lotus is conveniently in Portland?" I raise an eyebrow at that.

"More like you were conveniently in Portland," Fen says. "Our mansion is there because it's a useful location for our work with other beings in addition to the humans. It's likely what drew your mother to that area. Portland has a pull for those embroiled in the otherworldly, which your mother certainly was, even if she was only human."

"I'm going to pretend, for the sake of our relationship, that you didn't just say *only human* in relation to my mother. Them's fighting words, mister. Prince of hell or not." I'm still so tired, and so weak, and in so much pain, and things are still so bleak for us all, but I do my best to bring some levity into our situation. To laugh. To tease. To find some semblance of normality in all this.

Fen's face is tight, and strained by worry and anger and tension, but he sees what I'm trying to do and relaxes, if only marginally. He bows graciously and uses the same light tone I employed, though there is still a seriousness in his eyes when they lock with mine. "Please accept my apologies, Princess. I have only the utmost respect for humans."

I smile at his attempt. "Apology accepted. But don't let it happen again, or my royal punishment will be swift and merciless."

Fen laughs.

Dean clears his throat. "Do you two want a room? And some company?" He winks at both of us. "Could be fun."

"Ugh, you're gross," I say.

"You won't be saying that when our month is through, Princess," Dean says seductively, his teasing transforming into something serious. I can feel his pull, the hormones or pheromones or whatever magic makes him irresistible, but it doesn't make me lose my way. Dean is not the one I want.

The cavern we are in fills with the sound of running water. And it glows with crystals infused with some kind of magic. They hang from above us and jut out from the walls in all manner of shapes and sizes. A waterfall flows over them and into a small pool. It's a magical sight.

"The Mirror is behind the waterfall," Dean says, as he strips off his shirt and steps into the pool of water.

"Really?" I ask, eyeing his torso. "You know the shirt's going to get wet whether you wear it or hold it."

He grins like a mischievous boy. "But it's more comfortable off than on. And how could I deprive you of this view?" He flexes his muscles for me and I can't help but laugh. Fen just grunts.

"I thought there were no mirrors in the seven realms?" I say.

Dean laughs. "Not officially, but we are demons. By our very nature we don't follow rules. So each Prince keeps a secret mirror in his realm. For emergencies."

Fen smirks. "And I still wish you never knew about mine. You seem to have a difficult time with the word... emergencies."

"Hey? When have I ever dropped by without good reason? Except for that one time. And that other time. And the time with the drinking doesn't count. Drinking's important."

Their playful banter puts me more at ease, and I step into the pond. The water is warmer than I thought it would be. Almost hot. And it eases the cold aches in my bones and washes off the stink of the dungeon. I stand under the waterfall for a moment longer than necessary, letting it soak through my hair and cleanse me as much as it can. I can feel the grime and dirt peeling off my skin, and I sigh in temporary happiness. Now I just need some soap and proper toothpaste. When I remember we are returning to my world, my happiness soars at the prospect of plumbing and modern conveniences, assuming The Black Lotus has such things.

Fen pulls me past the water until we face a mirror built into the rock. It looks like it's made of some kind of reflective crystal. My image is distorted, looking as if from a surrealist dream, and of course Fen and Dean don't appear in the reflection at all.

Dean grabs my hand and squeezes. "Ready, Princess?"

I nod, and the three of us walk through, with a wolf at our heels.

...

Baron has never traveled with us to my world, so I don't know what to expect when we arrive. But we couldn't leave him behind this time, not when we are Inferno's most wanted. I'm relieved to see he managed the trip safely, and transformed just enough to blend into my world. He's smaller, looking more like a wild dog than an oversized wild wolf.

I smile and pat his head. "You're strong, aren't you boy? You need to teach Yami that trick. When he returns."

Fen looks at me curiously.

"I'm told when his magic is stronger he'll be able to take a form in other worlds, but not yet. Now he turns into jewelry. Really cool jewelry, but still, jewelry." I put a hand on my throat, the ache of missing my little dragon a physical pain.

"And Baron?"

I shrug. "He's been with you for many years. He's already very strong. So are you, I imagine. Once you practice. He should grow even more powerful. He should also be able to disappear around those he does not wish to be seen by. Has he done that yet?"

"Um, I don't know. I didn't ask."

I laugh and Baron barks and walks in a circle before settling between me and Fen, who no longer acts quite as grumpy that his wolf seems as loyal to me as to him. Right now I'm glad of that small comfort. I wish I knew what became of Yami. Surely he's not gone for good? He can't be, not while I yet live.

I look around, taking in the rundown alley we've found ourselves in, noticing the cheap looking strip club across the street. "We're in Portland?" I ask skeptically.

Fen nods.

I don't recognize this part of my home city. But then, this isn't the kind of neighborhood I usually hung out in. I wrap my arms around my wet body, shivering. It's cold here. The sun has already set, and it's recently rained by the looks of the wet cement, though the sky is blessedly dry now.

Dean leads us to a large black door carved out of what looks suspiciously like bone—but what species of bone is anyone's guess. In the center is the design of a lotus made of skulls.

My eyes widen. "Is that—?" My hand lands on a small skull, expecting it to be clay or metal. But I can feel the energy of something dead that was once living pulse through my body, and I yank my hand away, my heart ricocheting in my chest.

Fen takes my hand and tucks it into his, the warmth of him pushing out the chill I feel, not just from being wet and cold, but from that door.

"Best not to ask too many questions about the things you'll see in The Black Lotus," he says. "You won't like the answers."

Dean turns one of the skulls in the lotus, revealing a large eyeball with a black iris. I suck in air through my teeth and squeeze Fen's hand more tightly, and Baron puts himself between me and the door, growling menacingly at the eyeball.

A voice booms from the bones of the door. "Who dares enter?"

Dean answers. "The Princes of Hell request entry. We come in peace with no intent to harm. We need to speak to Sly."

"Which princes?" the voice asks.

"Dean and Fen," Dean says.

The voice is silent a moment before answering. "And someone else. Someone quite powerful."

The princes both look at me, then Fen speaks. "She is under our protection."

"We welcome Lust, as always, and we extend an invitation to the Midnight Star. We do not allow War."

"I am not here to start a war," Fen says, and I can tell his patience is stretched thin. "I'm just here to get help."

"For war." This isn't a question. And I wonder what magic the door holds that it always seems to know the intent of those requesting entry.

"But not for war here. Just information. We are in trouble and injured and need a safe place." Fen pauses, but the door doesn't reply. Dean gives Fen a meaningful look, and Fen sighs. "Please let us in. If Sly can help me, then the Prince of War will owe him a favor."

"Your promised favor has been accepted, and will be called upon in time. Welcome to The Black Lotus," the door says. There is a series of clicks as bolts grind and move within, then the door swings open of its own accord, revealing a dark and smoky hall with walls of blood-red velvet and gold accents.

I sniff the acrid air and wrinkle my nose in disgust. "That's not cigarette smoke. And it's not weed. What is it?"

Fen chuckles darkly. "You don't want to know. Just don't breathe too deeply and you should be fine. The first time I came to The Black Lotus I had a hangover for a week just from breathing the fumes of this hallway. It's coming from the adjacent rooms, but that's not where we're going. The smoke will die down soon."

Dean, on the other hand, smiles and takes a deep breath, holding it in for a moment, before exhaling. "Ah yes, I do so love this place."

Fen shakes his head in silent judgment as we descend into The Black Lotus. There is a power here, a thick magic that wraps itself around me, pressing on my lungs, pushing into my body like an aggressive virus. Dean doesn't seem as affected, but Fen's jaw is clenched, and I can tell he feels it too.

"It's never been like this before," he says.

Dean furrows his brows when he sees our struggle. "What's going on?"

"Well, well, well..." A deep, booming voice says from the shadows before we enter the room. "It looks like someone went and got themselves all magicked up! How delightfully wicked." The body that goes with the voice seems to materialize from smoke and appear before us.

We stand at the entrance of a large ballroom draped in more red velvet and gold. Spread throughout are chairs and sofas of velvet. There's a bar in one corner and tables full of food lining the walls. Some of the food is still moving. On stage, a live band made of creatures straight from a science fiction movie play instruments that look to be part of their body, creating an eerie, organic, fleshy musical sound. I'm about to ask about them, but my eyes continue to roam the room and I realize there are more creatures than I originally realized.

In one far corner a mermaid floats in a huge tank of water. Her blue hair billows around her like an ethereal halo. She has green tinted skin and green and blue scales and is one of the most beautiful things I've ever seen. Her eyes catch mine. They are large blue-green orbs that nearly glow. Then her gaze shifts to Fen and she smiles, revealing shark-like teeth. When he notices her, she winks at him, and he looks away and frowns. I'll have to ask him about that later.

"Hello, Sly," Fen says.

The mysterious man's face curls into a smile. "Hello, Prince of War. You've changed some since we last met, haven't you?" His eyes turn to me before Fen can reply, and his face lights up. "And who do we have here? The epitome of loveliness and innocence, but so much more lurks beneath, does it not? The Midnight Star, returned to her people at last. So the rumors were true." He takes my hand and brings it to his lips, kissing it gently. Fen tenses beside me, but I ignore him, my eyes glued to this strange man.

"I'm Arianna Spero. It's nice to meet you." I'm pleased to note my voice is firm, and not as wavering as I feel under the dark gaze of Sly. "But it's not very nice to use this forceful magic on your guests, is it? That's hardly a proper welcome."

From the corner of my eye I see Fen grin at my cheekiness. But he still looks worried. I know I'm probably playing with fire, but it's getting harder to breathe and the magic he's placed on us is making my bones hurt.

"Forgive me, but one can never be too careful with powerful magic wielders. I assume I have your word that neither of you will use your gifts to harm any of my guests while here?" Sly is still holding my hand. His words are light, but his gaze is heavy.

"You have my word," I say.

"And mine," Fen says. He looks at me. "The penalty for breaking this rule is death," he informs me.

"Oh. Okay then."

Baron growls, but sits between us calmly.

Sly smiles down at the wolf and pulls from somewhere unknown in his silky black robes a raw steak. "Here you go, boy. Enjoy a treat."

He drops the meat at Baron's feet. The wolf sniffs it once, looks up at Fen, then back down, and devours the steak greedily.

Sly looks at me for another moment longer, then uses his index finger to draw a symbol into the air. All at once the tension I felt within me subsides, and I can breathe deeply again. I see Fen suck in oxygen and relax a fraction as well.

"Thank you for removing the spell," I say.

"Anything for a beautiful lady such as yourself," he says, his black eyes holding my gaze with a level of intimacy that is beginning to make me uncomfortable. I get the impression this man can have anyone he wants, whenever he wants.

Fen drapes a protective arm around me, and I roll my eyes, but I don't pull away.

Sly looks at us both and smiles. "There must be some terrific story in this. I will insist on hearing all about it. But first, let us fix this state you're in." He wrinkles his nose delicately in distaste at our appearance. Probably at our smell, too. The waterfall helped slough off some of the dungeon grime, but not all.

Sly pulls a black wand made of bone and crystal out of his robes and studies us a moment. He then snaps his fingers and grins. "I have it now. Stand still, you three. This will only sting a moment."

Before I can object, he waves the wand over us and mutters an incantation of some kind in a dark language dripping with magic. My body burns, and Fen stiffens next to me but doesn't move.

I bite my tongue to keep from crying out as the magic digs into me. There is smoke, light, pain, and then it all disappears, and the three of us are no longer dripping wet. We are dry, but not just dry, we are all wearing new clothes, and my body is fresh and clean—even my teeth. I look down at my dress in admiration. It's long and dark with feathers cresting my shoulders and chest and a silver crystal pendant hanging at my throat. On my head sits a crown of crystal and silver. Fen is dressed in black leggings and tunic, a fur cloak emblazoned with a silver wolf hanging from his shoulders. Dean is draped in black silk, his chest mostly exposed, of course.

Sly claps his hands. "Much better. You are all dressed properly for your stations. Now come, join me for a drink. Tell me what you want, and I'll tell you what it will cost."

Sly leads us through the large room, greeting each guest by name with a smile and a witty quip. He's the epitome of charm and style and everyone either loves him or has a very healthy respect for him, it seems. He looks quite human, save the black eyes that look like pits to hell—well, the dungeon part of hell at any rate.

When we pass the mermaid swimming languidly in the spacious water tank built into the wall, she places a hand on the glass. Behind her, beautiful fish and sea flora decorate the chamber. Her voice echoes through some kind of speaker system. "Fenris Vane. You haven't come to see me in ever so long."

Fen glances at her, frowning. "Hello, Marasphyr."

Sly stops to watch the exchange, a knowing grin playing on his lips.

Marasphyr smiles, her sharp teeth making her beautiful face much more sinister. "Want to come swim with me, Prince? I've missed you."

Fen glances to me, then back to the mermaid. "Afraid my swimming days are over."

Dean chuckles. "I'll come play, sweetheart. I'm a lot more exciting than my brother, I assure you." He winks at the mermaid, who hisses at him.

"Seems I'm not the only one your charms fail to seduce," I tease, a grin tugging at my lips.

"I never fail, Princess. I have the patience of the immortal. I always get what I want eventually."

Fen nudges Sly in the shoulder until the demon continues escorting us to wherever we are going.

"Who's she?" I ask as I increase my pace to catch up. Now that I'm dry and properly—if extravagantly—clothed, I'm starting to feel the pain of my injuries more.

"An old acquaintance," Fen says gruffly.

"Is that what we're calling past dalliances these days?" Dean asks. "I'll keep that in mind."

I have so many questions. The most pressing is actually one of biology. How exactly does one have a 'dalliance' with a woman who's half fish?

Sly stops again and opens the door to a parlor, escorting us in. I table my questions about the mermaid who was clearly more than an acquaintance, and look around. This room is more subdued than the flamboyant hall we were just in. It's got floor-to-ceiling bookshelves of rich mahogany lined with mostly leather-bound books, a desk in one corner, and a couch, two overstuffed chairs and a love seat in the middle with a fireplace crackling to the other side.

I walk to the bookshelf first, admiring the selection of titles, until I come to a section with modern covers of scantily clad men and women. Sly joins me and smiles. "I see you've discovered my greatest treasures," he says.

"Your books?"

He pulls a novel out and admires the image of a woman being embraced by a topless man. "Romances. I just adore them, don't you? The love, the drama, the scandal when propriety comes head to head with good, old fashioned lust. Extraordinary."

I shake my head, half smiling, as I join Fen on the love seat. Dean takes a chair, and Sly sprawls out on the couch after making himself a drink. He offers us one; Fen and I decline. I have the strong suspicion it's best to keep your wits about you when dealing with a demon named Sly Devil.

Dean obviously doesn't have the same reservations, and pours himself a double of something yellow with smoke coming out of it. I don't even want to know.

"Now, pray tell, what can old Sly do for you?"

Fen speaks first, giving Sly a very short version of what's happening on Inferna. "We just need a safe place to stay until we figure out a plan for defeating Levi and taking back Stonehill. And Ari's been injured. She needs medical treatment."

"I'm fine," I say, more out of reflex than truth. In reality, I'm not fine. I'm weak, tired, sore, malnourished, dehydrated and I have open wounds all over my body. The more I think about it, medical treatment might not be a bad idea.

Fen knows this too. He frowns at me and I shrug, relenting to his idea.

Sly crosses his legs and sips his drink, staring at the two of us. "This is just so intriguing. There hasn't been a good war in Inferna for all too long. Your lot has become complacent in your power. That's always dangerous. Every empire falls eventually."

"I don't want their empire to fall," I say carefully. "I want to remake it. I want to create a world that is fair and just to vampires and Fae, where both can live in harmony."

Sly studies me. "That seems quite impossible. But if anyone could do it, I do think it might be you." He stands and holds out a hand to me. "May I escort you to your quarters, Princess?"

Fen frowns as I take Sly's hand, and then I am the one frowning as the world spins around me, then edges away like a view just out of reach. Strong arms catch me, and I find myself cradled against Fen's chest. "She needs a healer," he says gruffly. "Levi fed on her after she'd been left to rot in the dungeon for weeks."

I try to insist I'm fine and can walk, but my mouth isn't working right. My brain is so fuzzy, and everyone is suddenly surrounded by halos of light.

"Why are you all glowing like angels?" I ask through slurred speech.

Sly's eyes widen, and his halo glows brighter. "Follow me."

"Follow the devil!" I say, trying to raise my arm in salute. But I think it comes out more like "swallow the lever" and everyone looks confused.

I give up and sink back into Fen's arms, letting darkness steal me away.

...

A beautiful white wolf stares at me when I wake. As soon as my eyes peel open, Baron licks my face.

"Ew, come on, dude. Not a great way to wake a girl up." I wipe the slobber off and pat his head. "You're a good boy, aren't you? Where's Fen?"

Baron whines and jumps off the bed, then scratches at the door. Before I can rise and open it, Fen walks in. He smiles at me when he sees me awake. "You've been asleep longer than the healer expected. You had us all worried."

He sinks into the bed next to me and I scoot over to be closer to him. "I feel amazing," I say, stretching. The bruises and cuts on my body are mostly healed, and the pain that has lived inside me for weeks is nearly gone. For the first time since the dungeon I almost feel like myself again. "Whatever they used on me, we should take it home with us," I say as I lay my head on his lap.

"I'll see what I can do about that." His hand falls gently to my head and his fingers wind into my hair.

The muscles in his thighs flex as I adjust my position so I can look up at him. "I've missed you. We haven't been alone since before…everything."

He cups my face. "I know. When they dragged you away after the trial, I've never felt more like waging war on everything and everyone there. I killed four guards before they could get me back in my cell."

I suck in a breath. "None of ours, I hope?" I don't know the exact moment I began identifying Fen's realm and people as 'ours' verses 'his.' I don't know when it began to feel like home more than anywhere else in my life. But it happened. I can feel it in me, this shift. He is mine. I am his. Those people are ours to protect.

"No, not ours. Levi's." He growls his brother's name with so much pent-up aggression I could almost feel bad for the Prince of Envy, if he wasn't so deplorable.

I clutch Fen's hand harder in mine, and then pull myself up so that we are facing each other. I search my brain for the perfect thing to say. For the exact right words to make this moment perfect. We are finally together. Finally alone. Finally safe.

And what comes out of my mouth is…"I have to pee."

My bladder is suddenly on fire and about to explode. I don't know how long I've been sleeping, but it could have been a month based on how urgently I now need a bathroom.

Fen laughs at my abrupt change of topics. "Washroom is there," he says, pointing to a door. "Do you need help walking?"

I shake my head no, but then realize I actually have no idea. I crawl out of bed slowly and take small but urgent steps toward the door Fen pointed to. It's dark, but the light of the ever-burning fire gives enough illumination to keep me from falling on my face and pissing myself.

There is nothing more instantly gratifying and pleasurable in the most basic way then relieving yourself when your bladder is close to busting.

When I return to the room, Fen is already standing. I walk to him and wrap my arms around his waist.

He holds me, and we stand there for I don't know how long, just being.

"Stay?" I ask as he eventually pulls away.

He looks down at me, then leans in. I stand on my toes to reach his lips. The kiss starts sweet. Gentle. Then deepens into something that makes my whole body wake up.

It ends too soon. "I can't. If I did, we'd do things."

I grin. "And that's a problem because…?"

"Because you might feel better, but you still need rest. I don't want to hurt you." He leans in and whispers in my ear. "I don't want to have to hold back our first time together."

Heat pools in the center of my body and I crave him so badly I can hardly contain myself. "You don't have to hold back now."

He shakes his head and steps away, putting space between us. "I am not human," he says. "I'm much stronger. I have…more stamina and endurance."

He dances around the words, but I get the picture. "If that's supposed to dissuade me, I'm afraid you've failed miserably."

There is a long pause as we stare at each other. Then he turns and opens my door. "Soon. Very soon." He pauses, his hand on the knob, his eyes locked on mine. "I'm just across the hall if you need me…for anything else."

He leaves, and Baron trails after him with his head hung. I close the door behind them and sink into my bed, suddenly exhausted by the effort of walking and talking and containing all the pent up sexual energy between us.

I can feel sleep stealing me away within moments. I guess Fen was right. I am more tired than I thought.

...

When the door creaks open, I awaken, my body instantly on alert. He came back. My heart beats wildly in anticipation of what is about to happen.

I roll over, about to say something to him, when a knife lands in my pillow where my head just was.

I scream.

My attacker backhands me and tries again with the knife, but I knee him in the groin and use my body to flip him off me. His sharp blade grazes my cheek, leaving a crimson stain behind, but I barely feel it. My body is pumped with adrenaline and I am ready to fight. I reach for my sword under my bed and stand to face the man in black just as my door slams open.

Fen is there, wearing only pants, his eyes wild. He raises his sword and attacks the man.

They fight. Blades clash.

The attacker's knife is wicked sharp, and it lands a few blows against Fen. Each time the blade hits his skin I feel the pain inside me.

But it's all over fast. Fen waits until the moment is right and then raises his sword and swoops it down, cutting off the attacker's hand. It falls limply to the floor along with the knife.

The man screams as he stares at the stump left at the end of his arm.

Lights turn on.

Sly appears as if from smoke, wrapped in a black silk robe. "What the devil is going on in here?" he asks.

Fen, whose sword is dripping with blood, points to the attacker. "He tried to kill Ari."

Sly turns to the man. "Is this true? Have you defiled the sanctity of my haven?"

The man shakes his head in denial. "He attacked me. I'm the one missing a hand."

Sly stares at the man—who is still masked—long and hard, then laughs. "We'll just have to see who's telling the truth, won't we?" He pulls out his wand and speaks words in a strange language.

There is a booming sound and the air rips open around us, revealing a new scene. It is the past, the recent past. It is me, in bed. Everything plays out as it happened, only I'm seeing it from an omniscient point of view.

The attacker shakes from fear, or maybe blood loss. Sly stalks over to him and pulls off his mask. He's a ruddy man with a bulbous nose and a mean mouth. No one I recognize. "Who sent you?"

"The Prince of Envy," he says without hesitation. He is clearly scared out of his mind. What kind of reputation does Sly have, I wonder? I fear I'm about to find out.

"Toward what end?" Sly asks.

"To kill her. Then capture him," he says, pointing to me then Fen.

"You know the penalty for harming anyone under my protection at The Black Lotus?"

The man lowers his head.

"They never learn," Sly says as he waves his wand.

Nothing happens for a moment, and the man looks almost relieved despite missing his hand.

But then...

Oh God.

I've never seen anything so awful.

The man screams again, and this time it's a gut-wrenching sound that tears out of his throat. His body begins to convulse, as his skin peels off bones and muscles essentially turning him inside out.

It seems an eternity before the man finally lays silent in a pool of his own insides.

I'm still standing in stunned shock as blood spreads across the hardwood floors, staining my bare feet red.

Sly puts his wand away and sighs. "I'll have another room prepared for you. Please accept my apologies. It's rare for anyone to risk my ire by breaking the rules, but it does happen on occasion. The Prince of Envy must be truly desperate."

"He doesn't like me very much," I say.

"Sounds like he likes you too much, but realizes he will never have you," Sly says.

"No, he covets me. There's a difference."

Sly nods. "You've spoken truly, Princess." Sly turns to Fen. "There will be no punishments levied against you since you were defending yourself and another guest."

Fen nods.

Then collapses to the floor unconscious.

4

TAVIAN GRAY
Kayla Windhelm

"You cannot make too many enemies and still rule."
—Kayla

The messenger came early that morning, before our raiding party had risen from slumber, before we'd broken camp and headed out. It was a short note, sent from Levi—excuse me, *Prince Levi*—demanding we return. Saying we were needed for war. Saying Fen and Ari were scheduled to be executed—I mentally tick off the days, and my heart stops. Today. They are scheduled for execution at sunrise, today.

I look up into a sky just starting to lighten, casting long purple shadows into the twilight. I frown and chew a lip in frustration. There's no way I'll make it back in time. I'm at least two day's ride from Stonehill, and that's if I don't care if my steed survives or not.

I'm already too late. But I have to do something. I crumble the letter in my fist and look around for Salzar, snow crunching beneath my fur boots. He's not in his tent. I head to the rear of our party and find the section I know he'll be in.

Here, there are many awake. They belong to the night in their scantily clad costumes as they use all their charms to lure the desperate into their arms. I disturb a few outraged "couples" before I find him. He's laying there with his eyes closed as a young woman...services him.

I pull the girl off of him and toss the crumbled letter at his naked lap. "We've got to go back. Now. Ready the troops."

"It's the middle of the bloody night," he screams, spittle flying from his mouth as he scrambles for something to cover himself. "I'll do no such thing. Now get back to your tent, Mistress Kayla Windhelm. And remember your place. You're not a princess here."

"I was never a princess," I hiss. "And when I outrank you, it will not be because of my birth. It will be because I'm not a lecherous asshole with zero ability to lead a crowd of vampires to blood, let alone a troop to raid villages of Fae. This is dangerous work. Deadly. And they need someone who will protect them. Not someone like you. We leave tonight, with or without you."

I storm out, my heart pounding frantically in my chest. I can taste the rage on my lips, like it's a poison soaking through me. For the last fortnight I have suffered the abuse of this vile man in an effort to keep our troop undivided and effective. But I am done placating that ass.

What I do next can be considered treachery, turning on my superior. But I am the one following an order from a prince of hell, and Salzar is not.

The company bell stands in the middle of the sleeping quarters, and it rings throughout the makeshift village. Tired bodies pitch out of their tents to see what the emergency is.

I summarize quickly, then give my commands. "We leave now. Pack only what is necessary to make it to Stonehill safely. Leave everything else. We have no time."

Not all follow. Some are still more loyal to greed and rage than fairness and justice. But many—most—do. I release a long held breath. For all I knew, every soldier could have decided to stay with Salzar, decided to continue raiding village after village. It was easy work. Full of reward. I had gone on two raids myself, and though at first I was driven with thoughts of vengeance for Daison, they soon turned to thoughts of shame. These weren't soldiers we were fighting, but innocent men, women and children who could barely hold a sword.

I argued with Salzar to turn our attention to military strongholds. He said we didn't have a force big enough. I think he grew too fond of the slaughter and spoils.

But now, with an official message from a prince, I have most of the troops traveling back with me. Hopefully, my good luck continues. By the Spirits, I'm going to need it before this is all said and done.

I'm faster than most, and I'm ready with bedroll and minimal provisions in hand, mounted and wearing light armor. I set the pace for the day's march, and we make good progress come early night. But it's not enough. So I push us more.

I push past the recommendations of my advisors.

I push past my own whispered reservations.

I push past what is safe, as night falls in darkness. As a new moon keeps us shadowed. As we are blocked by a lake that we must cross.

"We must trail back and go around," my advisors say. "It's the only way. The Druids will punish us if we enter the water."

The map lies between us on the rough earth, firelight casting shadows over the parchment. I lay a rock on the narrowest part of the river. "We cross there. We shave off days of travel." I look at each of them pointedly. Daring them to contradict me. To challenge me. To tell me we should abandon my brother and friend to a false hanging.

None do.

But I alone bear the burden.

Of the thing that happens.

When we cross.

When the wind lashes at us, and the waters rage in violent waves. I see a horse pulled under before me.

And then I follow.

Drowning. Feeling the water fill my lungs. It burns. It incites the most animalistic instincts we have. That of survival. *Breathe.* I must breathe.

I am dying.

They are dying.

We are all dying.

The water turns colder. The pain turns numb. It all turns numb. My mind flicks in and out.

I am a breath away from breathlessness.

From the great beyond.

From nothing.

From death.

I muster a last bit of fight. I lift my arm and pound against the ice freezing between me and air. Me and sky.

Pain shoots through my wrist. The ice doesn't move. It is unbreakable. It surrounds me.

Warmth.

Like a small ball of fire at the pit of my stomach. But it spreads, reaches out for my extremities, filling me with delicious heat. I look up, into the ice, and I lift my hands. They glow a silver light, and they send their heat outwards—breaking through the ice and bringing me to air.

Breathe.

In. Out.

...

Breathe!

Choking.

Gagging.

Lungs burn. Throat burns.

Someone is holding my head. A voice, deep and strong, is telling me to breathe. To live. To stay.

I vomit all the water that ever was out of my mouth.

And then I can breathe. And his face is over mine, a wry smile on his lips. His green eyes crinkled in humor. "Good girl, Princess. Can't have you dying on me yet."

...

I don't know how much time has passed, but I awaken in a dark space. My body shudders, ice still penetrating my nerves, despite the fire that blazes beside me.

...

There is an animal here with me. But I don't feel scared. He is big. Fierce. A white tiger with black stripes. I think he even purrs.

...

The tiger is gone and the man with the secret eyes is back. He always smiles when I open my eyes, and his voice always soothes me. Warm. Caressing. Safe.

...

"Where the hell am I?" I push myself up from the hard ground and nearly knock myself silly on a stone protruding from the wall of a cave.

I could swear I saw the tiger, but when I blink it is the man, sitting with a stick beside the fire, watching over me. "Who are you?" I demand, trying not to get too lost in his green eyes. Dear gods those eyes. Where do you even get eyes like that? Is it some sort of spell? Where can I learn it?

Doesn't matter. I need answers. I need to find my troop. If anyone else survived.

When I sit up, the furs fall off me, exposing my nudity.

The man with the eyes does not avert his gaze.

I glare at him, but don't attempt to cover up. "Where are my clothes?" I ask.

He points his head to the side of the cave where my clothes are strung up on cords to dry near the fire. He stands, though he can't stand all the way up—he's too tall and would knock his head—and walks over to the clothes, testing them before pulling them off the line. "They aren't fully dry, but they're better than nothing," he says, his voice deep and smooth. "For now."

He tosses them to me and turns around while I dress. I hate putting on damp clothes, but I have no choice at the moment, so I finish as quickly as possible.

"You can turn around now," I say. "Besides, I assume you're the one who undressed me, since we're the only two people here."

He faces me again and nods. "You would have frozen in your clothes. I saved your life."

I blink, and remember the feeling of drowning. Of freezing. Of breaking through the ice. Then, nothing.

I believe him. "Thank you. I didn't want to die just yet."

"Better places to be?" he asks.

"As a matter of fact, yes." I glare at him. "I must return to Stonehill as quickly as possible. It's life or death. And I must find my people. The troop I was traveling with. Surely I can't be the only one to survive?"

He's silent, his gaze unwavering.

"I'm the only one who survived?"

He nods once. "I'm sorry. You were the only one left to save by the time I arrived."

I look around as I pull on my cloak. "I must leave. Now. Where's my sword?"

The man pulls my sword out of the scabbard hanging from his hip and spins it in his hand. "It's a beauty. True artistry and craft went into the making of this."

I cross my arms over my chest. "I know. I'm the one who made it."

He raises an eyebrow. "Impressive. I'd heard rumors the bastard daughter of the King had a knack for metal work. I didn't put much stock in it."

My laugh comes out like a croak. "You really have elevated ideas of who I am. I'm nothing. A Shade like the rest."

That's when I take a closer look at my savior. At the white fur cloak spilling down his back. At his ears. "You're Fae."

He bows. "At your service, Princess."

"Stop calling me that. I'm no more a princess than you."

"Surely someone misses you?"

"The only one who'd miss me if I was gone is about to be hanged, if he hasn't been already."

Something changes in the man's face. "Would this by chance be one of the princes?"

"Yes. Fen, Prince of War. My brother."

"And he's dead?"

"He's scheduled for execution. Which is why I need to go. Now." I hold out my hand for my sword, but he doesn't move to hand it over.

"Here's my dilemma, Princess. You're my ticket out of this shit hole. I was going to take you to the Seven Realms and sell you back to your family for a nice profit. But if what you're saying is true, then it's not the vampires I need to be negotiating with."

"What are you talking about?"

The kindness on his face vanishes. "I need money. You're that money. If your family won't pay for your return, I know one other who will. A certain newly awakened Water Druid who, rumor has it, would pay a hefty ransom to have you in her dungeon."

Metsi. "She's psychotic. You can't take me to her."

"I can, and I will. Now get up. We leave shortly." He sheathes my sword and begins rolling up the bedding I was laying on.

"Who do you think you are, telling me what to do?"

"I'm the man with the weapons. The man with the horse. And the man with the provisions. How long do you think you'll survive the Outlands by yourself with nothing but your clothing...if I let you keep even that?"

"And if I refuse?"

He grins, and I want to punch him. "You're coming with me, one way or another. You can ride on your own, or I can tie you up and strap you to my horse. Makes no difference to me, but might make a big difference to you after a few hours. You decide."

With that he strides out of the cave with all our supplies. I look around, but all that's left to do is put out the fire. I'm fuming when I get outside, but he's got his horse packed and ready to go. He's just waiting for me. "Which option will the vampire princess choose?"

I hiss at him with fangs revealed, something I never do. "Better sleep with one eye open, jackass. I hear your kind are particularly tasty."

He laughs and throws a leg over his horse, then holds out a hand for me. I ignore it and mount by myself. This isn't a surrender, I tell myself. It's me buying myself time to figure out a plan. Being tied up won't help me.

But when he chuckles again, I can't resist the urge to smack the back of his head. "Shut it."

At our first rest stop, I'm no closer to answers than I was three hours ago. He hands me bread and dried meat and I devour the food greedily. As I sip on the water he gives me, I look at him again. He's a handsome man, and he knows it. Tall, skin the color of dark honey, and those eyes. His hair is dark and disheveled and he has a shadow of dark stubble across his jaw. "What's your name?" I ask.

"Tavian. Tavian Gray," he says, his eyes teasing me about something. "And of course, I already know yours, Kayla Windhelm. Was Windhelm a name chosen at random, or did it belong to your mother?"

"Yes," I say curtly, not wishing to discuss my mother or myself at all.

"Yes it was random, or yes it was your mother's?"

I sigh. "Yes it was my mother's. Now, can we not talk please?"

He raises an eyebrow. "Touched on a sensitive subject, have I?"

I stand, dusting off my pants. "Isn't it time to get going? We only have a few more hours until dusk."

He shrugs and stands. "If you say so, Princess."

"My name's not Princess," I hiss at his back as we both mount the horse once again.

He just laughs.

Infuriating man.

It's a long ride to wherever he's taking me. We travel through woods, avoiding roads and open areas. He's hiding from someone, or being extra cautious. But we're in the Outlands. He's Fae. What's he got to hide from? My questions yield nothing but more questions from him.

"Do you feel more loyalty to the Fae or vampire?" he asks.

"Neither. I'm loyal to myself and those I love." Included amongst that list is a vampire, a Shade and a human girl, though I don't tell him that.

"Why do you not support your own people more?" he asks.

"I assume you're talking about Fae? But how are they any more my people than the vampire? I wasn't turned. I was born this way. And while I might not have much position in the vampire world, at least I'm not outright shunned like I have been from those who are Fae. Your race is elitist and unwelcoming to anyone not pure blood," I say. "Perhaps you should be asking why my people aren't more supportive of me."

Tavian clicks his tongue and his horse responds, taking a left toward the sound of running water. "It is true, our people have not always been the most...tolerant, shall we say? But it seems as if that might be changing, if the new Midnight Star is any indication."

"There's a new Midnight Star?" That's news to me. I know the stories, more or less. That the Midnight Star is one born of Royal Fae blood, and it's their magic that awakens the Druids and the magic of the Fae. But the Fae haven't had a Midnight Star since the Unraveling, when the last of the Royal Fae were killed and all the Druids disappeared. I was born well after that time, so it's all just stories to me.

Tavian nods and turns his body to look at me. "I'm surprised you don't know. The story of the half-Fae Princess has spread through my people like wild-fire. And it was your people who brought her here. The girl from the other world, half human, half Fae, here to unite the world and bring the magic back to our people. Legends already abound about her."

I nearly fall off the horse at his words. I'm shaking and my thoughts form in pieces. He stops the horse and helps me dismount. "Are you ill?" he asks.

"This Midnight Star? What is her name?" I ask.

"Arianna. I think that was her name, yes." He hands me a bladder full of water and I drink deeply as he talks. "She was rumored to be with the vampires, but the Fae made a strong case for her ascension. She's the daughter of the last known Fae Prince, who was exiled to the human world many suns ago. She is a new hope for my people, or so they say. I have little care for Fae politics."

I look up at him, my eyes burning. "She's likely already dead," I say. "That's who I was trying to save when you captured me." My voice is bitter. Angry. "She was executed this morning in Stonehill, at least according to the letter I received." And now I know why. Levi, that bastard, must have found out what she was and had her killed. I will destroy him when I find him, that I vow. But why Fen? Why was he killed too? He probably did something stupid in defense of her. Stupid man.

I will my tears away and stare at the other stupid man in front of me. "Looks like your people have lost your hope," I say, praying my words act as a dagger in his gut.

But he doesn't look upset. He looks mildly bemused, which just pisses me off more. "She's not dead," he says.

"How would you know?" It's a hope my heart still clings to, but I don't trust my captor.

"Her magic yet lives. Those of us connected deeply to ourselves can feel the awakening. Midnight Star is alive. So your friend must be as well. I would know if she had died."

Our break is short lived, and he has me back on the horse and clipping along at a fast pace, presumably to make up the time lost on my near breakdown. "Truly?" I ask him again, for the fifth time.

"Truly," he says. "I may be a vampire-killing, princess-capturing bastard, but I am no liar."

I choke out a half laugh at his words. "At least you have standards," I say sarcastically.

But he nods gravely. "A man's word should be trustworthy. For when we are stripped of all that made us what we were, we have only our word left." He turns again to look at me. "I promise you this, Princess...I will sell you to whoever will give me the best price. I'm not claiming to be a good man. But I'm no monster. I will protect you on this journey. I will not harm you or let harm come to you. And I will not lie to you."

"I could almost like you," I say, "if you'd just drop the part where you sell me to the highest bidder like a slave."

He turns around abruptly. "War breeds a necessary kind of evil in all it touches. It turns even good men into raiders, killers, thieves."

His words sound much like my thoughts of late, and I look down, memories of burning villages and crying children filling me with shame and sorrow.

We travel a few more hours in silence before stopping for the night. My feelings are spilling all over each other—spiraling into a cacophony of fear and hope. If Tavian is right and Ari is still alive, does that mean Fen yet lives? Did they escape? That's the only thing I can figure. Levi wouldn't have altered their sentence once he'd taken a public stance. Which means there might still be time. To help them. Save them. To do something.

I have to get back to Stonehill, and right now we're going in the wrong direction. I do my part to help make camp, which includes collecting dry wood for the fire. I could run now, but I would have no supplies. So I plan.

Later, as we sit around the fire, I pass Tavian his dinner, a stew made from fresh meat he caught cooked with vegetables I foraged.

And then I wait.

It takes longer than it should.

Perhaps I underestimated the dose. Tavian is a big man, all muscle and brawn. But eventually he begins to slur his words and slant to one side, unable to sit up straight. I move to him and help him into a sleeping position. Then, once he's fully unconscious—thanks to some herbs I slipped into his meal—I tie up his feet and hands.

Part of me hates leaving him here this way. Drugged. Tied up. Without a horse, since I will take his to get back to Stonehill.

But I shrug off my guilt. He's Fae. He'll find help. And he tried to kidnap me and sell me to my enemies. Surely he doesn't deserve my sympathy.

Still. He saved my life. Nursed me back to health. And he has treated me kindly. For that, I leave him some food, the bed roll, and his sword. He'll be able to work out of the knots eventually, leaving me enough time to escape.

I stoke the fire and add wood to it, to keep night critters from getting to him. As I do, my hand plunges too close to the fire, and I pull back, expecting the bite of a burn, but instead, I feel nothing. I see nothing. I turn my hand back and forth, waiting for the tell-tale redness and swelling to show, but it doesn't. As a blacksmith I've had my share of burns, and I know this should have hurt. I wave my hand through the fire again.

When the fire does not react to my skin, I plunge my hand deeper into the flames, then pull it out. I'm covered in sweat, but not from the heat. My hand is perfect. Not a mark on it.

I don't know what this means, but I don't have time to dwell on it now. Instead, I retrieve my sword, pack some supplies, and mount the horse. I've lost too much time already. I must be off before the drugs run through Tavian's system and he awakens.

It's slow traveling in the pitch of night, despite one of the moons being near full. The coverage of trees keeps everything cloaked in heavy darkness, and I have to walk my steed slowly to avoid breaking his leg.

So I hear it right away.

The crunch of twigs in the distance.

The sound of a large body moving through tree and brush.

The heavy breathing of an animal far larger than me.

And then there is a great roar, and the horse whinnies and bucks, throwing me to the ground as it darts off into the night.

"Blast it all to hell!" I whisper through my shaking teeth as I try to right myself. There's another roar. I pull out my sword and squint, trying to see something other than the silhouette of trees in the darkness.

It comes closer, and it's huge.

By the time I see it, it's too late. A giant claw flashes toward me, swiping at my head. I duck just in time, and swing my sword blindly, hoping to hit something critical.

I think I just hit a tree.

Cursing, I scramble up and put my back against the largest trunk near me. It's the best cover I can find. Raising my sword, I wait for the next attack.

The beast is fast, pushing itself through bramble and bush without concern. Its girth shakes the ground beneath my feet. It throws itself toward me, a beast made of teeth and fur and muscle and claws. A black bear of the Outlands.

My sword nips at the bear's shoulder, but doesn't slow it down.

Then something else growls in the night.

And the beast I'm fighting shrieks in pain as some-thing attacks it.

I scurry away and keep my eye on the bear as I walk backward toward safety.

A white tiger with black stripes fights the bear.

The tiger is big, but nothing compared to its foe. But it's fast. And deadly.

They fight viciously, and I know I should run, but I'm frozen in place, unsure of what to do. This tiger is familiar. I remember dreaming about it when I was unconscious. But it was only a dream, wasn't it?

I scramble to find any supplies that might have fallen off of the horse, but find nothing. At least I kept my sword on me. I continue backing away from the two beasts, sword still up, when the tiger swings wide, exposing its chest while trying to get the kill.

The bear doesn't hold back, and bites into the tiger's shoulder. The white beast groans in agony, but doesn't falter. It claws through the bear's throat.

They both crash to the ground, and suddenly the forest is silent. The bear remains still, but the tiger makes a pained noise and tries to stand. It falls again, and then scoots itself away from the bear and toward me, until it can no longer move.

It is so still.

I wait, holding my breath, to see if it will get up.

It doesn't.

Instead, the tiger slowly turns into a naked man.

It turns into Tavian Gray.

5

SLY DEVIL

"Things aren't always black and white. Not in your world, and certainly not in mine."

—Asher

"What the ever-loving Hades?" Sly says with exasperation as I run to Fen.

I feel his pulse, which is still strong. There's a wound in his side that doesn't look fresh, but reopened and is bleeding heavily. "He was tortured before coming here. He should have had a healer."

Sly shrugs. "That man has to be unconscious for my healers to get at him."

I raise an eyebrow. "So now would be the perfect time to summon one, don't you think?"

Dean nudges open my door, wearing nothing but a very skimpy pair of underwear that leaves little to the imagination. "What's all the noise?"

He notices Fen unconscious and the pile of man-goo on my floor and shakes his head. "I miss all the fun. I assume he's still alive?" He asks, looking at Fen.

"Yes, help me get him to bed."

Dean grins like the fool he is. "I thought you'd never ask. I wasn't kidding about that threesome."

"My no wasn't a joke either," I say pointedly.

Sly glances at each of us, then sighs. "I'm back to my slumber, kittens. Healers will be here shortly. Let's meet in my office at some later point to be determined by my level of awakeness."

The demon turns with a swish of his black gown and saunters out of the room as if he had no care in the world. I stare at the man-goo splattered across the floor, bile rising in my throat. Dean sighs dramatically but then lifts Fen in his arms as if the Prince of War is weightless.

Baron whines and stays at Dean's heals, nipping at him from time to time.

"Back off dog, or I might drop your master," Dean says.

Baron growls and I nudge Dean. "Don't rile him. His teeth are sharper than yours."

Dean winks at me. "You've never felt the bite of my teeth, Princess. But we can change all that. I promise I'm not a savage like Levi. You would enjoy it."

Levi wasn't the first to try to forcibly feed on me, and the idea does not elicit happy thoughts. I glare at

Dean as I open the door to Fen's room, but the Prince of Lust ignores me. He's laying Fen on the bed when a very short woman with tiny horns on her head hobbles in. She must be three feet at most, and mostly human-like, other than the horns and blue skin.

"I'm Cavery, the Black Lotus healer." Her voice is surprisingly high pitched and airy...not what I was expecting based on her looks. "Move over, let me tend to my patient."

Dean and I both step back as Cavery holds her hands over Fen and closes her eyes. Her hands begin to glow blue, and waves of light flow over him. She hums and creates intonations from her vocal chords not possible for humans.

Her song seems to mold the light, transforming it into different colors and shapes until it settles into Fen's body. His skin heals quickly, closing up the wound and even whisking away the blood. But still he sleeps.

"Why isn't he waking?" I ask, when she drops her hands to her side.

"The magic is still healing his innards. He needs rest, and the only way someone like him will rest is if he's unconscious," Cavery says.

"So you're keeping him asleep deliberately?" I ask.

She nods. "For now. Someone stay with him. He should wake naturally when he's healed enough, but even then, try to keep him from pushing himself too hard."

Dean laughs. "Good luck with that, Ari."

"Me? You could help, you know. He is your brother," I remind him.

"Yes, but he's much more susceptible to your charms, than mine," Dean says.

The healer leaves, and Dean follows her out the door, then stops before closing it behind him. "If you get too lonely, Princess, I'm just down the hall."

I roll my eyes. "Good night, Dean."

He winks at me, a mischievous smile on his lips. "Good night, Princess."

As the door closes behind Dean, I stare down at the man I love. He's pale, still, almost lifeless, but if I watch carefully I can see a gentle rising and falling of his chest. He's still alive. Healing, presumably. Safe, for now. I familiarize myself with his room, which is similar to mine, and use a remarkably modern bathroom to wash the grime and man-goo off me. Then I rummage through Fen's clothes until I find one of his shirts to sleep in. I don't want to go back into my room just yet. Not with the mess still on the floor.

Baron is asleep at Fen's feet when I crawl into the bed and scoot close to the unconscious Prince of War. He smells of pine and wood. His body is warm, but not hot. I place a hand gently on his abdomen and close my eyes. I'm not sure what I'm doing, but I open myself up to my magic, the way Varis taught me.

There, just at the edges of my grasp I can feel a trickle of power, but I can't reach it. Why can some use their magic here, but I can't? There is so much I still don't know. I need to find a way to be stronger, better. I need to find a way to help retake Stonehill and save everyone from Levi's evil rule. I need to find a way to end this war and bring peace to both the vampires and Fae.

...

Fen is already up and dressed when I wake the next morning. "You should be resting," I mumble, trying to shed the cobwebs from my morning brain.

"I've rested plenty," he grunts as he shrugs on his cloak. The thick brown fur seems too hot for indoors, and I wonder if he's wears it more out of habit than necessity.

"You were badly injured last night," I say, sitting up. "We aren't safe here."

Fen signs, then sits down next to me and lays a hand over mine. "It was just a scratch, and this is the safest place we'll find."

We lock eyes, and for a moment I believe him, for a moment I feel safe.

Then the bedroom door creaks open, revealing a fully clothed Dean on the other side. "Good morning, Princess...brother. Ready for another exciting day of guess who's here to kill us?"

"Too soon for jokes," I say, remembering the man-goo from last night. "Speaking of, I need a change of clothes. Last night's are ruined."

"Clothes are overrated," Dean says with a smirk. "I can think of a better look for you."

Fen walks over to the door and kicks it closed. "Go away, Dean. We'll be out soon."

"Such unkindness," Dean says through the thick wood. "And here I was, just coming to tell you Sly is ready to see us."

There is silence for a moment, then the sound of heavy boots stalking away. Fen tosses me some clothes from his dresser. "These should cover you well enough for now. Undoubtedly Sly will just transform them to something he prefers regardless."

"He likes dressing his guests, I take it?" I ask, pulling on oversized pants and using a leather belt to keep them up.

"It's one of the necessary evils of coming to The Black Lotus," Fen says with a frown.

I laugh. "There are worse things than nice clothing," I remind him as we leave the room and head to Sly's office.

Fen side-eyes me. "I'd rather deal with the worse things," he says.

The hallways are long, wide, and elaborately decorated with art and artifacts that look foreign to our world: A carving of a creature that looks half-snake, half-bird. A statue of a stumpy beast resembling both a turtle and a mouse. Not like anything I've seen in Inferna or Avakiri. "Where is all this stuff from?" I ask.

"Different worlds, different realms," Fen says. "Sly's a bit of a collector. It's considered courtesy when staying as a guest to bring something from your world to gift him with."

"Did we bring something?" I ask.

"Not this time, but we've given him many artifacts from Inferna."

Sly and Dean are sitting in front of a fire sipping drinks when we arrive. Sly stands, arms outstretched, greeting us as if we haven't seen one another for months, rather than hours. "So good to see you both well and refreshed, if so poorly dressed." He pulls out his wand and without another word, spells us into new clothes.

Both of us now wear the same regal costumes he put us in last night. "I'm surprised," I say. "I didn't think you were the type to wear an outfit twice in a row."

He laughs. "You know me well, already, my lovely kitten. But you had so little time in this beautiful ensemble,

it seems only fitting." He hands us each a drink and ges-
tures to platters of food on the table. "Help yourself to
anything you fancy. I apologize for the unpleasantness
of last night." His smile slips and his eyes glow red for
a moment. "The Prince of Envy has some explaining to
do," he says with a fair bit of menace.

Fen and I sit, with Baron at our feet. I notice Fen's
glass contains a dark red liquid that I'm guessing isn't
wine. I sniff at my glass, but it seems to be ordinary
orange juice. I sip it cautiously, just to make sure.

"The Prince of Envy is my problem to deal with,"
Fen says. "He won't live long enough to explain anything to you, Sly."

I purse my lips and as I take another drink. I don't
disagree with Fen, but I hate that after so many years of
immortal life, their family is falling apart and going to
war because of me.

"Be that as it may, I've taken the liberty of increas-
ing security here," Sly says. "No one gets in without my
permission."

"So we're safe?" I ask.

Sly nods.

But Fen doesn't look convinced. "There are always
ways to get to someone," he says.

"That is true," Sly says. "I can only control The
Black Lotus. Are you vulnerable in other ways?" he
asks, addressing me.

"What do you mean?"

"Is there anyone else Levi can use to get to you?"

Blood drains from my face as his meaning settles into me. "My mother," I whisper. "He could go after my mother's body at the hospital."

Fen shakes his head. "Won't happen. The contract protects her. Levi can't break the contract."

I let out a deep breath. "Are you sure?"

Fen and Dean both nod.

"Okay then. That's good. But...what about my friends? Es and Pete?"

Sly shrugs as he pulls out a cigar from his black silk robes and lights it. "In his position, I would target them."

The smell of pine and smoke fill the room as Sly puffs on his cigar. It's a musky scent, but not unpleasant.

"I need to warn them."

Dean shakes his head. "And what good would that do? Your friends know how to fight a Prince of Hell?"

My hand tightens around my drink, my brain scrambling for ideas. "Can they come here? For protection?"

"No," Fen says.

"Of course," Sly says, cutting him off with a smile and a flourish of his hand. "For a price."

Fen looks at me. "Don't bring them here. It's not worth it. Sly always takes more than he gives."

Sly clutches at his chest. "Please...you wound me."

I ignore him and turn to Fen. "Can you promise me they will be safe if I don't?" I ask.

I see him struggling to answer, because I know what he will say if he's being honest, and he knows what I will do with that answer. Finally, he speaks. "No."

"Then I have no choice." I look at Sly. "I will owe you a favor, if you keep my friends safe until the threat against me is eliminated."

Sly claps his hands and grins from ear to ear. "Wonderful. You must summon them at once then."

I nod. "Great. How? Do you have some kind of portal or spell I can use?"

"Oh darling! We aren't in your prince's Middle-earth anymore," he says, reaching into one of the many hidden compartments of his robes. "We have cell phones here."

I look down at the shiny silver device he hands me, enjoying the smooth polish of glass and metal. It seems like so long ago that this was a daily part of my life. I turn it on and type in Es's number first. When she answers, all I hear is the sound of shouting.

"You best be getting your ass out of here if you know what's good for you," Es yells in her fake southern accent to someone in the background.

A man lets out a string of expletives, and I hear glass shattering. Someone calls for a broom.

"Es? Hello?" Did she even mean to answer or have I been butt-answered? Is butt-answering a thing? I imagine it must be. The opposite of butt-dialed.

"Hello, one moment. I'll be right with you," she says into the phone, before she continues shouting at whoever crossed her.

She's on speaker, and all the guys in the room listen to the exchange with a range of facial expressions. Sly is entertained. Fen bemused. Dean amused.

"Thank you for holding," Es says. "Some twat-weasel thought he could stiff us the cost of his meal and harass the staff, all in one glorious hour. He's now on the Wall of Shame. Who's this?"

"Es, it's Ari. I'm in Portland—"

"Oh my god, oh my god, oh my god!" Her pitch rises in decibels that threaten to blow my eardrums. "Ari. Where are you? How are you? Where have you been? I've been so worried about you. You've been gone longer than normal."

That's true, I realize. My time in the dungeon was extensive. It felt like a lifetime. "I have a lot to tell you, but first I need you and Pete to pack a bag and let your jobs know you had an emergency come up. I'm sending a car for you."

There's a pause, where all I hear is her breathing. Finally she speaks. "Ari, what the hell is going on?"

"I'll tell you everything when you get here. I just need you to trust me. I'm in danger, and you might be too. Because of me."

"Everything? You'll tell me every goddamn thing? No secrets? No lies? No half truths or evasions like last time?"

I suck in a breath, make eye contact with Fen, who nods, and answer her. "Yes. Everything. Just be ready."

Sly has already sent a driver to the address I gave him when I hang up the phone and hand it back to him.

"Thank you, Sly. I appreciate this."

"You're more than welcome. I look forward to discovering what kind of favor I can extract from one as talented and lovely as you," Sly says.

Fen growls under his breath, and for a moment I wonder what I've gotten myself into, but I can't worry about that now. The most important thing is that my friends will be safe.

"They should be here within the hour," Sly says. "Do they know about...them?" he asks, with a raised eyebrow at the princes.

"In a manner of speaking," I say. "But I'll need to explain a few things." Like...how I signed a demon contract and live with vampires and am half Fae and have to pick one of the princes to marry...and how they are now in danger from a vampire prince because of me. Yes, there will be a lot of explaining to do.

"In the meantime, let us get to the crux of the matter, shall we?" Sly asks, looking at each of us. "As much as I adore your visits, you are making the other guests nervous."

Fen stands and pours himself a drink. "Are you kicking us out, Sly?"

Sly holds a hand to his chest in mock shock. "I would never dream of it, but we must discuss how to fix your situation at home. Sooner rather than later."

I remember my fight with Oren. How I wasn't fully myself. Somehow, my powers had taken over, and I had defeated an ancient Druid. "If I get more training, if I learn to control the powers within me, that could give us an advantage in a fight against Levi," I say.

Fen frowns at me. "This isn't your fight."

"Are you serious right now?" I ask him. "Of course it's my fight. It might be more my fight than anyone else's, all things considered. I may not have asked for it, or known what I was getting into when I signed that contract, but the fact is, my blood woke up powers in your world that are leading to a war, and I can help."

"She's not wrong, brother," Dean says. "We need her."

Sly stands and walks to the door. "You do need her, that is true. And I have someone else you'll need." He opens the door to a familiar face.

I jump up and run to the man standing there and throw my arms around him. "Varis, what are you doing here?"

The Druid pats my back awkwardly and then lets me go. He whispers into my ear. "I had to flee Avakiri after taking a stand against Oren." Then he speaks louder to the rest of the room. "Most of the free Fae have rallied behind Metsi. I am no longer welcome amongst my kind."

Dean stands and reaches for a sword that's not there. "You're not welcome amongst our kind either."

"Stop it," I tell him, and I glare at Fen before he can argue. "Varis is my friend. He's the Air Druid. He was kind to me, and he helped us in the last battle. We need him." I turn back to Varis, and Baron approaches the Druid and pushes his head against him. Wow. Didn't expect that to happen. By the look on everyone's faces, they didn't either.

Varis pets the wolf gently as Fen watches with a frown.

"Are you all right?" I ask the Duird. "Have you healed?"

He smiles. "Yes. I'm well." He glances over at Fen and then back at me. "I see things have changed since I last saw you."

"Yes, it appears they have. Varis, this is Fen, Prince of War...and the Earth Druid, as it happens." I reach for

Fen's hand and pull him over. "Fen, this is my teacher, Varis."

Dean frowns and stands as if ready to break into fight at any moment. "I know who Varis is. He's one of them. He fought us once upon a time."

Varis sighs. "I didn't fight against you. I just…"

"Guys, it doesn't matter," I say. "You all live too long to hold grudges like this. If you hate everyone who's ever been on the wrong side of a disagreement with you, you'll have no friends or allies ever. Varis is one of the good ones. I vouch for him."

Sly puts out his cigar and downs the last of his drink. "Varis can complete your training. You can defeat Levi. And you can all get the hell out of my hair and get back to your own worlds. It's a win/win for everyone."

"There's one problem," Varis says.

"Just one?" Fen asks with a raised eyebrow.

"We can't train here," Varis continues, ignoring the irritated man at my side.

Sly frowns. "Of course you can. I can keep you safe long enough to get our girl here up to snuff."

Varis shakes his head. "This world is too removed from the source of her powers, from where the Midnight Star first originated. Even Yami isn't strong enough to manifest here yet. We must return to…"

He pauses and I realize he can't talk about Avakiri here. Dean and Fen don't know about it, though at minimum I need to bring Fen up to speed. He is Fae after all.

"Return where?" Dean asks.

"To our world," Varis says, evasively. "To complete the training."

"We are wanted on our world. It's not safe," Fen says.

"There is a place that could be safe for her. A place she can train," Varis says.

Dean claps his hands. "Great, when do we leave?"

"The invitation wasn't for you," Varis says. "Just Ari."

Dean shakes his head. "No can do. She's mine for the month. Bound by a blood oath. No breaking it, isn't that right, Princess?"

I look at Varis, frowning. "I'm afraid he's telling the truth. I have to stay with Dean."

Fen crosses his arms over his chest. "And she's not going anywhere without me."

"That won't work," Varis says. "I can't possibly bring two princes of hell to...this place. It would be instant war."

"Then we stay here," Fen says.

"We could go to my realm," Dean offers.

Fen turns to his brother. "Where Ari and I will be hanged upon return?"

"No one knows I helped you escape, and they will hardly suspect me at any rate," Dean says. "You'd be safe in my realm, at least long enough for Ari to train."

"Until someone recognizes us and reports us to Levi's men," Fen says.

"There are ways to remain unseen," Dean assures us. "Disguises. Illusion. It's the perfect solution. We get home, assess the damage, make plans, train up the princess until she can kick ass, and off we go."

"No," Fen says. "We don't go back until we're strong enough to defeat Levi. We can't risk it."

Sly yawns and opens the door to his study. "Okay boys and girls, you're boring me. Go sort this out elsewhere. I have matters I must attend to. This club doesn't run itself, you know. I—"

A loud screech interrupts Sly, who smiles. "Ah, Lopsi is awake. Time to feed my sweet pet."

"Your pet?" Dean asks.

Baron whines and stands closer to Fen and me.

There's another screech, and I shiver, wondering what kind of pet can make such a sound.

"Indeed. A darling little beast. I collected her as a gift from a realm known for their remarkable creatures. We're getting along smashingly." With a bow, Sly leaves, and the energy seems to get sucked from the room.

"What do we do now?" I ask.

Dean stretches and puts his drink on the table. "I'm off to enjoy some of the perks of being here. This is all too dry for my liking." He saunters out and Fen frowns.

"He needs to learn to take life more seriously," Fen says.

Varis turns to me, his face unreadable. "How is… Asher?" he asks softly.

"He's fine," I assure the Druid. "Caught in the middle of this, but unharmed last I saw him. Missing you, undoubtedly."

Fen raises an eyebrow at the exchange, but says nothing. Does he know about his brother's relationship with the Druid? It's not something we've ever had a chance to talk about.

"Varis, can you help me get Yami back? He was injured and disappeared. I haven't seen him for days." I've been holding in my fears about Yami for so long, it's a huge relief to talk to someone who might know where my baby dragon went and how to find him.

"He is young and weak," Varis says. "When injured, threatened or scared, it's not unheard for Spirits to retreat to an ethereal form while they recover. It shouldn't be hard to reunite with him once we return home. We cannot summon him here, however, not until you have much stronger control of your magic."

"Then help me."

Varis stares at me a moment, then looks at Fen. "So…the stories are true then?"

"What stories?" Fen asks before I can.

"When the last Earth Druid died, she was pregnant, this was common knowledge. It was assumed her child died in the battle, but there were rumors. Rumors that he yet lived and was raised by wild wolves." Varis looks down at Baron and pats the wolf on the head. "Rumors that he was taken by the vampires and used as a blood sacrifice to their gods. And one barely whispered rumor that he was the heir to the Earth Druid's Spirit."

"Did you know her? The woman who gave birth to me?" Fen asks.

I notice he doesn't say 'mother.' He clearly still isn't ready to accept who he is. I guess it makes sense, given how long he's been alive and how long he's been living with his current identity. He could argue that time makes this transition harder for him than it was for me, but I don't know. At least he already knew that all these beings and worlds existed. My entire worldview flipped and turned inside out when I met him.

Varis nods. "I did, of course. We were bonded by the Spirits, just as we three are now bonded to each other, and to the remaining Druids of Water and Fire."

"But—Oren's dead, right? He can't come back, can he?" Sweat breaks out on my forehead and under my arms at the thought of the Fire Druid coming for me. The way he cut into me with his blade of fire. The pain that ravaged my body. It's a terror that lives deep in me now, burrowed into my core memories. Fen reaches for my hand to calm me as I take a deep breath.

"He is dead, yes, and the Fire Spirit will have chosen someone new, someone worthy. So we have Metsi, who has her own agenda for the Fae, and one unknown who we must find," Varis says.

"Tracking down wayward Druids isn't my job or priority," Fen says gruffly. "We need to reclaim Stonehill and stop Levi before he destroys both of our kingdoms."

Varis tilts his head. "I think you'll find that to do one we must do both. But first, we must travel to a place where Arianna can access her magic. Without further training, she will not be useful in the coming war. And you, Fenris Vane, must move past your blindness and embrace who you are. You are not only the Earth Druid, but the blood heir to the most powerful Wild One we've ever seen. Your mother was highly revered for her ancient magic and knowledge of the Old Ways. You have her blood and her Spirit...you are stronger than you know. Your people need you."

"And who are my people?" Fen asks. "I've been raised a Prince of Hell, a vampire demon hated and despised by your people. You think they will accept me as a Druid after my kind nearly destroyed your world?"

"Times are changing," Varis says softly. "Our Midnight Star is half human and aligned with the vampires. Our

Earth Druid is a turned vampire. We don't even know who our Fire Druid is. There are many of the Fae who resist these changes, who want our blood to stay pure, but they don't understand the truth of the magic that flows within us. It is not bound by blood alone. For our people to survive...all of our people, we have to broaden our minds and embrace a new world. I think we need to rethink our choices." Varis looks at me, and I nod.

"Tell him," I say.

Varis nods. "You think the Fae have been decimated. That all who remain exist in the Outlands. But you're wrong."

"What do you mean?" Fen asks.

"There is another kingdom, one mostly hidden from your kind," Varis says. "It is called Avakiri. It is Ari's birthright as promised ruler. It is your birthright too, as a Fae and Druid."

"If you could see it, you would understand," I say. "It's magical. Beautiful. They have their own tribes, their own stories and cultures and communities. There's more to this world than you know."

Fen looks at me with an unreadable face. "When did you go there?"

"When they kidnapped me," I say. "That's where I trained with Varis. I wanted to tell you about it, but we've had a lot going on. You travel there through the Waystones. I tried to call you there with your demon mark."

He looks down at his wrist. "I think I found a Waystone. But I didn't know how to work it. But…it's a futile conversation. Even if I was willing to walk into the center of Fae power—which I'm not—Dean was right about one thing. He has to stay with Ari."

Varis nods. "Until we know his loyalties, he can't be given access to this information. We'll have to find another way. Another place to train."

Fen does not look happy by this conversation, and the clock is ticking. Plus, Es and Pete will be here soon, and I need to get to them before anyone else does. Lest they go into shock.

Fen and Varis trail me as I leave Sly's office and head to the door we first came in. "Would they arrive through here?" I ask Fen.

"There are other entrances," he says. "But this one is most used."

When we turn a corner, I hear Sly's voice coming from the main ballroom. "Well, well, aren't you a lovely creature full of feistiness. The princess failed to mention how utterly delightful her friends are."

"The princess? What are you talking about?"

I recognize that fake southern drawl! I run around the corner and into the ballroom, and see Es and Pete standing close to each other staring around the room wide-eyed. When Es sees me, she gasps. "Ari? What happened to you?"

Crap. My illusion spell isn't active, so my Fae ears and hair are on full display. And I'm dressed like a medieval princess from a fairytale, thanks to Sly and his obsession with costumes and playing doll with his guests. "Es! Pete! I can explain. Kind of."

We three crash into each other in a mingle of arms and hugs, and the feel of these two solidly real, relatively normal people I've known for so long calms my soul in a way nothing else does. But they are here—and in danger—because of me.

"What is this place?" Pete asks, running a hand through his red mop of hair. He scans the room, mouth agape, taking in the strangeness of it all. "Is that—"

He's staring at Marasphyr. "Yes, she's a real mermaid. This place...it's a safe place for people from all over," I say awkwardly.

"Like a domestic violence shelter?" Es asks, though I can tell from her tone and expression she knows this isn't a shelter.

"More like a neutral zone for paranormal or magical beings from different worlds," I elaborate.

Fen walks over and holds out his hand. "It's nice to see you again, Es." He turns to her boyfriend. "Pete. Nice to finally meet you. I have heard so much from Arianna."

Es shakes his hand, firmly. "I like you, Fen. I told Ari that too. But if you're getting her mixed up in something dangerous..."

I nearly choke at that. Then I start laughing, because what else can I do but laugh at the absurdity of this? How do I tell my best friend everything? About the contract and my mother and Inferna and Avakiri and my bloodline and that I'm to be queen of two kingdoms. How do I tell her I'm wanted for execution, that I spent the last several weeks in a dungeon, that I thought I would surely die and never see them again? How do I tell her she is now in danger because of the people who want me dead?

The words are resting on my lips, waiting to be spoken, when Dean saunters in, somehow once again missing his shirt.

Es stops paying attention to me as Dean's charms light her up and turn her to jelly. And he notices. His smile spreads over his handsome face as he glides to us, his perfect body glistening under the lights of the ballroom.

"Why, hello. I'm Prince Dean, but you can just call me Dean. Who might you be?" He's holding Es's hand to his lips when Pete smiles and holds out a hand to shake Dean's.

"I'm Pete, this is my girlfriend Es. We're friends of Ari's."

I stifle a laugh as Es regains her focus and steps back, allowing Dean to reluctantly shake Pete's hand.

"So, what's this about a princess?" Es asks, eyeing my pointy ears. "What did they do to you?"

"Well, I—"

Something screeches.

Someone screams.

Fen reaches for his sword, but it isn't there since Sly changed our clothes.

He stands closer to me, and Baron growls, pacing in front of us.

Es reaches for my hand. "What was that?"

"I don't know. It kind of sounded like…"

"Lopsi!" Sly sounds worried. Too worried.

"Who's Lopsi?" Pete asks.

"Sly's pet," I say. "I haven't met her, but I think we're about to."

More screaming, and then…the room fills with darkness that blocks out all light. I look up and see a creature of black fur and rotting flesh, wings spread, its massive body taking up half the ballroom, its head bent slightly to avoid hitting the very tall ceilings. The beast resembles a bat with huge ears and wings stretching from its front limbs, but its face is twisted and vicious, a face torn from nightmares. It hisses, and thick saliva drips from its razor teeth.

"What the hell is that thing?" yells Es.

"A Drakar from Vandaris," says Sly, stepping between us and the beast. "This pretty beast is worth a fortune, so no harming it." He turns to the bat and speaks with affection. "Now, Lopsi, how did you get out of your cage? Someone forget to close it? Come on, let's just take you back there and—"

Lopsi screeches, and I have to cover my ears to block out the piercing sound. Sly steps back, frowning.

Varis holds up his hand, about to use magic, but I pull him back. "Don't. You're not allowed to harm anyone here, remember? Or Sly will turn you into goo."

"Let me handle this, my dears," says Sly. He walks slowly toward the monster bat, clucking in a calm voice. "Good girl, Lopsi. You remember your daddy, yes?"

Lopsi replies by spitting something from her fanged mouth—a viscous yellow substance. Sly dashes out of the way and the liquid hits a chair instead.

The chair hisses, fizzes, then melts to the ground.

Crap. "I'm guessing that's doubly dangerous on human skin?"

Sly speaks with his back turned to us. "Only if you enjoy having skin."

I flinch. "I'm pretty attached," I tell him.

"Just stay very still," Sly says. "Everything will be fine."

"And if it's not?"

"No one lays a hand on Lopsi. Or they will lose said hand."

Fair enough. The giant venomous bat can do what she wants to us, but we have to play nice. I stay as still as I possibly can, but as Sly approaches his pet, she

121

hisses and stretches her wings, then makes a screeching sound that nearly deafens me.

Then she lunges.

And we all run.

"Blasted princes," says Sly. "You show up and everything goes to hell."

Fen says nothing. Dean grins. Stupid man. He actually seems to be enjoying this.

I most definitely am not. The princes are fast, and Es, Pete and I barely keep up. The beast starts to close the distance between us.

"How about some of that magic, Sly?" I say between panting breaths.

"How dare you," he yells. "I'm not turning Lopsi inside out. What kind of cruel demon do you think I am? You'll be fine, and if not, well, it was nice meeting you. I will make sure none of your flesh goes to waste." Sly veers off to the side, whether to escape without us or to lead Lopsi away, I'm not sure. If he's trying to help, his plan utterly fails. Lopsi follows us.

"Seven Hells," yells Dean, punching a wall. "Dead end."

We turn around, facing the giant beast. I look for passages, but see none.

Baron growls, preparing for a fight. Fen positions himself in front of me. I push Es and Pete to the back of our group in hopes of keeping them as safe as possible.

Dean grabs my hand. "I know a way out," he screams over the beast's war cry.

He runs forward…

Toward the beast.

I curse, then follow.

Then I see it. Next to Lopsi, half hidden by her wing, a door.

Dean rams himself in the entryway, bashing the way open. The rest of us follow just as Lopsi turns, swinging a giant claw behind us. She misses, hitting the wall and shattering stone. We're almost safe—

Something flies by me.

And then pain tears into my arm.

Lopsi's venom singed my dress, burning it above my elbow. My skin is scorching and red, but I've had worse.

Dean and Fen slam the door closed behind us, then keep it shut with their strength as Lopsi tries to push it open.

I look around. "Where are we?"

"It's the Way Room," Fen yells, spit flying from his mouth as he strains to keep the beast away.

Mirrors of different sizes and shapes fill the room, shimmering in a splendor of colors. Scenes flash in them: a swaying tree, a raging storm. "This is how Sly travels to different worlds," Dean says.

He points to a silver mirror on the left. "We can get back to Inferna with that one."

Fen shakes his head. "We'd be walking into a death sentence."

I have to agree with him.

Until the bat spits venom at the door and it rots away. Fen jumps to me, holding up his bare hands like claws, ready to fight.

"I don't think we have a choice!" I scream.

Dean runs for the mirror. "Everyone grab a hand, we go now!"

My hand lands on Baron as Fen reaches for my arm. I make sure Es and Pete grab onto me, and we rush through the mirror.

And step out in a familiar realm. Out of instinct, I glance back at the mirror, fearing Lopsi will follow, but see nothing but my reflection. I turn away, scanning the city ahead of us. It smells of wine and expensive oils, and though it is late and the moons are high in the sky, there is music and dancing and scantily clad men and women serving food on golden trays.

Dean smiles. "Welcome to my Pleasure Palace, Princess."

6

YOU KNOW SO LITTLE
Kayla Windhelm

"You are a dog, And you will know your place at your master's heel."
—King Lucian

It takes a moment to steady my breathing. Adrenaline pumps through me, making my limbs shake. My sword is still clutched in my hand, ready to kill or maim, but there is nothing left to fight. The bear is dead. And the tiger...the tiger is somehow Tavian Gray.

This shouldn't be possible. This kind of magic doesn't exist.

Tavian is silent. Still. His caramel skin is striking against the white of the snow, even in the dark. Blood leaks out of his wounds, staining everything red around him. This is my chance to escape, to find out what happened to Fen and Ari—but if I leave he will die.

That's not my problem. He intends to sell me to Metsi as a prisoner.

But he also saved my life. Twice.

Bloody hell. This man is making my life impossible. Because I cannot leave him to die, but saving him means risking my own life.

I swear a string of expletives under my breath as I grip under his arms and half lift—half drag him back to the cave. He's heavier than he looks, a solid build of muscle, and it takes a lot to move him.

Once back in the cave, I kindle the fire and cover him with furs to warm him, then I set to examining his wounds. They are deep, but not fatal. Still, he's losing a lot of blood. I clean them as best I can with melted snow, then pull out my crystal pendant. Clutching it in one hand, with the other laid gently over his chest, I whisper the words I know will aid in the healing.

When I'm done, fragile pink skin tentatively holds together his wounds. He will need to take care not to rip them apart again.

Now all I can do is wait and keep him warm.

At some point in the night, the horse that abandoned me comes back, more loyal to his master than me, I guess. I tie him up at the edge of the cave and give him food and water, then return to my patient.

I keep telling myself I should leave. But as he fights imaginary foes in fevered dreams, his brow drenched and body twitching, I can't bring myself to walk away from him. I lay a hand on his face and note that he's finally cooling.

When I lift the furs to check his wounds, a large hand grabs my wrist. "You know, Princess, if you wanted access, all you had to do was ask."

I drop the furs and scoot back. Tavian props himself up on his elbows and flinches only slightly at the pain caused by his movement.

My witty retort dies on my tongue as he stares into me with his emerald eyes. This man is entirely too mesmerizing for my liking.

He smirks, as if he knows what I'm thinking. "I'm surprised you stuck around, Princess. Could have left me for dead and saved yourself."

"Could have," I say. "Probably should have."

"Why didn't you?" he asks as he slowly sits up.

I resist the urge to help him, crossing my hands in my lap instead. "I needed answers first," I say.

He raises an eyebrow. "Really? What kind of answers?"

"You shifted into a tiger? How? I've never heard of this kind of magic."

"Says the Shade who has lived with vampires her whole life." He grins as he stands. The fur drops away and my eyes are glued to the hard lines of his body as he dresses.

"And living in the Outlands would have taught me more?" I ask.

He chuckles. "You know so little of your people. Of your magical ancestry. You think the Outlands, as you call them, are all that's left of the Fae?"

This is news and gives me pause. "What are you talking about?"

"Come with me to meet Metsi, and I'll show you," he says. "There's a whole other world out there. The vampires don't know about it. Some Fae have even forgotten. But it is the way we have survived since the Unraveling."

"Not possible. We've raided every inch of this world. If there were a secret group of Fae living somewhere, we would have found them," I say.

"You vampires think you know everything. Makes you blind to the obvious. You believe you have the world mapped out, and so you have stopped exploring." He puts out the fire and packs his bag. "I'm going to Metsi. She will have information I need. And she may have a place for you. A purpose." He pauses. "Our people are at war. The vampires fight each other. You are as much Fae as you are vampire, don't you want to at least see what might be?"

"Are you giving me a choice?" I ask. "So I can leave if I want? Back to Stonehill?"

"You saved my life when you could have left me for dead. I'm not a monster. But...the horse, the pack, the food...that goes with me. If you leave, you're on your own. If you leave, you'll never know where your people are from. You'll never know what you could be. You'll never know whether Metsi could be a powerful ally or not."

"Are you still going to try to sell me to Metsi?" I ask, crossing my arms over my chest.

"If I can get money for you, yes. But only if you want to stay." He holds out a hand to shake mine. "Deal?"

"And if I leave?" I still have Ari and Fen to consider.

"If you leave now, I won't stop you. But how far do you think you'll get alone, without a horse, without provisions, without someone watching your back?" he asks.

He has a point, and it irritates me to admit it. The weather is harsh. I am alone with nothing but the clothes on my back.

"How do we get there? To the Fae?" I ask, stalling.

"We travel by Waystone. There's one close by. Come, see for yourself."

And so I follow him, but I don't commit. Not yet. Not until I see the Waystone. Not until everything begins to click.

Because the Waystone is familiar. I've seen it before, or one just like it. With Fen, when Ari was missing and we went in search of her.

It is a wall, hidden deep within a damp cave, decorated with symbols of the Fae, a handprint in the center.

I run my fingers over the carved stone. "How does it work?"

"Are you coming?" he asks, raising an eyebrow.

I sigh. "I guess I have no choice, do I?"

He grins. "There's always a choice, Princess. But I like to make it a hard one."

"What about the horse?" I ask as Tavian presses his hand against the center stone print, against the spikes there, and his blood flows into the carvings.

"He doesn't like the travel."

I soon understand why.

The stone grinds open revealing a slab that Tavian leads us both onto. And then it begins to move, dropping into the earth, moving us quickly through the core of our world. "Where are we going?" I ask.

"Avakiri. The Fae kingdom on the other side of this world."

"Other side?"

"You'll see soon enough." Tavian grabs my hand. "Prepare yourself."

"For what?"

Too late.

Gravity ceases to function and I barely contain a scream as we both begin to float. Tavian demonstrates how to flip over so that his feet are facing what was the ceiling. I do the same, and then gravity hits us hard and we both fall against stone, the floor now above us. "What was that?" I ask, rubbing a new bruise on my shin.

"We are half way there," he says.

Half way to the other side of the world I thought I knew. Surely someone must have discovered these secrets, but I can see why they would be so closely guarded. The vampires made the Fae almost extinct, save those kept as slaves. The Druids were put to sleep, the Midnight Star and all blood ties killed...and yet the Fae found a way to survive. To live. To regrow.

And now they have Ari.

It's still so much to absorb. For so long we have lived in this one routine, existed with our ways intact. Then this human girl shows up and everything I know about my life is twisted into something different. I don't blame Ari, of course. If anything, she's more a victim in this than anyone. But it makes me wonder...how have I become so complacent with the injustices I see? How have I grown so jaded in this world? And what will this trip to Avakiri do to me? To everything I believe in?

When the Waystone stops moving, the doors swing open, and we emerge into a different cave, filled with sparkling green crystal. I can hear running water and smell the scent of fresh grass. Tavian reaches out and waves a hand over me. I feel a shimmering of magic, then it fades. "What did you do?" I ask.

"I cast an illusion over you, to change your appearance," he's says. "I don't know how many would recognize the illegitimate Fae daughter of the vampire king, but likely Metsi would."

I'm touched by his concern and begrudgingly thank him.

We step outside, and into a different world.

No longer covered in snow, this land is a lush growth of tropical jungle, the sun bright and hot upon my skin. Before us flows a waterfall, hiding the cave with the Waystone. I run forward, eager to see more, skirting around the water and climbing a rock covered in green vines, overlooking a pond.

The water is so clear I can see the bottom. Colorful fish swim around as light flickers against their scales. The trees here are tall, with vines growing between them like ropes. Tavian leads us to a stone path decorated with ancient symbols and dotted with moss. Critters scurry through the undergrowth, and the sound of birds and other creatures fills the silence with hoots, chirps and whistles. It's a cacophony of life.

The trail narrows and turns into stone steps, placed so close together I have to be careful not to trip on my own feet. Walking up the steps—it seems there are hundreds—is its own kind of meditative exercise.

I'm entranced by the beauty and serenity of it all until we reach two carved sculptures that act as guardians to the entrance of a garden. When we walk through, it takes me a moment to understand what I'm seeing. At first, I'm taken in by the many waterfalls and pools of clear water dotted throughout, surrounded by explosions of floral color. But the sounds of nature are drowned out by the sound of dying men and women.

Bound to the trees by the rope-like vines are dozens of vampires, stripped nearly naked. They hang over the pools of water, branches curling around their flesh, piercing their skin, fusing with their veins. The enchantment drains away their blood, releasing it through the roots and into the water. The pools swirl with red as the cries of my people carry on the wind.

And not just vampires. There are Shade there too, dying in the clutches of the trees. I prepare myself for the smell of rotting flesh, the smell of death, but none comes. The air is sweet and calming, the scent of flowers. How twisted that such cruelty is masqueraded as beauty.

I stop, my throat dry, my jaw clenched so tightly I might break my teeth. Tavian grabs my hand, but I yank it away. "Is this what you wanted to show me?" I hiss at him.

"No. I have never seen the likes of this. I swear to you, this wasn't my intention."

By the look in his eyes, I can tell he speaks truth. I'm about to suggest—nay demand—we leave, when four Fae arrive wielding swords and spears. They wear masks that cover their faces and blue and green armor that covers their bodies, shimmering like scales.

"The Wild One requests your presence," one of the soldiers—a woman—says.

Tavian shoots me a worried look. It appears we have no choice but to walk with them.

We reach a massive and ancient palace made of stone and carved with more of the glyphs I saw on the steps. Inside, the walls are decorated with tapestries and silk curtains of blues and greens, and everywhere there is water. Fountains, pools, indoor waterfalls...the sound is soothing, and the air fresh.

Fae mingle about, talking, laughing, drinking and eating, reclining on colorful pillows and stone chairs. Their skin is dark, unlike most of the Fae I meet. None seem concerned by the dying vampires and Shade outside their door.

When we enter the throne room, a woman who could only be Metsi sits upon a raised throne, ancient and covered in vines. She wears a long gown of silk and satin, blues and whites. Her skin is dark, like that of the other Fae here, and pale blue tattoos cover her long arms and bald head. Her serpent, Wadu, curls around her left arm. She smiles when she sees Tavian. "It has been far too long since we've been graced by your presence. What brings you to our corner of Avakiri?"

"The realms have heard rumors of the Midnight Star's return, of power being restored. Of war being waged against the vampires. I came to seek the truth," Tavian says.

I remain quiet. Waiting. Worrying. He could easily betray me. Tell them who I am. Get the money he so desperately wants.

Metsi flicks her hand and someone brings her a silver goblet with drink in it. "So much talk. So many rumors. Some have merit, others less. We will soon have the Midnight Star in our control. And the vampires, well, they will meet their end. Their time has come. It's our turn now. Our turn to reclaim what is ours."

"I've seen the Outlands. People speak of your defeat at Stonehill while they cower and drink away their sorrows, and yet you speak of victory? You are not prepared."

I glance at Tavian, wondering why he speaks so freely. Who is he to question a Druid?

Metsi laughs. "We have many weapons and soldiers here. We have Druids coming back into power. We have a spy amongst the enemy's midst. And...we have an ally. One of the princes is on our side. He will ensure our victory from within."

Tavian and I both flinch at her words. A prince is working with Metsi? Who? I cannot think of even one who would side with the Fae.

Metsi smiles, probably in response to our faces. "I would very much love to include you amongst our supporters," she says. "Come, Tavian. Join us. Give up your vagabond ways and I will make you wealthier than you can imagine. I will give you anything your heart desires. Join with your kin once more and help us defeat our enemies."

Her speech is persuasive, but I won't fight my brothers. Tavian however....

"I appreciate the offer, but I am done with war, Metsi. You know this." Tavian sounds casual, but I see the tension in his muscles. This does not seem to be the conversation he expected.

Metsi rises from her throne and walks down the steps to stand closer to us. She stops a few feet in front of Tavian. "Have you not brought me anything then?" she asks. "Do tell me, who is this friend of yours? Has she a tongue?"

"This is Darnsa, my apprentice," he says without missing a beat. "We were just passing through and wanted to pay our respects. I have nothing to offer this visit, but if you have a request, I will do my best to oblige."

He's smooth, but she's looking too closely at me. I resist the urge to clutch the sword at my hip, but my hand is twitching. I'm ready.

"Oh, Tavian Gray. How you disappoint." Metsi raises her hand and waves it over my face. "Look here. Not a mere apprentice at all, but rather Kayla Windhelm. The bastard Shade of the late king. And a pretty prize, indeed."

A low growl forms under Tavian's breath. "She's with me, under my protection."

Metsi flashes a look at him, her eyes narrowing. "I will pay you handsomely for her. Rumor has it you are in want of a small fortune. I can provide that, no strings attached. Leave the girl here and you may leave with what you can carry."

I suck in my breath, waiting. This is what Tavian has wanted. And even if he refuses, why would that stop a Druid? I look around, searching for windows and doors, searching for a way to flee, wondering if I can find my way back to the Waystone. I see no options.

A moment. The air thickens between the three of us.

Tavian takes three measured breaths before answering. "Metsi, you do not wish to press me. We leave now."

"Guards!" the Druid screams, and dozens of armed soldiers surround us.

I pull my sword out, but Tavian lays a hand on mine. "Trust me, please," he whispers.

I don't sheathe my sword, but I lower it slowly.

All eyes are on us.

Tavian growls again, and the room grows dark. Candles flicker out. Smoke fills the space around us and the air crackles with lightning. His voice sounds louder, deeper, when he speaks. "Have you forgotten who I am? Do you take me for a common Fae? You do not wish to challenge me, Druid."

Metsi's eyes widen, and she takes a step back. Her serpent recoils. With a flick of her wrist, Metsi signals the guards, and they disappear from sight. Only then does the light return and the air settle. Only then does the tension fall from Tavian's body.

Metsi walks slowly back to her throne and sits gracefully. Despite her mannerism, I can see the fear on her face, though I do not understand what a Druid has to fear but a prince of hell. "Now, now, Tavian. No need for all that. It was just a friendly request. Of course you and the princess are free to go."

The look Metsi gives me sends a chill up my back. Then it fills me with anger for the vampires and Shade outside, and I clutch my sword harder. But Tavian wastes no time. He grabs my hand and pulls us out of the room.

We speak no words as we make our way through the garden and back to the Waystone. It isn't until we are behind the stone door and moving back to the Outlands that I finally ask. "Who are you, Tavian? Who are you, to scare a Druid?"

He looks at me, his emerald eyes hiding so many secrets. "I'm not one to be trifled with."

7

THE PLEASURE PALACE

*"You will wake the ancient powers of our kind and
bring balance back to the Four Tribes. And then we will
free our people and rule our world once again."*
—Madrid

I sit on a stump calming my breath after our escape, keeping my eye on the mirror. A part of me still fears Sly's pet will follow us, finish what it started, but then I remember it's not the mirror that is magic, but the vampires who brought me here.

Es bends over, puking and cursing between bouts of vomiting. "What just happened?" she mumbles, leaning against a tree in the moonlight. "What was that...that..." She collapses, and Pete barely catches her before her head hits the ground. He pats her face, calling out her name, but she doesn't respond.

Fen walks over to them, Baron at his side. "She has witnessed too much too soon. I have seen this happen before. It will pass in time, but she needs a healer." He reaches for Pete's shoulder, to comfort him.

Pete smacks his hand away. "Get off her. Where the hell have you taken us? She'll be fine back home. Back where—"

"You cannot go back," says Fen. "Not if you want to live."

Pete clenches his jaw. "Fine. A healer then."

Dean leans over to me, whispering, "What's wrong with the redhead?"

I roll my eyes, "How about the fact that his girlfriend just passed out? Or that they almost ended up as dinner for a giant bat? Or maybe it's the fact that they're in a new strange place, surrounded by things and creatures they don't understand, with no way home?"

Dean raises an eyebrow. "You sure he didn't just have a bad lunch?"

I groan and push him away, then stand and walk over to Es. "Here, I can help."

Pete looks at me coldly, the same stare he gave Fen, but then his face calms, and he nods.

I hold my hands over Es's chest, and whisper incantations Varis taught me. My energy flows through me, and I feel a presence I have not felt in a long time.

Yami.

I turn my face, seeing the little dragon perching on my shoulder, his skin like moving stars in a dark sky. His company fills me with happiness, and I channel that bliss into Es.

She gasps, then breathes in deeply, steadily. Her eyes do not open, but she is stronger than she was.

"Thank you," says Pete, avoiding eye contact with me. I'm waiting for the questions, but whatever he's thinking, he doesn't ask. I'm sure he wishes I'd never brought him and Es to The Black Lotus, never gotten them involved. I wish that had been an option. I wish I could explain it all to him in a way he'd believe. And for a moment, I wish I had never come to Inferna myself.

Fen takes Es by the shoulders. "May I?"

Pete nods, and Fen lifts Es up in his arms, carrying her to the glowing city.

Varis and Dean are arguing about something at the edge of a river. The Druid turns to me. "We cannot stay here."

Dean grins. "Well, I'm not leaving, and your precious Midnight Star goes where I go, so…"

"You are far too happy," says Varis to Dean, sighing. He turns his attention to Fen. "Do you not fear retaliation from your brothers?"

Fen nods. "The Druid has a point. We can't be seen gallivanting around Inferna. We escaped hanging and are still wanted."

I shudder as I imagine being locked in the dungeons again, and Yami trembles on my shoulder. Oh, how I missed my baby dragon. I scratch his chin, soothing him, and he purrs and rubs his head against mine. No one seems to notice the behavior, so I assume Yami is keeping himself hidden again, invisible to all but me.

Dean laughs. "No one in my realm cares about politics. You're safe here. Now, let me show you why the Moonlight Garden is the most popular city in all of the Seven Realms."

"The most popular city?" I raise an eyebrow. "And you think no one will report us to Levi? Not even someone passing through?"

Dean growls, clearly done with this conversation and ready to return to his palace.

Varis sighs, rubbing his tired eyes. "If we must stay, I can cast an illusion to hide who we are. Only a powerful wielder of magic could see through it, and only if they knew to look."

Dean grins. "Well, why didn't you say so earlier, my good friend? You know, this illusion thingy seems incredibly useful. There's this lady friend of mine, absolutely gorgeous. We didn't leave things off so well, if you know what I mean. She still hates the sight of this pretty mug. So, maybe we could alter it for an occasion. Just keep it beautiful though, okay?"

Varis ignores the prince, addressing everyone else. "Each of us will be able to see through the illusion, but strangers will not. Understood?"

Fen purses his lips, looking down at the woman in his arms. "Cast the spell on Arianna's friends as well. I don't want the vampires here tempted to feed on them."

"And no illusion for me at the moment," says Dean. "My people must see their prince."

Varis nods and pulls a stone from a pouch around his neck. He mumbles words in a language I recognize as ancient Fae but don't understand, and a glimmer of magic shimmers over us, like a light rain on a warm day. For a moment, I see what Varis, Fen, Es, Pete, and even Baron will look like as someone else. Then the glimmer fades, and they return to normal. Pete's eyes are round and scared but he's still not saying anything. I think he's in shock.

"Neat trick. You'll have to teach me that," I say.

The Druid rolls his eyes. "I've been trying to teach you things exactly like this. Pay better attention."

Dean chuckles at my expense and leads us into his glowing city.

...

When we enter the Moonlight Garden, I lose my breath, and fall deep into its wonders. This is nothing like the rugged Stonehill, nor even the elegant Crystal Palace. This is like a dream, one in which everything moves slowly, for everything is too beautiful to experience in haste, and in which you are happy without even knowing why. It is a dream from which you do not wish to wake. It begins with the gates, carved from pure white wood, resembling a tree and branches that you can see between. It continues in the white and purple flowers, filling the air with scents I can only call intoxicating. Scents that makes me glance at Fen and wish we were alone. It follows in the cobbled paths, and the people that fill them, scantily clad in silver and black clothing, dancing to a primal beat that reverberates through the city, stirring my body to movement. It is found in the piper sitting on a beautiful boat as it glides through the canals, and he fills the passages with the sweet melody of wonder and bliss. It is there, when we arrive at the palace. A structure of the colors of night, glowing like the moon in the darkness, its spires vanishing in the pale blue clouds. Purple vines spill from its balconies, running into gardens where naked women and men swim in glorious fountains, spouting water that glows when disturbed. There is no place like this dream. No place like the Moonlight Garden.

...

We enter the main hall of the Pleasure Palace, and I raise my arms to the ceiling so far above I can barely make it out. Purple clouds drift there, fooling my mind into believing we are still outside in nature. "An enchantment of my Keeper, Baldar," says Dean, noticing my gaze. "Ah, look, he is here to greet us." Dean motions to the Fae before us, his face perfect and pristine, his white beard short and well kept. He is a short man, the shortest I have seen in these lands, and his face is kind.

"Prince Dean," Baldar says, his voice loud and jolly. "How splendid it is to witness your return. May I prepare a bath or—"

"My friend needs healing," says Dean, gesturing to Es. "Take them to the eastern wing and use only your best potions."

Baldar nods and motions to a nearby servant, a shirtless Fae with ivory skin and long, elegant limbs. The young man takes Es into his arms, then Baldar guides him and Pete into a grand hallway, out of sight.

"I should go with them. Explain things." I step forward, and suddenly my knees buckle and I fall backwards.

Fen catches me from behind. "Let the Keeper do his work. Later, when Es is awake, you can explain. Right now, you need to rest." He glances at my arm, where Lopsi's venom burned my dress and left a red mark.

"Fine," I say, knowing he's right.

Dean waves us over. "Come, I'll show you to your rooms."

He guides us up a marble staircase, into floors even higher than the grand hall. There are so many steps, I grow exhausted, and Fen lifts me into his arms. I don't even bother protesting. It feels too good to be this close to him. To feel his body. I lean my head against his chest, taking in his scent, and listen to the strong beat of his heart.

Dean glances my way and rolls his eyes. "Here you are," he says, motioning to a room with the largest bed I have ever seen. Silk sheets and purple pillows cover the mattress. Four wooden posts surround the wooden bed frame, and see-through curtains spill from their tops, like a dress that shows more than it hides.

The entire back wall of the room is missing, leading to a grand balcony overlooking the city, making way for soothing aromas and wistful songs.

"Varis, you will find your room next to hers," says Dean.

Varis nods, looking at me. "Call if the vampires cause problems." Then he disappears into his room.

"And this," Dean points to the door opposite mine, "Is my room."

Fen grunts. "Where do I sleep?"

"Down the hall. Four levels down. To the right. Behind the kitchens." Dean's face is pure seriousness.

"Can't have you sneaking into the princess's room now, can I? It *is* my turn after all."

Fen puts me down and mumbles something about "not wanting to be king" and "bloody contract." Then he cups my face in his hands and kisses my lips softly. "If you need anything, call my name. And I will come."

He turns away and disappears down the hallway, though Baron takes a few more moments to follow, and I wonder if Fen truly can hear so far. If he was bluffing in front of his brother, I can always draw his mark to summon him. The thought fills me with a sense of security, and I fall into the bed, letting myself sink into the soft mattress, Yami curling up against my neck. The aches in my body seem to fade instantly, and my mind starts to fall into sleep.

"Sweet dreams, Princess," says Dean as he closes the door, and I rest comfortably for the first time in a long time.

...

I dream of fire and pain. Of buildings crumbling around me and leaving nothing but ash. I see Daison before me, half his body blackened and dead, the other half innocent and pleading. Pleading for me to save him.

But I cannot.

I cannot.

I cannot.

No matter what I do, he is gone. He can never return.

I turn away, and now, amidst the burning ruins, I see Es and Pete. They stand together, their eyes filled with tears and rage. "How could you bring this upon us?" says Pete, his voice cold.

"You were our friend!" yells Es. "You were our friend and you let us die!"

No. No. No. You're not dead. There's still time.

Time.

Time.

It seems to stand still.

I run forward. To reach my friends. To save them. But I cannot move. I cannot stop the flames.

They reach down, tendrils of smoke and heat, curling around flesh and bone and burning hair. I watch as their faces melt. As their bodies turn to blood and bone and ash.

I watch.

I watch.

I watch.

And I can do nothing.

...

I wake with a gasp, covered in sweat and a stench. For a moment, I can't remember where I am, and panic begins to grip me, but then I recall the Moonlight Garden, the Pleasure Palace. Fen.

I slip from my bed and undress, throwing my sweaty dress across the room, and go the bathroom. It's bigger than the room I grew up in, and the shower proves warm and soothing. I use various soaps laid out on the counter, and they fill the air with a sweet, orange citrus scent. Next, I find an armoire to the side of the balcony and scan it for something new to wear. Everything seems more undergarment than actual clothing. Figures. Finally, I settle on a plain white dress that is only *slightly* see through. I slip it on, and it feels smooth and cool against my skin. This is not a material I have ever felt before. It's lighter than feathers, and more comfortable than a warm embrace. There are beauties to this realm that are indeed to be cherished.

I think of returning to bed, but my nightmares still haunt me, so I leave my room and wander the halls, searching for something to distract. After passing many closed doors, I come upon an open library, with shelves higher than I can reach, and ladders taller than I dare climb. Lanterns hang on the walls and sit on tables, illuminating the room with warm orange glows. I hear shuffling of paper and realize I'm not alone.

A Fae looks up from his book, a monocle covering one of his eyes.

"I'm sorry. I didn't mean to disturb you," I say, crossing my arms, hoping to find more modesty in my dress.

"Disturb me?" says the Fae, and I realize it is Baldar, Dean's Keeper. "You bring an old man company. Come, come sit."

I take his invitation and find a plush chair across from him. I glance at the book he was reading. Something about herbs and their proper uses.

"Can't sleep?" asks Baldar, raising a giant grey eyebrow behind his monocle.

"Just wanted to look around. I..."

Before I can even finish speaking, he pulls out a bag from under the table and begins rummaging through the contents, mumbling to himself. "Not this one, no. This one? No. No. Definitely not that. Oh, yes. Here is it." He pulls out a small vial filled with a white liquid and holds it between us. "Two drops before bed, and it'll keep the bad dreams away. Make you sleep like a babe full of milk."

I take the vial from his hands. "Thank you."

"Ah, it's no trouble, my lady. No trouble at all. But...when you run out, come visit my show by the lion fountain. I have all manner of potions. To cure the cold, treat the aching head. Even something to entice the man of your dreams."

I chuckle. "A love potion?"

"Like I said, I have all manner of brews. Perhaps you require something for Prince Fenris..."

"Thank you, but we're fine. Wait." A shocking thought comes to mind. "You know who I am?"

"Apologies, Princess, but I can see through the illusion. I am a Keeper, after all. But I promise, I won't tell anyone who you are." He reminds me of Kal, and that puts me at ease.

"Thank you."

"Is he here right now?" asks Baldar, looking around thin air.

"He? Oh, Yami. Yes. He's on my shoulder."

Baldar's jaw drops so low it almost hits the table. "It is truly an honor to be in his presence. And yours, Princess. I've just...please, forgive my excitement. I've just never met a Midnight Star before."

"It's fine. But I'm just a normal girl. Well, mostly."

"Of course. Of course." He doesn't look like he believes me.

I try to recall what we were speaking of, and a dark thought crosses my mind. "How effective are these love potions?"

He leans back, casually relaxing in his wooden chair. "Depends on the herbs and the craftsman, but in the right hands, very."

"So someone can slip me one of these, and I'll just, I'll just—"

"Calm yourself, princess. These potions have limited effect on one already in love, and I suspect you are."

I let out a long breath, grateful I won't have to pick Levi as my husband just because he poured some magic herbs in my drink. "Are Fen and I that obvious?"

He chuckles. "Yes. But, even if it were not so, the rumors of your...partnership...have spread far and wide."

"What do people say?"

"That the princess has already chosen her king. That Fenris Vane will soon rule all seven realms."

Man. No wonder most of the princes seem to hate me. They haven't even had a turn, and already they hear of their failure. But the people are wrong. Even if I wanted to pick Fen, he would not forgive me for placing the crown upon his head. "I don't know what I'm doing."

Baldar laughs. "And who does? Please, do let me know. I must study them. Create a potion to replicate the effects."

His humor brings a smile to my lips. "I just...I feel like the seven realms are in the palm of my hand, so delicate and fragile, and if I squeeze too hard, if I move too fast or stumble, I will crush them. Nothing I do feels right, and every choice feels on the brink of bringing ruin to everything."

Baldar nods sagely. "Wait a moment. I know just the potion." He pulls out a goblet from his bag and places it on the table. He fills it with golden liquid.

"What is it?"

"Eighty percent alcohol. Twenty percent something nearly as strong."

I laugh so hard I snort, and then laugh some more at my ridiculousness. Once I've settled down, I grab the goblet and try a small sip, fearing the concoction will burn my throat. Instead it fills it with sweetness and warmth, like honey coating my tongue. "Wow. This is amazing."

"Thank you. Thank you. Tis my own brew. Nectar of the Elder Ones, I call it. It's the twenty percent that makes the taste, you see. Secret formula. The eighty is for the kick."

I take another sip, a big one, and already I feel the effects numbing my mind and body. "This could make a fortune."

The Keeper looks down, his face suddenly dark and melancholy. "Yes...yes it could."

"Did I say something?"

"No. No. You just remind of another time. Another place. I was not always a Keeper, you see. Once, before the vampire came to this land, I lived free, not far from here. My parents were of the Earth Tribe and owned a small home in one of the mighty trees that once stood in Inferna. They made a modest living, but worked hard, constantly. I spent most of my days at, well, I suppose you would call it an inn. There I would talk with the locals, and hear the most wondrous stories from the barkeep. I spent so much time there, eventually, he hired me on as an apprentice. I didn't take much to cleaning tables and floors though. No. I had more devious pursuits. The mixing of drinks and liquors. At first, only the truly brave and adventures tried my concoctions. But, as time passed on, and my skills and ingenuity improved, even common folk would take a sip. Eventually, I became the most famous brewer in all Inferna. I'd pour drinks that'd fill your dreams with visions of grand adventures and trials. Mixtures that'd wash away all cares in the world and bring you back to your lover's arms.

"I made a fortune. More than one thought possible in such a trade. And when I had saved up enough, I bought that whole tree that my parents had raised me in, and I put them up in the fanciest room, with the most glorious of views. They told me I'd done them proud then. And I told them it was because of their work and love that I got where I did. After, I was busy with work, so busy I never saw them again.

"For the Unraveling came. And when the vampires raided our city, they set the forests on fire, and the tree

I grew up in, the tree where my parents lived...it lit the night up in flames. I still remember the shadows the fire cast. Of faces screaming. Screaming into the night."

Baldar wipes at his eyes, turning away, wearing an embarrassed expression. "Excuse me, Princess. I must have partaken too much in my own wares."

I reach out and take his hand. "I'm sorry for what happened."

"No. No. I have it far better than others. Keeper to the Prince. And I still get to brew my mixtures, even if they are more potion than drink now." He sighs heavily, looking at the goblet between us. "I think it is time for me to go, Princess. Time for rest."

"Thank you for the potion," I say as he stands up and puts out the lanterns.

He smiles at me, though whether it's genuine or not I can't say. "Sweet dreams, Princess."

It takes me a while to find my way back to my room. Once back in bed, I take two drops of the white potion, and it fills my body with calming numbness. It is only then that I see him.

"Varis?"

He stands on the balcony, his fur cape flapping in the wind. "We cannot stay here. The vampires will use you until there is nothing left."

I sit up, though the motion is difficult with all the herbs and eighty proof alcohol running through my blood. "Varis, I trust Fen. He won't let anyone hurt me."

The Druid shakes his head. "You will be safer in Avakiri. There you can rally the Fae. Give them hope again. Hope for peace. Not the rage and fear that Metsi feeds them. If the Prince of Lust must come with you, so be it. I know herbs that will make him more docile. We can bring him with us."

"I can't leave. I must go back to Stonehill. It's my home."

He looks away, seemingly unconvinced.

I pause, thinking of what else I could say to sway him. "I know the way you feel about Asher. I see it in the way you look at him, in the way the two of you talk. So I know you understand vampires are more than just beasts. They are people. Some I deeply care for. And I will not abandon them."

Finally, Varis nods. "Very well. We stay here for now. I will train you, and hope it is enough to keep you safe."

...

The sun is bright when I wake. And Baldar is standing over me.

"Apologies, Princess," he says. "But I was told to deliver a message as soon as you awoke. Prince Dean and Prince Fenris request your presence in the training yard today."

I nod, reminded of my early days in Stonehill, when I didn't yet know what I would do in this world. "How's Es? Is she okay?"

Baldar nods. "She is well. Resting. They both are. I gave them a stronger sedative to help them sleep. After a shock such as the one they've had, they'll need time to rest and process."

"Okay, well, please make sure someone notifies me when they wake. I need to talk with them." To try and apologize...to explain.

Baldar agrees, then waits outside the room as I grab another white dress from the armoire, and slip it over my current one. It's a little less see through this way. More or less.

Yami finds purchase on my shoulder, and the Keeper guides us outside the palace, to a courtyard filled with flowers and warriors, honing their swordsman skills on wooden and stone columns. Fen and Dean stand around a wooden table, pointing at a large map and taking turns speaking.

"We can use the secret passageway behind the waterfall," says Dean. "Sneak into Stonehill and catch Levi unawares."

Fen shakes his head. "He knows of the passage. Would have had it caved in by now. Or worse, set with traps."

"Valid point. Well, that only leaves a frontal assault. But no great army. I have few men left after the battle against Metsi and Oren, and most of them are deserters."

"They will have to be disciplined," says Fen, massaging his knuckles.

I join them at the table, wrapping my arm around Fen's, and smiling. "They fled a battle that wasn't worth fighting. We shouldn't blame them."

Fen grunts. "They fled because Yami made them shit themselves."

My baby dragon stands a little taller, roaring into my ear with pride. I giggle.

"He's back, isn't he?" asks Fen.

"Yes. And he misses Baron. Where is the wolf?"

"Hunting." The way Fen says it, he seems quite jealous.

Dean steps up to me, uncomfortably close as he scans my shoulder. "Where is the beasty? Come on boy, you can come out. I need to congratulate you for pushing the Fae back. I was surrounded by fifty men, near my wits end when you roared in the sky and sent them running. Ah, there you are."

I flinch. "He revealed himself?"

"I see him too," says Fen, grinning.

I turn to Yami and pet his little scales. "What a good boy. Such a good boy."

Dean takes a turn petting as well, and my baby dragon purrs with joy. "You train up and get big now," says the prince. "We're going to need you." Yami nods, squinting and trying to look serious. "There you go. Good little beast of mass destruction. Now, back to the plans. We need a bigger army."

"Best keep your voice down," says Fen. "Back in Stonehill, I discovered there was a spy in the castle, reporting back to the Druids. They may have ears here as well."

Dean nods, lowering his voice to barely a whisper, sounding like an old woman on her deathbed. "Very well, then. Let's all talk like this. It totally won't draw attention."

I chuckle, then look around, seeing vampires train, but no others. "What about the Fae? We could recruit the slaves?"

Fen sighs, leaning down on his elbows. "Slaves make for poor warriors. They either join the enemy as soon as possible, or fight with so little vigor they lose you the battle."

"Okay. Well, what if we motivated them." An idea forms in my mind, and I start to tremble with excitement. "What if we offer them freedom after a certain term of service?"

Dean looks more serious than usual. "Might actually work."

"Maybe," says Fen. "But the masters won't be happy, if we send their slaves off to die."

"Then we lose support of the vampires," adds Dean. "Maybe even the Shade."

I chew my lip thinking. "Maybe we compensate anyone whose slaves leave to fight. We could pay them."

Dean whistles. "And who has that kind of coin?"

"Niam," says Fen.

"Right. The person least likely to help us." The Prince of Lust sits down on a chair, running his hands through his golden hair, mumbling about stupid vampires and Fae. Seems Fen and Dean have something in common.

Someone yells outside the courtyard. Then others join him. "What the bloody hell is going on?" asks Dean, already up and running.

Fen and I follow him out to the streets. Three men, vampires wearing leather and carrying swords, tie a rope around a man's neck. "You stole my dagger, you dirty Fae!" says the biggest vampire, his face dirty with mud.

"No," pleads the Fae, on his knees, his neck red and straining against the rope.

"Yes, you did. Don't lie. You know what we do to lying and thieving scum like you?"

"No. Please."

"String him up, boys."

The other two men grab the end of the rope and begin to tie it on a branch of a nearby tree, withered and barren of leaves.

Fen growls and rushes forward. "Stop. Now."

The vampires look his way and laugh. Continue their torture. How? And then I remember, the illusion. They don't recognize Fen as the Prince of War.

Dean raises his arm. "Cut him down. Now."

This time, the vampires do pay attention. They pause. "Apologies, your Grace," says the big one. "But this one is my slave. I can do what I like with my property."

"You will cut him down," Dean says, and intensity in his eyes I've not seen before. "Or I will take your hand with my blade."

"Maybe we should, Roge," says the smallest of the three.

Roge, the big one, nods. "Very well. I meant no offense. Release him." They untie the rope, setting the Fae free.

I run to the man's aid, helping him stand and whispering an incantation to help with his pain. He is covered with purple bruises, and my spell does not do enough. "I need to take him to a healer. Is there one nearby?"

Dean points to a tree in the distance. "There's a healer in the building there. Faster than trying to find Baldar."

I nod and help the Fae forward as his accusers disappear down an alley.

"I'll come with you," says Fen.

"No. I'll be fine. You're of more use here, planning how to retake Stonehill."

He pauses, then nods and returns to the courtyard with Dean.

I venture forward with the Fae, making small talk, and learn his name is Lars. The sky grows grey as we walk, and mist begins to form around our feet. "A storm be coming," says Lars. The words send him into a coughing fit, and we rest for a moment before continuing.

As we approach the tree, I see it's far larger than I imagined, towering over the nearby houses. It is grey and dead, and I wonder if this is one of the great trees Baldar spoke of. I notice holes and passages carved into the trunk high above, and I wonder if that's where he lived.

At the base of the tree stands a structure of white and gray stone, built so part of it wraps around the trunk. It's a large location and full of space. Inside, I see dozens of beds filled with men and women suffering from various injuries and ailments. There are vampire, Fae, and Shade. It seems all are welcome here. Healers scurry about, their white gowns grey with dust and sometimes red with blood. One woman catches my eye. "Seri?"

She finds my gaze, her short bob pinned away from her face. She was the one who taught me basic healing in Asher's realm. But..."What are you doing here?" I ask.

She blinks twice. "Excuse me. Do I know you?"

Right. The illusion. I want to tell her who I am, but I can't be sure who's listening. Any one of these patients could let the information spread. "I helped to treat the wounded at Sky Castle. You taught me how."

"Oh. I'm sorry. I don't remember."

I shrug, smiling. "I wasn't there very long. This man, he needs help."

"Of course," says Seri. She helps Lars to a bed and gives him a tonic for pain. I bring clean sheets and examine his wounds. The whole time, her face seems confused, and I think perhaps she is sensing I am more than I appear.

After a minute, Lars doses off, resting with the remedies we gave him, and Seri turns to me. "You want to stay a while? I need more like you."

"Sure." I know Varis will not be happy, since he needs to train me, but I need to feel helpful in the moment. I need something to ease the pain of my nightmares. Of what I allowed to happen to Daison. Of what I may allow still.

"What's your name again, I don't remember?" asks Seri.

"Um...Diana."

"Very well. Nice to meet you Diana. Come, I need help with another patient."

I nod, following her to another bed, and help set a woman's broken leg. "So many injured," I say later, sitting on an empty cot, looking around.

Seri leans against the wall, eating some kind of leaves from the pack tied around her waist. "Most were injured in the battle of Stonehill, fighting against the Fae. Others are just unlucky or careless."

She offers me a leaf, and I accept. The chewing is difficult, but the taste is nice and it's surprisingly filling. "What brought you here?" I ask. "Aren't you Keeper to Prince Asher?"

Seri sighs, leaving a leaf half eaten. "Things are changing up north for Fae and Shade. People are being hung and beaten for no reason under Levi's rule, and his influence is spreading. Asher allowed me to travel south for my own safety."

I think of Lars, almost hung on that tree. He healed enough to leave a few minutes ago, and I wished him well. "It seems, even here, Fae are in danger like never before."

Seri shrugs. "Times have been hard for our folk before. We always survive."

Her words touch me more deeply than she can know. For I am the reason things are changing for the worse, and I am the one who must make it better. Instead I sit here, talking, eating tasty food. "Seri, I—"

Someone screams, and we both turn, looking at the man being brought in through the back. I stand up, and the healers lay him down on the bed as I examine the wound. His belly is covered in blood, cut deep by some-thing. A sword.

Seri gives him a tonic for pain and a piece of wood to bite down on, something to stop the screaming and help prevent him from biting his own tongue.

"Someone assaulted this man," I say, continuing my examination. "Fairly recently. They missed the major organs, or he'd be dead, but he could still bleed to death. I need string and a needle and—

Something catches my eye. A tattoo of a serpent. A tattoo I saw only in Avakiri.

"This man is a raider."

Seri nods, bringing the string and needle. "He must have never escaped back to the Outlands. Must have gotten lost and found his way here."

I step back, my hands shaking. The raider. He would have been part of the attack on Stonehill. Part of the reason Daison is dead. "We can't help him."

Seri grabs my hands. "We are not warriors. We are not lords. We are healers. And we help all those who need our aid." She turns back to the raider, the patient, and begins cleaning off his wound.

I catch my breath, the shock of my memories wearing off, and join her, preparing the stitches. Once we are finished, Seri wraps the wound with clean bandages, and then washes her hands. "You did well," she says, glancing at me. "The first time is always difficult. Treating someone who has caused you pain."

I lean back against a pillow, sighing. "It should have been easier. I don't care for pain. Only peace. Only healing."

"That is how it should be. But all of us have darkness within. Sometimes it comes to the surface. A reminder of why we must keep it at bay."

I think on her words. Perhaps there is a reason behind the suffering and pain, a purpose to my thoughts of vengeance against Levi and Metsi. Perhaps they remind me to do better, to be good.

"Thank you," I say.

"For what?"

"For reminding me I can still do the right thing."

...

The sun is setting by the time Seri tells me to go home. "I'll need you tomorrow, so get some rest." I try to argue, but she runs this Healing Tree, and so I leave, traveling back to the palace, admiring the gold hues on the horizon. Something catches my eye.

A tree.

A man.

A rope.

Lars hangs from a withered branch, his face pale and blue, his body still. They hanged him. When no one was looking. They killed him. And I could do nothing.

Nothing.

Nothing.

How could you bring this upon us? The voices echo in my mind. *You were our friend! You were our friend and you let us die!*

I push away the thoughts and climb the tree, then untie the rope. I take what remains of Lars into my arms, and I weep for what has been done. And later, when the sun has set, and my tears are gone, I carry his body to the palace, to Dean's room, and I lay the body at his feet. "You will give him a proper burial," I say. "You will give him the respect of a free man."

Then I head to the east wing and find my friends.

I stand in the doorway of the room, uncertain if I should go in, but they both look up and smile at me. "Oh darlin'," says Es, half-awake, laying in a white bed with Pete at her side. "I had the nastiest dream. My hair was all messed up."

I smile and cross the room to hug her.

And then I tell them everything.

From the beginning.

About my death.

About the deal my mother made to save me.

About the deal I made to save her.

They're both more shaken than shocked by the story, maybe because they're here in Inferna, seeing the truth with their own eyes.

"You could have told us," says Pete, his eyes cold. He reminds me of the way Ace looked when he learned that Fen tried to kill their father. And I decide to never hide the truth from people I care about again. I only hope I still have time to remedy what has passed.

"I tried to protect you from this world," I say. "I didn't want anyone sacrificing their life, their happiness, to try and help me. But I know, now, I should have told you. I should have let you make your own decision."

Pete nods, and then a warmth enters his eyes I haven't seen since we reached Inferna. The tension leaves his body and he begins to weep.

And so I hug him.

And hold him.

And the three of us talk through the night, laughing about the past, and remembering how good it feels to have friends.

8

THE PRIMAL ONE

"I want to be king. Out of all my brothers, I think I would be the best choice. Out of all of us, I alone want peace. I alone want to end this war. And with you, I know I can."

—Asher

Dean does as I ask, and Fen holds me as we attend the funeral for Lars the next morning, Es and Pete at my side. It is a quiet affair. Only the five of us.

Later that day, Varis resumes my training.

We study at the library I stumbled upon, pouring over books. Varis shows me a spell to translate the language of the Fae into any language I know, and I begin to make quick progress on my reading.

"The amount of knowledge here is astounding," says the Druid, as he studies the different shelves and their contents. "I thought the vampires would have destroyed such volumes. Some of these have even been lost to Avakiri."

I think on it, grateful for the distraction from mathematical spells. "The Princes of Hell still rely on magic for ease of life. They have Keepers and others who cast spells. These Fae must learn somehow."

Varis rubs his chin, studying a particularly dusty volume. He seems enthralled by the writing. "Yes, I believe you are right. I suppose I always thought the knowledge was passed down orally, through storytelling and lessons."

"It usually is," says a new voice. Dean, standing in the hallway, his shirt off again, his muscles glistening under the golden hue of the lanterns. He looks a god amongst his domain. Perfect and powerful.

"My brothers burned most of the Fae texts they came across," he continues. "But I would not part with such knowledge, such beauty of language." He walks forward and pours himself a drink from a bottle on the table. He offers me one, but I shake my head.

"We are studying," says Varis.

Dean grins. "And I'm offering to make it a little more exciting."

The Druid shakes his head.

I sigh and reach for the drink. "Why not? I've studied all day, and yet I've learned nothing to help me fight."

Dean's eyes go wide, and he turns to the Druid. "What are you teaching her, old man?"

"Old what—"

"Yami needs to learn combat, tactics. Don't you Yami?" The dragon nods, licking his lips at our wine. "You see?"

Varis sighs, sounding very old indeed. "There are basics to be mastered first."

I take a sip of the wine, enjoying the sweetness of the drink, and make sure to keep it away from my rebellious dragon. "But I have fought with Yami before. Once, when Oren nearly killed me, Yami changed, grew larger than this room, and fought off Riku, the Fire Spirit, himself."

Varis sits down, closing his book. "Spirits can muster power when threatened. But it is a dangerous form."

Zyra, his silver owl who sits on a nearby shelf, nods.

"How do we access it?" I ask.

"You don't. Not intentionally. Not unless it is absolutely necessary and awakened on its own. Like the time you describe."

I groan, closing the boring spells before me. "There must be a way."

"No," says Varis, not skipping a beat. "There is none." He glances at the book in his hands. Then back at me.

I study the volume. It is pitch black with a unique leather binding. Ancient Fae glyphs decorate the spine. "That one looks interesting."

"It's not. Well, not for you anyway. It is a history of the fifth Air Druid and is primarily a description of his many political meetings."

Somehow, I just don't believe him.

Varis clears his throat. "It is late. And time for rest. I will be in my quarters if you need me." He stands and leaves the library, Zyra on his arm. Though he tries to hide it, I see the black volume peeking out from under his robes.

Dean pours me another cup of wine. "Now, how about we have some fun?"

I glance between him and the mathematical tome before me. "Fun it is."

...

It's dark by the time we leave the palace, Dean dressed in a black vest, me in my two layers of white. "We should find Fen?" I say.

Dean raises an eyebrow. "And pull him away from training?"

"Right. Fen does prefer swords over...well...anything."

"Then let him have his fun while we have ours." Dean bows and offers me his arm. "Come, the games are about to begin."

"Games?"

"You'll see, Princess." His eyes sparkle with excitement. "And then, you'll wish you could stay here forever."

I chuckle, taking his arm and letting him escort me forward. On the way, various women wink and purse their lips at Dean, their delicate clothing revealing perfect bodies with long legs and smooth skin. "Come visit me later," they say in voices that remind me of song. "And who's the new girl? Moving on already?"

Dean addresses them each by name, promising to…visit…with them later. If, of course, he's not taken. He winks at me.

And I roll my eyes. "I see you get around."

"My realm has a very open view of sexuality," he says. "The focus is on enjoyment and consent, a beneficial experience to all parties. The things some of these women can do. You should see one day."

"Um. No thank you." I have no interest in his offer, yet a part me wishes my world was more like this one. Where woman don't have to struggle with consent and assault throughout their lives. I've known a few, back at the Roxy, who fought every day to protect themselves from abusive boyfriends and nasty bosses. It scarred them. Perhaps, if they could have grown up here, things would be different.

We leave the women behind, and the streets begin to clutter with more people, all pushing toward one destination: An arena, at least ten stories high, built from white pillars covered in purple vines. Dean escorts me in, to the second level, and what appears to be the best seating, a private box overlooking the area below. "The perks of being a prince," he says, as we take our seats on a plush burgundy couch and slaves bring us grapes and wine on silver platters. I hate benefitting from the injustice, but I know I can do nothing yet, so I accept the food graciously, thanking the Fae and making sure they know they are appreciated. A part of me wants to resist, decline everything they bring me, but I know that will make them more worried than happy.

Plopping a grape in my mouth, I study the arena below. It is a pool of clear water, dotted with islands of white rock. An announcer calls out, "And here she is, lords and ladies, the unmatched champion of Moonlight, the Dancer of Waves, Callisia!"

The crowd, hundreds of men and women and children, roar in applause, causing the very sofa beneath me to shake. The energy is intoxicating, but I worry for what's about to happen. "These aren't gladiator games, are they? Where people kill each other? Because if so, I'm not interested."

Dean smirks and gives me a wink. "Don't worry, Princess. This is far, far more interesting."

I frown, still skeptical, and turn my attention back to the arena. Callisia enters through a steel gate, wearing black armor that hugs her curves and reveals her legs and stomach. Of course...so practical. She hops from stone to stone, leaping further than any mortal human could, and, once in the center, pulls a long red cloth from her belt.

"And now," says the announcer, "the Reaper!"

Suddenly, a giant fish leaps out of the water, it's large mouth and razor sharp teeth aimed at Callisia. The performer dodges, her red cloth drifting behind her. The fish falls back into the water. Its body reminds me of a shark, but its fins are long and wide, making me think of a manta ray.

Dean nudges me. "First time seeing a Windshark, huh?"

"Yeah," I say, my eyes glued to Callisia as she avoids attack after attack, luring the Windshark with the red fabric. It reminds me of bullfighters back on earth. But because Callisia is a vampire, she evades and maneuvers in ways no human can, leaping over the arena, twisting and twirling in the sky, a streak of red and black.

"They live in the oceans of Inferna," says Dean, pointing at the Windshark, "but sometimes they travel upstream, through the rivers. The fact that they survive in fresh water makes them one of the deadliest predators in the land. A live one sells for quite the fortune."

I nod, clapping as Callisia jumps into the water, then back out as the Windshark bites at her feet but never touches flesh. The event fills me with adrenaline, and I barely stay in my seat.

"Isn't this fun?" asks Dean.

"There's a beauty to it. And I can't even imagine the skill it takes to survive. I had imagined something far more barbaric."

"I never fail to surprise. How about—"

"Prince Dean!" a young Shade runs into the private box, panting. "I'm sorry Your Grace, but I have urgent news," he says.

Dean stands, concern flashing in his eyes. "Tell me."

"The north-eastern caravan…"

"Yes?"

"It's gone, Your Grace. Raiders. Took all the goods and killed all but a few men who escaped."

"But that's a new route. There is no way they could know…" Dean rubs his chin, his eyes growing dark. "Make sure the families of those who perished are provided for. Now go."

The man bows and leaves, as Dean sits back down, trembling with rage. "It appears Fenris was right. There is a spy in my realm. How…how could I have allowed this?"

I touch his hand, hoping to calm him. "Don't blame yourself. The spy could be anyone in a realm of thousands."

He shakes his head. "Only those with power knew about the route. And Keepers know more than most."

My jaw falls. "Baldar? You think it was him? But he's so kind."

"And he's a Fae. A Fae who lost his home and family when we took over his lands. Why wouldn't he betray me?"

"Just…don't do anything you'll regret. Everyone is innocent until proven guilty."

He chuckles. "It's not that way here, Princess. Though perhaps…perhaps it should be." He sighs, and I see some happiness return to his face. "Very well, I won't punish anyone yet, but I will keep a close eye on Baldar and the rest of my servants."

I smile, letting him know I approve.

He smiles back, then looks disappointed. "I'm sorry, Princess, but I've lost interest in the match. Perhaps, you'll accompany me somewhere else?"

I blink, surprised the Prince of Lust could grow tired of something as exciting as a fight, particularly one involving a woman in sexy armor. Perhaps he's more complicated than I gave him credit for. "Sure."

He escorts me outside the arena, away from the crowds, and into a maze of bushes and vines. "Are we going to play hide and seek?" I ask, as Yami flies off my shoulder and looks around.

Dean grins. "As fun as that would be, no. The maze hides something more precious." He guides me through a series of turns, until we reach an ornate white door. We step through.

And into a grove I did not believe could exist.

Giant trees, reaching past the clouds, surround a clearing of grass and flowers. These are behemoths of nature, blocking out the stars, making me seem inconsequential in their presence. I wonder if these are the trees Baldar spoke of. The ancient forests that burned.

Dean guides me down into the grove, and we lay on the soft grass that smells of mint and honey. The Prince lays a hand on one of the trees, caressing the bark. "When my father invaded this land, he set fire to the forests and buildings, burned all in his path until victory was his. Somehow, this grove survived. It was when I discovered it that I decided to fight for this realm as my own."

I lean up. "What do you mean fight?"

"The seven realms were not always so. After the invasion, the land had to be divided up, and my brothers and I were all allowed to make a case for which we preferred. I requested this land, because of the grove, because of the beauty that remained here. Niam talked about using it for cheap wood, Levi for burning it down as a symbol, but I would not have it. These trees are more than bark and leaves. They are a part of this land's history, a part of its culture, and that must be protected."

"Fen would have been a child at the time, yes? So did your father pick his realm for him?" I ask. It must have been such an elaborate dupe for everyone to pretend Fen had been one of them all along.

"Fen's realm didn't exist at the time," he says. "It was part of the Outlands. It was wild, which is why his realm sits at the edge of our kingdom and is the most desolate and untamed. High Castle was considered a realm, and my father was the seventh prince, the seventh curse. Have you not figured it out yet? Fen isn't cursed, not with what we are. There's a reason he's the Prince of War and not the Prince of Wrath, as the seven sins would have him. My father, the prince turned king, is the true Prince of Wrath."

I have so many questions, about Fen and his brothers and Lucian. "So what happened when you claimed this realm?" I ask.

"I was sure my father would side with one of my brothers, but he surprised me. Though it was thousands of years ago, I still remember clearly. I remember when he told me the news. He grasped my shoulder and said, 'Though we no longer live in the Silver Gardens, I would never wish to see them burn,' and then he left. It was one of the few moments, I think, that we truly understood each other. And because of that, I will never forget."

"It's beautiful," I say, motioning to the nature around us, this private sanctuary, this secret.

He looks up, deep into my eyes. "Not as beautiful as the woman before me."

I can't help it. I blush. Probably just the wine. "Please...I saw those women ogling you back in the city. I don't even compare."

"Beauty is in the eye of the beholder. If I claim that leaf is perfect in its form, who's to say I am wrong? If I say that rock brings me joy, who is to question me? If I confess, you are the most amazing women I have ever met, who will change my mind?"

"Dean..."

He leans forward. Closer. Closer. Until our lips almost touch.

His scent is sweet and intoxicating. His warmth consuming.

He breathes in deeply.

He moves closer.

And then he pulls away.

"You are under the influence of drink," he says.

I am. So drunk I might have let him kiss me. So drunk it's hard to think. "And?"

"If there is to be anything between us, you should be of clear mind. I wish no regrets upon you."

This is the last thing I expected the Prince of Lust to say. In many ways, Dean would make a better king than his brother. He wouldn't focus on fighting and accruing wealth, but on bringing joy and comfort. Isn't that the sign of great ruler? One who could bring upon a golden age?

"Thank you," I say. "For being a gentleman."

He grins, though I see in his eyes he wishes more could have happened between us. He stands, offering me his hand to help me up. "If you would indulge me, Princess. I have one more surprise left."

I nod and take his arm.

He guides me to the outskirts of the city, to a tunnel built by man. I raise my dress, trying to keep it from dragging in the mud. "I must say. You surprise me once again. What are we doing?"

"The Fae lived here for millennia before we arrived, and who knows—perhaps there was something even older once. I have seen things in my travels, artifacts brought to my museum, that are neither Fae nor vampire, but relics of an ancient age. So, I've tried to find more."

We descend deeper into the tunnel, and it grows hotter as torches cast hot yellow lights at us. Dean wipes his brow and removes his shirt. "I've had my servants digging for artifacts for years. And a few weeks ago, they uncovered this."

He motions me to stop, then grabs a torch from the wall and dips it into some black liquid. Oil. It lights on fire, streaking across the darkness, illuminating the giant cavern we have reached.

Before us stands a giant stone door, cracked open in the center. It is dark green and covered in ancient glyphs. It reminds me of a Waystone, and for a moment I fear Dean has uncovered Avakiri. But then I look past the door, and see that it doesn't lead into a Waystone, but a garden. "What is this place?" I ask.

"Not sure yet. I've held back on exploring, waiting so we could do it together. I needed something to impress the princess." Dean grins and grabs my hand, pulling me past the door.

And we emerge into a giant ruin, with ceilings as high as the palace, the walls around us withered stone covered in green moss. Tiles cover the floor, and a barren fountain stands before us, long dry. We walk forward, past doors and windows overgrown with vines and trees. Past a dirty pond filled with flowers. And then I see them.

The statues.

Five of them.

Tall and majestic, carved from emerald green stone. Two are men. Three are woman. Each carries an animal on their shoulder. "The Druids," I whisper, realization dawning on me. "These are the Four Druids and the Midnight Star."

Dean nods. "This must have been some kind of temple. Someplace to honor the Wild Ones. Look here behind them." I follow Dean up a wide set of stairs to a giant wall completely covered in ancient text. "Can you read it?"

I run my hand over the glyphs and cast the incantation to translate languages. Most of the words change, but not all. "It seems to be written in a form of Fae, but I don't recognize all the characters. This language must be ancient. More ancient than anything I've seen."

Dean smiles with glee. "Can you make anything out?"

"Yes," I say, studying the markings. "It's the tale of the Primal One. It's well known amongst the Fae, but this version is longer. There are details I've never heard." I'd heard children sing the tale of the Primal One back in Avakiri, but it was never this. I focus on the wall and continue reading.

"The Primal One was first of our kind. When he came to this world, he found it ravaged by the elements, in a state of constant chaos. At first he sought to fight them, but even he could not conquer nature. So the Primal One tamed the elements, taking their power within him and brining balance to the world.

"But it was so empty.

"So the Primal One used his power and created others in his image. The Fae.

"He told them how to live, how to be happy. And they listened. So powerful was the Primal One, that his words, his thoughts, became theirs.

"And the world was happy, and yet it was sad. It was full, and yet it was hollow.

"As the years went by, despite all the people around him, the Primal One grew more and more lonely. And in his despair, he drew something else to this world.

"Darkness." I shiver before continuing.

"A being that preyed upon weak worlds. It attacked Avakiri and Inferna, consuming all in its path. The Primal One fought the beast as best he could, using the Fae as an extension of his arm when needed, but he couldn't stop the Darkness.

"Though he was everywhere, a part of everyone, he could not focus on all things at once. It was then that the Primal One realized, by making everything a part of himself, he had created nothing. He had made the world empty.

"And it was then that the Primal One gave up the elements. He did not set them free as before, but instead gave each element to a keeper, creating the four Wild Ones.

"With the powers broken apart, the Primal One felt his connection with the Fae fade away, but what he saw was incredible. They began to develop thoughts and ideas of their own.

"They were given free will.

"Now, they did not fight as one mind, but hundreds of thousands, and together...

"They defeated the Darkness.

"It was then that they realized it could not be destroyed, only beaten, and so the Primal One tamed the Darkness like he did the elements, and bestowed it upon a new Wild One, creating the first High Fae.

"The Druids were linked, so that the power of the elements could keep the Darkness at bay. And the Darkness would keep the elements in control, keep them from consuming the world in chaos.

"Years of peace followed, and happiness, and sorrow. But it was happiness and sorrow created by free will. And after many, many ages past, the Primal One gave up his rule, and left the world, leaving his children to be truly free."

I pull my hand away from the wall, the story finished.

Dean frowns. "How is this different from the original?"

I turn to him. "In the common tale, the Primal One grows lonely, yes, and he divides up the elements creating free will, yes. However, he retains a connection to them all, and thus manifests Yami, who is all. And thus, the Primal One becomes the first High Fae. Eventually, he leaves, and his children, the next High Fae, continue to rule."

Dean raises an eyebrow. "So if this tale is true, then..."

I look at the dragon on my shoulder, his scales gleaming with stars. "Then there is a darkness within me. A darkness that can consume the world."

Dean notices my grim face and chuckles. "Don't give yourself too much credit, Princess. I, for one, have already destroyed a world. Well. I helped. There is no way to know if this story is true. If any of them are true."

"You're right," I say, sighing, letting tension escape me. "These tales were probably just created to explain creation and the beginning of life. In my world, there are many old religions that used stories to explain what can now be explained by science."

"Exactly." He snaps his fingers, and for a moment we don't say anything. Then Dean smiles devilishly. "I have a confession to make. I'm the one who let Lopsi out."

I throw my hands up in shock. "You freed that creature! Why?"

He shrugs. "I needed a way to get you to my realm. It was the only real solution."

I groan, rubbing my temples. "People got hurt. Someone could have been killed."

"But they weren't, were they? Hey, how about we focus on something else? Like that. What's that?" Dean points to something in the wall. A handprint covered in spikes.

I step forward. "I know what that is. I've seen its kind before."

"Well, what—"

Before he can finish, I stick my hand onto the spikes, letting my blood flow into the stone. The glyphs begin to glow silver, and then the wall with the story begins to open. Not a wall then. A door.

And behind it there's a smaller courtyard with a pedestal in the center. Upon it sits a shallow bowl of gold filled with clear water.

Dean looks into the vessel, his eyes lighting up. "This can't be. It can't."

"What is it?" I ask, walking to his side, and then I see it, my reflection in the water, and I understand.

I see myself in the water, back in Portland, at a graduation. My graduation. From law school. I see Es and Pete congratulating me. I see us go to dinner at a restaurant fancier than I could afford, and there is someone there with me. A man, tall and handsome, whispering in my ear. I laugh at whatever he says, and then we kiss.

I reach to touch the water, grasping at the droplets that run through my fingers, at the images that seem half memory. I can almost feel—

Dean yanks my hand away. "Do not touch the water. It's said if you do, you will be swept away into another reality, another existence."

I blink a few times, and the visions begin to fade. I begin to feel more like myself. "What is this?"

Dean looks at the bowl. "My Keeper told of such a thing, though even he thought it myth. The Mirror of Idis. It is said, at the deepest of his despair, the Primal One wept, and his tears created a pool, a mirror, showing how things may have been if he'd chosen differently."

So that could have been my life. If I had never taken the contract. If I had followed the path I was on. I could have been a lawyer. I could have been safe and happy with my friends. I could even have love.

But I could never have my mother.

She wasn't in the vision. Because her soul was still trapped. Trapped for all eternity.

That path is gone. I can never go back.

Dean touches my hand, pulling me away from my dark thoughts. He looks at me, his eyes filled with a sorrow I haven't seen before. "The mirror," he says, "the mirror showed me what would have happened if I had never let you go. If I had taken the first turn as was intended." He smiles, though his eyes fill with tears. "We could have been happy. Happier than I ever imagined. Perhaps we still can." He massages my hands with his own, caressing them with the softest touch. "I know what I want, Arianna. Do you?"

I step back, letting his hands fall away. Because I don't. I don't know what I want.

Fen, because he makes me happy.

Asher, because he can bring about peace.

Dean, because he reminds me that life can be thrilling.

All of them. None of them.

But I must choose.

And my choice will change the whole world.

9

UNCHAINED

Fenris Vane

"I can hear Fen mumbling his complaints. I ignore them."
—Arianna Spero

My skills have grown dull. For weeks I was tortured, barred and caged. Now, I wield a sword once more. I feel the weight in my palm, the leather grip on my skin. The blade is perfectly balanced, thick and sharp for piercing armor and bone. It is of Kayla's making. I strike at the wooden target before me, slicing through air, splitting the log in half. I move on to a stone pillar. The vampire blood coursing through my veins gives me strength, makes wood and flesh too frail. The stone will dull my blade, but I need something solid to practice on, something that won't break at the hint of my power. I side step on the soft grass, light on my feet, striking at the column. I cut into the stone over and over, and then I change my technique. I begin to stop my blade short just as it meets my target, practicing control over strength. I imagine a body where the pillar is. Head, torso, legs. Strike. Strike. Strike. I aim for where the major arteries would be. I aim for a guaranteed kill.

The training yard is near empty this time of night, but a few practice in the shadows far off. The smell of roses and peaches carries on the wind, tickling my nose, as I wipe the sweat from my brow. White flowers and green vines spill over the walls around the field, sprinkling the darkness with touches of light. There is no fancier training yard in all Seven Realms, and I wonder why Dean mixes combat and beauty. War is simple, brutal, devoid of art, and yet my brother approaches the two as one and the same. I've seen it in the way he fights, twirling through a battlefield, jumping over his foes, more dancing than cleaving. There is elegance to his technique, but foolishness as well. Too often he leaves his back exposed. Too often he strikes with more flair than speed. I see his methods in the others practicing here. The Style of the Rose, I hear them call it. Such a soft name for such a soft form.

Despite myself, I begin to adopt its stance. Upright, blade far from the body. Legs bent slightly and loose. I twirl, spinning my blade like a storm, ravaging the stone pillar. I leap, leaving myself exposed, but covering a far greater distance than usual. My heart rate begins to rise. There is some sense to this method after all. Perhaps I will never use it in battle, but it will be of use if ever I am forced to fight Dean's soldiers. If ever I am forced to fight my brother.

I whip the blade left and right, up and down, as if it were more string than steel. Clatter and clashing fill the air, but through it all, I still hear him, gliding over the grass.

"What do you want, Varis?"

The Druid's footsteps stop. He stands behind me. I can smell the fur on his clothes, the scent of places far away on his skin. Of Avakiri. It must be a world far different than my own, a sight to behold one day. If I live long enough to see it.

The Druid speaks softly, the wind stirring at his words. "You are fierce with the blade, Prince of War, but blind to the other forces at play. Blind to the earth and wind. Blind to the heat and water in all things."

"I see enough," I say, lowering my blade to my side.

He steps closer. "Let me train you. Let me do what your mother could not."

"You knew her." The words slip from my tongue. I do not wish to speak to the Druid, do not wish to know of his way, but I crave to learn more of her. More of the woman who haunts my dreams.

"She was my mentor," says Varis. "My friend. She was the oldest of the four Wild Ones. Our guide in peace and war. I would have given my life for hers if I had but the chance. I would give my life for her son..."

His words hang in the air, thick and heavy between us. This man, he sees me as more than foe, more than vampire. Perhaps even more than common Fae. But...I am a Prince of Hell, and he is but Druid. "We are not friends."

"No," says Varis. "We are not. But it does not mean we cannot co-operate, for prosperity, for peace." He pauses. "Your powers will continue to grow, and one day, you will lose control. Who shall suffer when the time comes? Asher? Arianna?"

"I am as I always was." It is a lie. I know. Something within me has stirred these past few days, something primal and dark. It slithers at the edge of my mind, hides by the side of my heart.

He steps closer once more. "I was once the same, you know. I was but a boy when the Spirit chose me. I had a family, a home. It was your mother who arrived to take me away. I would not leave with her. I would not leave my brothers and sister and mother and father. I did not want the gift bestowed upon me. I did not want the duty. I told your mother as much."

He pauses. "To my surprise, she did not force me, as I had heard was often done. Instead, she stayed at my home, pretended she was little more than honored guest, and allowed me to go about my days. First, I resented her presence, despised her like I didn't know I could. She was a hero, you understand, a hero of my people, and yet she was my personal enemy. For days, I did not look at her. Though we ate together and she shared words with my mother and father, I would not speak. I would not show her any kindness until she let me be. But, as all things, over time my resistance withered.

"I began to smile at her jokes. Laugh when her wolf Spirit licked at my face. Once, I even shared my meal with her. It was the next day, when it happened. My sister and I were playing by the Old Willow Well. Some boys from the village, older and bigger than we were, came by to play their own way. They smashed my face against the stone well. One held me down, for I was a small lad back then. The other took his hands to my sister. She was young, a little girl, but that did not stop him from running his hands over her. A darkness filled me then. Primal and hungry. I had felt it before, as hate for Lianna, your mother, but now it turned to rage. It poured from me like a river of blood and ice, and the wind bent in its wake. It tore through the air like a wave, knocking the boys back, slamming them against the tree and stone. It tore through my sister. She fell back. Back. Into the well.

"The screams still haunt my dreams. Her bloody face still scars my nightmares. It was Lianna who found us, who pulled out my poor sister. The girl yet lived, but her head had been crushed near the top, like an apple someone stepped on. Her words were slurred and strange. Her memories wrong and frightful. Lianna tried to heal her, but even the power of the Spirits was not enough. And after a few days, it was clear my sister would never be the same. It was then that I left with your mother. It was then that I began my training. I would never lose control again, you see. And I never did."

My heart pounds in my chest at his words. His story flows through my mind, and instead of him, I see myself playing by the well, instead of his sister, I see Kayla. And when she falls. When her head is caved in and scooped out, I see Arianna.

I drop my sword. It is only the exhaustion of my training, I tell myself. Only the fatigue.

Varis turns away. "When you are ready, I will be here for you. Always." He begins to walk, to slip away into the shadows.

For the first time, I face him. "Do you love him?"

He stops, shock in his voice. "Who?"

"Asher. Do you love him? Because he deserves to be loved. Even if it is by a Fae Druid."

Varis meets my gaze. There is certainty to his eye. "I do."

I nod. My blessing in a way.

"How did you know?" he asks. "You were not yet born when Asher and I first met."

"After the Midnight Star fell, it was still years before all Druids turned to slumber. I remember one night, when my mother...my Queen, had taken me to visit Asher's realm. After a night of feasting, I noticed my brother slip away in the cover of dark. I was a curious boy, and so I followed. It is strange. It is only now, in my memories, that I am a boy. Before, I was as I am now. But now I see the truth. I was a boy. And I wanted to see where my older brother was heading in the middle of night. So I kept to the shadows, tailing him through the castle, out into the forest. There, he met you. You did not speak for long, and though I could not hear what you were saying, I knew it was a form of goodbye."

Varis smiles, a glint in his eyes. "That was the night before I turned to slumber. Asher and I were enemies by then, but I had to see him one last time."

"And what are you now?" I ask.

He shrugs. "I do not know. I fought for the Fae. He fought for the vampires."

"But you turned on Oren. You protected me and Arianna."

"Yes, but is that enough? Asher and I have not spoken since before the battle. His mind and heart are his own. And I do not know if I will ever truly win them back."

I grin. "Perhaps if you wore a suit. Maybe grew some hair."

Varis runs a hand over his bald head and the silver tattoos there. He chuckles. "Perhaps. Times are shifting. Maybe we Druids can have a different look for once. But there are advantages. My hair never blocks my vision in a fight. You should try it some time—"

"I'm not shaving."

"But it's traditional for a Druid—"

"Never."

"But it symbolizes the eternal Spirits and—"

"Be quiet or my fist will symbolize eternal pain."

We both laugh.

"What'd I miss?" Dean walks out from the shadows, shirtless, a sword hanging from his belt.

I smirk. "Only the jokes we were making at your expense. Your fighters, I've seen Fae children with more strength."

Dean studies the men training in his yard. "You have a point."

Varis bows his head slightly. "I will see you two later. That is, if your vampire tendencies don't take over and you murder each other first." With that, he leaves, returning to the palace.

Dean throws a leather bag at me and I catch it. He grins. "Ready to return to Stonehill?"

I place my fingers to my mouth and whistle. After a moment, Baron rushes from the palace, falling in place at my side. He bares his teeth at Dean, growling.

And I smile. "Ready."

Together, we walk out of the palace, joking and laughing, but something tickles at my mind. I have never called Baron from so far before and had him heed me. Our bond is growing. Something in me is changing. I remember the tale Varis told me, and I tremble for what is to come.

...

I say goodbye to Arianna, and then Dean and I argue over going by boat or horse. My brother prefers the comfort of his barge, but I argue steeds would be quicker. Eventually, he relents, and we pick two horses from the stables and ride out into the night. The sun begins to rise before we slow our pace, allowing our animals to rest. Baron keeps stride with me.

"You're using illusion again," I say.

Dean nods, adjusting the black hood over his face. "How do you know?"

I just do. Something else I couldn't do before. My brother and I both wear cloaks, his black, my brown, and light leather beneath. We should look like travelers, likely nobility, judging by our horses and swords, but not very important. Important people would be on a barge after all. Baron would appear a black dog to anyone who would look. An odd companion, but not unheard of in these lands.

After I don't respond, Dean shrugs. "You scare me sometimes, you know. The things you can do. It's not like the rest of us."

I grin. "Saying I make you shit your pants?"

"No...but I'm not sure Levi can say the same."

"You've been part of the council since Arianna and I escaped. Tell me, how do the others stand on matters?"

Dean tilts his head to the side, grinning from ear to ear. "Oh, you should see the meetings. What marvelous entertainment they make. Niam and Levi bicker over Stonehill like an old couple. Levi controls the castle, without a doubt, and so his income has increased. Our poor greedy brother Niam just can't stand the thought. He's trying to split the profits, offer his consulting and manpower in return."

"Let me guess...Levi cares nothing for his help?"

"Levi cares nothing for any of us. Oh, everyone spoke of ruling their own realm in contentment, but what a pile of stinking shit that turned out to be. Everyone wants to be king. And now that Arianna is out of the picture, they're trying to figure out how to do it with maximum backstabbing and minimal honor."

I raise an eyebrow. "Even Zeb? I always figured him uninterested in politics. More concerned with food and wine."

Dean frowns, his eyes growing dark. "I know you have always liked him, but do not underestimate our dear brother. There is a darkness in him. I saw it during the invasion, when he lead the front lines against the Fae in battle. He tore men apart with his bare hands, did worse to the women."

"None of us are innocent," I say.

He looks away, shame on his face. "No. I suppose none of us are."

A moment. "What of Ace?"

"Unclear," says Dean. "He's colder than usual. Harsher. As far as I can tell, he's trying to stay neutral, but it is difficult in such times. I think, when you spoke of killing our father, he took it personally somehow, a betrayal. It hurt him most of all. More than Arianna being Fae. More than you being a Druid."

I sigh, the weight of regrets bearing on me. "He helped me search for our father's killer. I didn't wish it, but I couldn't turn his help down either."

Dean nods. And then he asks what I have dreaded. "Was it true? Did you really kill our father?"

"No," I say, studying his eyes, looking to see if he believes me. His gaze is hard, unyielding, so I continue. "I did not kill Lucian. But I did drug him. He spoke to me of freeing all the Fae, of making them our equals. It did not sound like him, and it did not sound possible without destroying our way of life. So I drugged him, intending to restrain him, see if his state of mind would return to normal. However, he did not go unconscious; instead, his symptoms were those of death."

"Symptoms?"

I nod. "Our father is alive. I learned later from Asher, and Arianna as well, our father took a potion to fake death. Then he fled to the Fae, with whom he has an alliance. Together, they plot to the bring the Fae to power once more, to restore balance between our people."

Dean frowns, chewing on his lip. "But why fake his death, why resign the crown? Why not be Vampire King *and* Fae supporter?"

"Arianna," I say, her very name warming my blood.

"Ah, of course. When he gave up the throne, the contract of his will came into effect. Then we did the rest, bringing Arianna to this world. With the Midnight Star returned, the Druids awakened, and the Fae grew in power. Our father truly is a genius. A madman, but a genius one. Still..." He looks out at the horizon, where the tips of Stonehill begin to appear. "Why the change of heart? Why care for the Fae?"

"Arianna told me he does not. There is some other game he plays. One that requires the Fae to be at full strength."

Dean laughs, slapping his thigh. "Now that sounds like good old father."

I see in his eyes that he believes me. That is good. I will need all the allies I can muster in the coming days. "So, what is your public stance on the council?" I ask.

"Publicly, I support hunting you down and sticking your head on a spike." He winks. "But privately I just want Arianna to pick me as the new king so everyone can stop acting like babies and just let me rule."

He chuckles, and I know he wants his words to come off as a joke, but there is truth in them he cannot hide.

"Arianna..." I say, the reality hard to muster. "Arianna will not choose me. I do not wish to be king, and now that Inferna knows I have Fae blood, they do not wish it either."

Dean snickers. "Please, none of that matters to Arianna. Hell, the Fae blood might even be a perk. Lucky bastard."

I know he seeks to cheer me, but it does not change the truth. Arianna must choose someone else. Someone who will save this world.

For a while, we do not speak, and I listen to the crunch of snow beneath hooves, to the winter birds singing in the trees. In time, men and women being to appear on the muddy road, most wearing gray rags and carrying bags. They travel opposite to us, away from

Stonehill and its walls. "Quite the exodus," remarks Dean as a woman avoids his horse. "Personally, I hope they're heading to my realm. Except that one. That one looks boring."

"Keep your voice down," I say, speeding up my horse. "To these people, you don't have a realm. You don't have a throne. To them you are but a traveler. Let us keep it that way, shall we?"

"Very well. Perhaps we need codenames then." Dean smiles, ideas playing in his eyes. "I will be Rump. And you can be...Dump."

I shiver. "Sometimes, I wonder if you even understand the things you say."

"What?" He recoils, looking shocked. "Something wrong with the names?"

"Everything, dear brother. Everything."

The gates begin to loom ahead of us. Many leave the city ahead, but a few try to enter as well. A Shade wrapped in blue robes and jewelry covered with rubies and diamonds is stopped in his path by a guard. The soldier is not one I recognize, not one of my men, though he wears my red colors. "No Fae allowed in the city," he says, raising a spear.

"Excuse me, but vampire runs through my blood," says the Shade, his speech of high nobility.

The guard spits at the man's feet. "Half Fae, all Fae. Turn around and leave before I make you."

My stomach twists at the sight before me. My blood runs hot. This is not the way of Stonehill. The way of my people. I reach for my sword, but Dean grabs my hand. He shakes his head in warning.

I clench my jaw, but do nothing as the guard kicks the Shade to the mud. Again and again. After a moment, the noble man finally crawls to his knees, and trudges away from the gate.

As the man passes us, I motion to him, and flick a coin into his hands. "For the journey ahead," I say.

"Thank you," he says. "I am glad there are some who still respect our ways." And then he vanishes into the mass of people on the road.

Dean leans closer. "I see the princess is rubbing off on you, dear brother. Hope she doesn't make you too soft."

I grunt, then dismount and lead my horse forward. The guard in red stops us as well.

"What business you have here?" he asks.

"Returning home," I say, showing my fangs as I speak.

The man seems skeptical, chewing his lip, and then Dean chimes in. "Bearing goods from Prince Levi's realm." He points at the supply packs on our horses. "For the event."

The man seems satisfied, and with a nod, he lets us threw.

"What event?" I whisper.

"Something Levi is planning for today," says Dean softly. "He would not tell me the details."

There does indeed appear to be something happening. The streets are packed with people young and old. Most are vampire. The few Fae I see tend to their masters, carrying around supplies or food. I do not see the Shade until we reach the center square.

There, a dozen men and women hang on wooden pillars, their arms and legs nailed to the wood. Their hair color ranges from blue to red to green like the Fae, but their teeth are that of vampires, their blood that of both.

"That monster," I hiss, trying to imagine what kind of madness compels Levi to act as he does.

One of the woman groans, and I realize she yet lives. She was hung here to bleed to death!

I rush forward, drawing my dagger.

Dean yells after me. "What are you doing?"

This time, I do not heed his warning. This time, I cannot. I jump into the air, grabbing onto the wooden pillar, and cut through the ropes holding the woman. I pull the nails from her limbs. She doesn't even scream, so weak is she. She falls into my arms. "Thank you," she whispers, her mouth stained with blood. I lay her down on the stone ground, and motion to Dean.

"Water."

He tosses me a jug, and I pour the liquid down the woman's throat. Then I wet a part of my cloak and gently wash away the crimson stains over her face and arms. Around me, the city turns quiet. As if all life has stopped in respect for this one tender moment. Many have gathered to watch in silence. I suspect it is because of what I have done in freeing her. I am wrong.

"Who dares disobey my will?"

I know the voice in an instant. Levi.

I stand, leaving the woman sitting against stone steps, and face my treacherous brother. He stands, draped in a cloak of red and gold, amongst a company of a dozen men. His armor glistens in the sun, and the ruby in the pommel of his sword speaks of newfound wealth. His long white hair billows in the wind. His face twists in anger.

I step forward, until we are but a few feet away. "The woman is a Shade. It did not seem fit to treat her as Fae."

Levi studies me, no doubt seeing if he recognizes me. But the illusion holds, and he seems frustrated. "Perhaps you do not know whom you address," he says, his voice full of fake pleasantry. "I am new to these lands after all."

I say nothing. I do nothing. He will get no satisfaction from me.

Levi sighs, disappointed I haven't yet figured out his importance. "You address Prince Levi, Lord of Stonehill and Crimson Castle." I know he expects me to be shocked. To drop down to my knees and beg for forgiveness.

I shrug. "Heard Fenris Vane is Lord of Stonehill."

Levi's eyes nearly pop out. "You fool. You—"

"Please, your grace," says Dean, stepping in front me. "My brother and I have recently arrived from far away. The lands of our Prince Zeb. We have traveled for days, and so recent news has not yet reached our ears."

Levi nods, as if this explains my behavior. "Then you best know," he says, addressing not just me, but the crowd of hundreds. "I am now ruler of these lands. All Shade within the city have been deemed traitors, complicit in the attacks on Stonehill. They are to be punished as if Fae and nothing more. All slaves must maintain the new curfew, and if caught without a written seal from their master, will be whipped."

He meets my eyes once again. "I will forgive you this once. But not again, understood?"

I cannot say the words, so I nod instead.

It seems enough for Levi, because he addresses the crowd once again. This time, his voice is unnaturally loud, amplified by magic. "People of Stonehill, we have all gathered here today for one purpose. To witness the punishment of those who have wronged us, betrayed us, fooled us." He points to the castle, and the giant stone gates grind open. A company of guards lead two prisoners outside. At the front is a woman. Her hair black and blue. Her eyes green. Her ears long.

It can't be...

I rush forward, but Dean grabs my arm. He whispers in my ear. "It's not her, brother. It's not Arianna."

I study the woman again. Her face. Her eyes. They are of Arianna. They are of the woman I love. But it cannot be. She is safe. She is at the palace. I look again, and as she draws closer, I begin to notice details I had not before. A lock of hair purple where it should have been blue. A freckle where there should be none. It is an illusion. A well done one. But whoever cast the spell did not know Arianna as intimately as I.

I scan the crowd, and behind Levi's retinue of men, I see a familiar face, smooth but wise, his beard long and white. Kal. His eyes are sunken and dark. His posture slumped and weak. His white robes are long, but not even they cover the purple bruises on his hands. He was the one forced to carry out this magic. Forced into helping Levi.

I turn my gaze back to the imposters. The man behind Arianna, the man who is supposed to be me, is an even better fake. His thick brown hair is mine, his eyes and nose are mine. Even the muscles of his shirtless body match my own. Kal knew me well, mentored me since I was young. It must have been easy for him to recreate me, and at the same time, unbearable.

I search for a hanging stage, the traditional pun-ishment for criminals, yet I see none. Instead, the imposters are led to a wooden block. The woman is pushed down to her knees, forced to lay her head upon the slab. Even from a distance, I see the tears in her eyes. Real tears of a real person. I do not know who they are. Fae or vampire, innocent or guilty, but I feel their fear within me. Feel the dread of their coming fate.

Levi walks up to the block and draws his large silver sword. I realize, he is intending to do the deed himself. He wants the world to know he personally killed the Midnight Star and the Prince of War. "Look upon the woman who lied to you, the woman who pretended to be your princess when in truth she is *their* princess, plotting with the Fae to take your very homes."

People begin to yell and curse and throw what they can at the woman they think is Arianna. They once loved her. How could this be?

"Look around," says Dean. "These are not people of Stonehill. They are Levi's men, crawled out from his realm." I do as he says, glancing around. My brother is right. There are few familiar faces, and those that are stay silent.

Dean seemed to have read my thoughts. My rage must be plain on my face.

"Today," continues Levi, "I slay the Midnight Star. Today, I end the war forever." He brings down his sword.

And chops off the woman's head.

It tumbles down the steps, staining them with blood, and lands near my feet. I do not look upon it. I do not wish to see Arianna's face torn from her body. I may strike at Levi if I do.

Next, the guards force the man down upon the block.

Levi grins. "Here is the one you thought your prince. The one you thought vampire. Instead, he is Fae. He is Druid. For millennia, he has deceived you. For millennia, he has used you. Now, his false reign is over. Now, the reign of Prince Levi begins." He strikes down with his blade, and Fenris Vane is no more. To the world, he is dead.

Levi walks down the steps, grinning like a fool, until he stands before me. "See, I rule Stonehill now. Tell all you see. Levi is the Prince of War."

I nod, meeting his eyes. I know he will take my look for sincerity, but it is filled with hate. Baron steps forward, baring his teeth.

And Levi recoils. On his face, I see even he does not understand why the dog scares him so. But I know. I know that Fenris Vane will return. And that, one day, Levi will find his own head upon the block.

...

The crowd disperses quickly as Levi returns to the castle. A few of his men stay behind to nail the woman I pulled down back onto the pillar. I do nothing to stop them, though inside I rage. It takes all my strength not to fight them. I can kill dozens. But I cannot kill every soldier in the city.

Dean squats down, studying the fake head with blue and black hair.

"Did the council approve this?" I ask.

"No." Dean shakes his head, no joy in him. "Like I said, Levi didn't share his plans."

I keep my voice low. "How does he intend to respond when people realize Arianna and I yet live?"

"You assume he's thought that far ahead." Dean pauses. "Perhaps he will claim you are using illusion to impersonate them. People will believe whatever it is that makes life simpler."

I grunt. I forget how simple the common folk can be, but I have seen it to be true. One speech can sway hundreds, one lie change the minds of thousands, and once they are seduced by their fear and lies and a charismatic charlatan who feeds on their basest instincts, no amount of fact or truth or reality will shake them from their madness.

"Have you heard from Asher?" I whisper. "Has he plans to fight this?"

"If he does, he has not shared them with me.'"
Dean stands back up, dusting off his black cloak. "He
does not support Levi however, that is clear. He will try
to expose this for the farce it is."

I nod, and then notice a man approaching us. His
cloak is gray and torn and covers his face. He keeps his
head tilted down, his identity hidden. He brushes by
my shoulder. "The Prince of War still lives," he says.
Then he stops, silent, and I realize he's waiting for a
response.

"The Prince of War still lives," I say.

The man nods. "Go to the Bloody Mare Inn. Tell
the man there what you just told me, and may the blood
bless you." He walks away then, slipping down an alley.

"Well, should we go?" asks Dean. "Sounds like fun."

"Or a trap."

"No one knows who we are—"

"A trap for those who still support Fenris Vane, no
matter who they are."

Dean pauses. "Oh, good point. Well, if it is a trap
in some rundown inn, we'll just fight our way out. We
couldn't do it out here in the open, but we could sure
do it there."

I nod, and then lead Dean to the inn. It's still early,
but the clouds turn dark with a coming storm, and rain
begins to fall. The Bloody Mare stands in the oldest

part of town, the rotten corner by the wall where beggars and whores dwell and bandits practice their trade. I make sure my cloak doesn't cover my blade to keep the hungry and desperate away. People will turn into beasts when all human things are taken from them. And I do not blame them.

A man and woman scuffle down an alley. At first, I think it a brawl, but then I see the blood on her neck. He's feeding off her. I charge forward and ram my fist into the vampire's gut. The woman, a human with pale skin and dark eyes recoils away. At first I do not know why, but then I see it. She fears me. Even more than him. She thinks I beat him so I can take her for myself. The very thought disgusts me. "Leave. Both of you." As the man scrambles away, I turn to the woman. "Get somewhere safe. Not all have forgotten the way things were. Soon, Stonehill will be a place of peace once more."

She nods, though I can see in her eyes she does not believe me. Then she runs.

Dean puts a hand on my shoulder. "Do not blame yourself, brother. This is Levi's doing."

"It is my failure that gives him the power." I look away, the human blood in the mud drawing at my senses. I have prohibited human feeding in Stonehill for ages. And Levi has desecrated even that.

Before the pull of blood grows stronger, I continue on, and reach the inn, where a sign of a red mare hangs.

I knock on the door just as the sky turns dark and thunder crashes. Someone opens a slit in the wood. "Closed we are," says a man. "We be making repairs."

I lean in closer and speak softly. "Fenris Vane still lives."

The man closes the slit in the door. Then metal screeches as a lock is unlocked and the inn opens. "Welcome, brothers. Welcome!" The man wraps me in a hug so hard my spine cracks, and I see he is even larger than I. "I be Bolsten," he says. Then motions to the rest of the inn, a collection of men and women, some vampire, some Shade, drinking and smoking in the dim light cast by torches. "This here be all those who don't support that lying-son-of-a-whore Levi."

Dean raises a finger. "If Levi was born to a whore, what does that make his brothers?"

Bolsten shakes his head. "No way Levi and the other princes share a mum. Just no bloody way."

I can't help but grin. "I believe you're right, my friend. I believe you're right more than you know." Bolsten smiles and steps to the side, and Dean and I take seats at the bar. My brother orders drinks.

The liquid is thick with blood and alcohol and something sweet. I don't usually partake in drink, but after today? To hell with it.

After a while, the alcohol begins to take effect, and I begin to mingle more than I usually would. This does not seem a trap, for a trap would have already sprung. I drink some more and listen to the others.

"I can't believe they hanged the prince," says Mary, an elderly woman who was once human, but was turned many hundreds of years ago.

"No they didn't," says Roke, a tall, spindly Shade who pours the drinks. "I've met the prince. He's far taller than that bloke they beheaded."

"And where was his wolf?" says Veni, a Shade girl with bright green hair, smoking a pipe in the corner. "Everyone knows he never goes anywhere without his wolf."

"Trickery," says Bolsten, the giant vampire. "'Tis magic trickery. Keeper was always loyal, he was. But if you walk close enough to Stonehill, you can still hear the screaming."

I clutch my mug harder, praying I can do something to ease Kal's pain. Soon. Soon I will. I raise my drink. "Fenris Vane will return," I say. "And on that day, the very hounds of hell will ride at his heels."

Everyone at the inn throws back their heads and howls. "Aye," says Bolsten. "Fenris Vane be the greatest of all seven princes, you hear?" He reaches his mug out to my brother.

Dean speaks through gritted teeth, as if he were taking a vow of celibacy. "Yes...greatest of them all."

They toast, and I can't help but grin.

Then Bolsten leans closer to us both and lowers his voice. "You two seem on the right side of things, I can tell. So, I'm letting you know, there are plans in the making. Me and other folks, we're rallying. And not a small group either. I'm talking an army. We're getting ready. And soon, we're going to tear that bastard down from the castle, and string him up just as he done to the Shade."

I sip my drink, careful with my next words. "As much as I like drinking, I'd much rather be fighting. Tell us more, and we'll stand at your side."

Bolsten seems to think it over, then smiles. "Stay around a while. We have an important member arriving later. He'll tell you more then, if he deems you be right and all."

I nod. "Thank you."

In time, day turns to night, and Dean and I slip away to a private booth as we wait for the important member to arrive. I feel heavy with drink, and say things I perhaps shouldn't. "So why are you helping me, truly?"

Dean lowers his voice. He stares at the fireplace roaring across from us. "Believe it or not, I care about you, brother. I remember when mother brought you back home as a babe. The others, already cast out, already scarred by war, resented the idea of another sibling. But I, perhaps because of my own curse, was thrilled at the idea of a little brother. I could see the beauty in it, the potential. So I took you as my charge. You may think of me as your smaller brother, but I was bigger once. I remember teaching you how to cheat at cards. Sneaking you your first wine." He smiles and refills our cups from a bottle. "I care for you, Fenris. I always have. And I will fight for you to the end."

I try to remember the things he speaks of, but all I get are flashes. Flashes of a caring brother slipping me an ace under his sleeve. Tending to a wounded knee. I do not have words for what he has shared, so instead I raise a cup to Dean.

We toast.

I try to say something. Anything. "I—"

The door opens.

A gust of wind rushes in.

And I turn to see the two men who just arrived. The important guest we have awaited.

Asher.

10

SHADOW AND FLAME

"There will be many pits of ash this night. Many new graves
dotting the landscapes beyond, some marked, others not.
Many empty homes and hearts that once were full. And in
the end, there will be more war. This is what I have wrought.
I am the Prince of War. I am the Prince of Death."

—Fenris Vane

My days are filled with helping Seri in the Healing Tree
and my nights training with Varis. He teaches me spells
to enhance my senses, and we track a rabbit in the forest. It takes me half a day, but eventually I begin to see
prints where before I only saw mud. I smell fur where
before I could only make out flowers. And by the time
the sun sets, I find the bunny in a field, resting. We do
the same exercise the next day. And the next.

Sometimes, when I have time, I visit Es and Pete.

Their first few days in the Moonlight Garden, they stayed to the palace, but as time went on I noticed them exploring further. Es found the training yard and started practicing the sword. Sometimes, when Varis or Seri can spare me, I help her with the basics, and she learns quickly. I notice the soldiers taking a liking to her, and they help out with more advanced techniques, especially when I'm not around. Soon, Es is close to surpassing my level, and we boast about who would win in a serious match.

Meanwhile, Varis takes an interest in Pete, and I see them meditating together at dawn. Other times, I catch Pete in the library with Baldar, reading books on herbs and brewing potions. He's always had a sense about the magical, and now that he can experience it first hand, I see him happier than I have in a long time.

About two weeks after arriving in the Pleasure Palace, my sleeping potion runs out, and I find Baldar's shop by the lion fountain. It's a quaint little place, tucked away between a book store and a pottery shop. Green vines cover the white walls, and blue lanterns flicker inside. When I enter, Yami flying around me, a bell signals my arrival, and I'm assaulted by all manner of aromas, some pleasant and others less so.

Baldar stands on a ladder, placing a decorative dagger on a high shelf, when he notices me. "Ah, so good to see you again, my dear." The short Fae descends the ladder and greets me with a formal bow. "Anything I can help you with?"

"The sleeping potion. I'd like to buy more."

He nods, his face red and happy. "Ah, yes of course. I'll have to brew a new batch, but it'll only take a moment." He walks behind the counter, where lay all sorts of pestles and cauldrons. Then he grabs different herbs from various jars and begins to grind them into powder.

I study his shop as he works, admiring the different fossils that adorn his walls, and the ceremonial weapons on his shelves. Pots and already-made potions lay scattered on tables, labeled with their names and uses. I see more love potions than any other and roll my eyes.

The doorbell rings, and I turn to see three men enter.

The three men who hanged Lars on the tree.

My hands tighten into fists, and I clench my jaw, trying to resist attacking them then and there. The big one, Roge, grabs a potion off a desk and sniff at the contents. "Bloody hell!" he says, making a disgusted face. He drops the vial and it shatters, spilling blue liquid on the floor. His friends laugh.

"How dare you!" I yell.

Roge turns, noticing me for the first time. He grins. "Oh, a fiery one. I like them fiery. You looking for any work, Shade?"

Shade. He refers to my illusion. "You will apologize to the shop keeper this instance and pay for that potion."

"Or..." Roge pretends to be dumbfounded. "We going to be in trouble? Oh, no..." His friends giggle at his antics.

That's it. I've had enough.

I draw my sword, Spero. Half white and half black.

Yami screeches on my shoulder, though I know they can't see or hear him.

The vampires laugh at my display.

They don't laugh for long.

The room grows dark around us. The wind picks up. The earth begins to shake. Vials and pots shake, some crashing to the floor. A chill picks up in the air. And something stirs within me. Something dark.

"My lady!"

I barely hear the words.

"My lady!"

A little louder.

"My lady!" Baldar grabs my arm, and whatever possessed me begins to pass. The lights return and the wind dies down. The cold recedes and the trembling stops. I look around at the destruction I have caused, broken potions and cracks in the stone floor.

The vampires look too, and then they run.

I bury my face in my hands. Tears well in my eyes. "I'm so sorry. I don't know what happened."

"It's alright, my dear. It's alright." He takes my hands into his, smiling fondly. "Those vagrants were about to destroy my entire shop, maybe even assault me. You stopped them."

I motion all around me. "And nearly ruined your entire shop."

"But you didn't. You stopped yourself."

I take a deep breath, processing his words. "You're right. Thank you."

Yami licks my face, trying to cheer me as well. It works, and I giggle.

Baldar places a vial in my hands. "To help you sleep, my dear." I reach into the pouch on my belt, searching for coins, but he stops me. "No need. Your company is payment enough."

I smile and thank him, then offer to help clean up. "No, but thank you. I have spells to aid in such things. Now, I believe you best be off. I think Varis expects you at this hour."

I glance outside at the sun. It's later than I thought, and the Druid won't be happy, indeed.

I thank Baldar and head for the door, and when I see he isn't looking, I drop a few coins on his desk and depart.

On my way back to the palace, I notice a forge where blacksmiths toil over roaring fires, forging steel and iron. A part of me wants to join them, but then memories of Daison return, and I keep walking, away from the forge and the flame.

...

When I find Varis in the library, he is sitting cross-legged on the carpet, meditating with Pete. I don't disrupt their trance, grateful for the delay before my training. Though I have learned some interesting and even useful things, none of my spells will aid me in the fight against Levi. I itch to do more, be more, to feel the thrill I felt watching Callisia battle the Windshark, and use that passion in combat.

Varis always preaches calmness and grace, but how can I fight and be calm? How can I fight without adrenaline pumping through my veins, fueling me like it fueled me when I fought Oren?

I slide into a chair, relaxing, when Es bursts in, shouting. "Pete, Ari. We've got things to talk about."

Varis groans, his concentration clearly broken. "Don't you have any respect for the sacred art of—"

"Sitting on your ass and seeing who falls asleep first? Not right now," says Es, flicking her blond hair. She wears a black leather vest meant for battle, and a thick broadsword hangs at her side, making her seem even tougher than I remember her being—not that she's ever had trouble taking care of herself.

Pete stands and stretches, his white fur robes nearly touching the ground. They seem likely borrowed from Varis and fit him well. Pete looks quite the Fae with his red hair. All he's missing are the ears.

"So," says Es, sitting down in chair next to me and crossing her legs. "When can we get back to Portland, darlin'? Because as fun as this pleasure palace is, I got friends and family who miss me. I also pray I haven't been fired."

"Me too," says Pete, sighing and running his fingers through his hair.

I fold my hands together in my lap, thinking. "Well, Fen left yesterday to scout out Stonehill. When he and Dean return, we should be able to make a concrete plan. Then once Levi is defeated, you'll be safe to return to Portland."

Es sighs. "This Levi is really that bad, huh?"

"My words don't do him justice. You really have to meet him. Or on second thought, don't." The three of us laugh, and Varis grunts, still trying to meditate.

After a moment, he finally appears to give up. "Arianna, when Dean returns, can you please ask him to show me the Mirror of Idis. It is a *Fae* artifact, a piece of *Fae* history, and I, as a Wild One, should have access to it. But instead he keeps it locked up in his room. And from what I've heard, gazing into it more and more by the day."

I bow my head, sadness filling me at the thought of Dean and what he told me. He still looks into the pool because he sees a happier life. A life that may even be possible, if I were to choose him as king. But my heart belongs to Fen.

"I'll ask him," I tell Varis.

"Thank you. Now, since it doesn't seem like we'll be doing any training tonight, I'll be off. I do however expect you to catch up on your reading. Good night everyone." He leaves with a flourish of his cape, and I roll my eyes, tired of my currently assigned text: *The History of Fae Cheese and Other Delicacies*.

Es looks over at me with a raised eyebrow. "Training going that bad, huh?"

I grunt. "Slow. Like molasses. I'm learning simple tricks and some useful incantations, but nothing that will win us a war. However, if you need to find a rabbit or change your appearance, I'm your girl." My voice is sarcastic, though the things I've learned have been interesting. It's just not enough.

"I take it you're frustrated?" says Pete.

"Yes." In so many ways. Fen is gone. I miss him. I want to explore our relationship more, but we're always stuck in one mess or another. I wish I could whisk him back to my world for a normal dinner and movie date. But that's not a life I will ever have if I stay here and fulfill my contract to the princes.

Es studies the shelves of books. "Is there nothing else he can teach you?"

My lips curl in a smile as something occurs to me. "There's nothing more he's willing to teach me, but... there might be something else I can learn. Let's go!"

I jump up and run into the hallway, Pete and Es at my heels. "And how will you learn this, exactly?" asks Pete, panting. He never did have the strongest constitution.

"There's a book. A book Varis hid from me the first day we studied. I bet it has something I could use."

"Have you considered there's probably a reason Varis doesn't want you reading that text?" asks Pete. "I know I haven't known him long, but he's shared some great wisdom with me, and I've yet to see him wrong."

I speed up, my excitement growing. "I'm sure he thinks he has good reasons, but he's holding me back, and we don't have time for that. People are dying!"

Pete is quiet the rest of the way, seemingly swayed by my argument. He could never stand the needless suffering of others.

Once we reach the correct hallway, I use illusion to make us look like the many scantily-clad servants who wander the halls and rooms of the palace day and night. We each carry a platter laden with food and drink and make our way toward Varis's room, as if we have every right to enter.

Once at his door, I enhance my senses and listen for any breathing. There is none. Instead of retiring to his room like he said, Varis probably went out to the local inn. I'd heard he was developing a taste for Baldar's Nectar of the Elder Ones.

I turn the handle and the door opens, unlocked so servants can clean, or in our case, more nefarious things.

His room is as tidy and neat as I would have imagined.

"I have a bad feeling about this," whispers Pete, but I shush him and look around.

My enhanced vision picks up traces of recent prints of dust, things Varis touched. His bed. His closet.

I look under his pillow, find nothing, and then check the closet. Stashed deep past layers of fur cloaks, I discover the black leather book he hid from me.

When I touch it, my hands fill with cold, and I hear something in the distance. "You hear that?" I ask, but Pete and Es shake their heads.

Strange. I open the leather and run my hand over the cover. The ice seeps into the bones of my hand, making them ache, my skin prickles, and my arm hair stands on edge. I slam the book closed quickly and shove it back into its leather cover, then replace everything as I found it.

"So what now?" asks Es.

"Now, I need to read it."

I guide them back to my room and drop our new illusions. Pete and Es stay with me as I peruse the pages of the old manuscript, using a translation spell to understand the glyphs. Most of what I come across terrifies me: human sacrifice. Nude rituals. "Guys, I really hope I don't have to do this stuff for Yami to grow stronger." I show them one picture of a woman being cut open from chin to groin, her organs pulled out to 'read'.

Pete recoils and Es bends over. "Think I'm going to vomit."

I flip the page and start scanning for something useful. The longer I have the book open, the worse the chill gets. The pages feel odd to me. Not like paper. And then I realize what they are. "Human skin."

Pete leans over the book to examine it. "There is precedent for that, even in our world."

Es wrinkles her nose. "Ew...this falls into the category of shit I don't need to know about."

I sigh and push on, reading deeper into the text. "Here. Finally. Something." I point to a section they can't read.

"It says the Druids and Spirits have a shadow form, that which taps into the Darkness. The power of light and dark. Life and death. Creation and destruction. Sometimes this form manifests when the Wild Ones are in grave danger. However, this power can also be summoned at will by those with the right knowledge." I close the book and put it back into the leather wrap. "Varis knew all this. He knew this is the information I needed, and he didn't tell me."

"How do you summon the shadow form?" Pete asks, eyeing the book with a frown.

"Under the light of the moons at midnight I must chant the binding words and connect with my Spirit," I say.

Es walks over to the door leading out to my balcony and opens it, letting in fresh air and a stream of sunshine. "It's sundown. We have time. What should we do until midnight?"

I shrug. "Hang out? Pretend life is normal? Catch up? We've hardly had time to just talk since we got here. Come on. Let's find somewhere in this pleasure domain to drink coffee and eat junk food and talk."

With that plan set, we leave the Pleasure Palace and explore Dean's realm, stopping at different vendors to try their wares and eventually settling on a little cafe by the water.

Once we have food and drink, I look at my best friends...really look at them...for the first time since I pulled them into this mess. "Are you guys okay? Is this completely freaking you out?"

Pete shrugs. "It's actually pretty cool. I mean, there are things I miss. Like phones."

"And television," Es says with an exasperated sigh. "What do people do here to relax?"

I laugh. "I don't know. I haven't had much time to relax since I got here. Unless you count my time in the dungeon relaxing."

Es shutters. "No, thank you. I can't believe that bastard did that to you. I'd cut his manhood off myself if I could."

"Thanks," I say. "But he'll get what's coming to him."

"Are *you* happy here?" Es asks. "Are you happy with *him?*"

"I could be," I say honestly. "When I spent my month with Fen in Stonehill...yeah, there were problems, and everyone here seems to be at war with someone, but we also found a routine. I trained with Fen in the mornings and worked with Kayla learning blacksmithing in the afternoons. At night, I would study everything I could about this place under the watchful gaze of Kal the Keeper. I made friends. I learned a lot. And..."

"And you fell in love with the tough-on-the-outside-soft-on-the-inside sexy Prince of War," Es says, finishing my thought for me in the way only she can.

"Yes, I suppose I did." I think of Fen and wish he were here with us now. It worries me that he's gone into enemy territory. But he should be back soon. "Without Fen, I'm not sure I'd want to be here, but I don't have a choice. I signed a contract. And...this is where I'm from, at least half of me."

Es shakes her head. "That must be so cray-cray! Being a Fae princess after spending your life thinking you're just a poor kid in Oregon."

"It is a bit surreal," I admit.

"There's something I've been meaning to ask. How do you handle...womanly things?" Es raises an eyebrow as if I should know what she's talking about.

"Womanly things?"

She sighs. "You know what I mean. I may have the parts, and sure, they don't all work. But I am familiar with the plumbing. You're young. Fertile. And prone to that monthly visit from every woman's most despised aunt. At least in our world you have the marvels of tampons and pain reliever. What do you do here?"

I laugh. "*That's* your big question? We're in a magical world with vampires and Fae and dragons and you want to know what I do for my period?"

"It's a legit question," she says. "Don't tell me it wasn't something you worried about too."

"To be honest, it hasn't been as bad as you might think," I say. "While this place looks very medieval, it's not. Not when you factor in magic and strong influences from our modern world. They can't replicate everything, but they've made a go of it with some things. And there's a potion I drink once a month that all but eliminates cramps and bloating. If I could bring it back to our world and patent it, I'd be the richest person to ever live."

"That's not so bad then," Pete says. "But...how much longer until you think we can go home?"

"I don't know." I don't know when we will defeat Levi. And if we lose, they might never go back. But I don't have the heart to tell them. "I'm so sorry I pulled you into this. Do you hate me?"

Es sips her drink and laughs. "Darlin', this is the first vacation I've had since I started working when I was thirteen. We are surrounded by eye candy galore and all the food and drink we could want. We're good."

"And I'm getting training I could have never imagined," Pete says, his face lighting up. "Varis is amazing." Then a shadow falls over his eyes, probably remembering the book we *borrowed*.

"Ha. Yeah. Slave driver, but amazing. Sure."

We spend the rest of the evening hanging out, exploring Dean's realm, and just talking. It feels good to have a semi-normal day with my best friends. I show them the grove of trees Dean took me to and explain their history. Pete, especially, is drawn to the magic of the forest, and convinces us to stay longer. Why not? We need someplace private to do the ritual, and the grove is about as good as it gets. We stay there as the moons rise higher in the sky and everything turns dark, save what we can see by moonlight. The ancient trees cast long shadows against us. It's a haunting scene, one that sends a shiver up my spine.

I start to have second thoughts, but I need an edge to defeat Levi. I must do this.

Yami looks nervous as I place him on the ground in front of me. "We're going to make this happen, okay, buddy? Don't worry, it's going to be fine."

I open the book and read the lines as instructed, then I close my eyes and focus. Something swirls deep within me, like liquid fire in my belly. I tug at it and pull it out, expanding it within me. It warms my bones and blood and pushes out the chill caused by handling the dark tomb.

And as I meditate the way Varis taught me, I feel the string of power that connects me to my dragon. Yami chirps nervously, and I try to sooth him through our connection.

I speak the final incantation.

And when I open my eyes, Yami's form evaporates and a darkness covers the light of the moons, blocking them from sight as a cold wind blows through the grove. Shadows form before me, coalescing into something much darker and larger than I've ever seen of the Midnight Star.

A surge of excitement spreads through my belly as I realize it's working. We did it.

Yami's form materializes into the sparkling midnight of stars, and he screeches loudly into the night, breathing a stream of blue flame across the sky. I reach a hand out to him, a smile on my face at his magnificence, but when he turns to me, it is not the Yami I know and love.

It is a different Yami.

Full of rage and darkness.

Then I feel it.

The shadows spreading through me like a cancer, infecting every part of my body.

The dragon screeches again and shoots more flames as his tail lashes out, hitting an ancient tree and cutting the bark in half.

No.

Pete and Es scramble to my side. "What's he doing?" Es asks.

"I don't know."

Yami roars again. Then turns his attention to us. His raises his talons, larger than a person. And strikes.

I push my friends out of the way and we fall into the grass. "Run!" I scream. "Run!"

We rush out of the grove, and behind us, a shadow loom over the sky.

Yami.

People scream in the streets. They run for cover.

And the dragon descends, breathing flame upon all in his path. He sets buildings on fire. And when I look behind me, I see it.

The grove.

Burning.

How could I have done this? How can I stop it?

"Yami!" I call out to the sky. "Yami, stop. Please. It's me."

The dragon tilts his head down at my form, and then he strikes. I dodge out of the way.

But Es isn't fast enough.

Talons graze her shoulder, and she screams in pain and falls to the stone tiles. Pete rushes to her side, blocking her with his body.

Tears fill my eyes. "Yami. This isn't you."

A gust of wind nearly knocks me down.

And the dragon lands before me. His purple eyes stare deep into my soul. Within them I see time and space and the end of all things. Within them I see death.

What have I done?

What have I unleashed?

Yami...

He lunges for me. To kill. To end.

And then a silver owl crashes into his side, ramming them both into a building. The stone crumbles around them, and the beasts roar and hiss as they fight each other with tooth and claw.

Varis glides down in front of me, his cloak twirling in an unnatural wind.

I nearly pass out from relief and fear and complete anguish. "Varis, I'm so sorry."

He doesn't look at me as he replies. "This is not the time. Focus. You and you alone can calm the Midnight Star and push back the Darkness. Close your eyes."

I feel gutted at his anger and disappointment, and my own failure to abide by his guidance, but I close my eyes and focus as he speaks. He takes me through exercises to calm my heart rate, to ease tension, to manifest the light in my soul and dispel the Darkness.

I can hear his owl, Zyra, fighting with Yami, struggling to pin him down and keep him from causing more harm. I can hear the screams of men and women as they try to put out fires and free others from rubble. I feel a wave of grief at what I've done, but I push it away and concentrate.

I push away the anger and fear and sorrow. I push away the thrill I sought after. I push until there is nothing left. But calm. But peace.

When I open my eyes, my little baby dragon is with me again, perching on my shoulder. And then I feel exhaustion overtake me, and I collapse. I look up, to the burning grove, to the ancient trees who groan as they die, and I weep. "I'm so sorry. I didn't know. I didn't know..."

Varis doesn't look at me. "I told you not to summon the Darkness. Now, you must live with the consequences." He turns and walks away, leaving me alone with shadow and flame.

11

SILVER FLAME
Kayla Windhelm

"We cannot let our enemies live."
—Lord Salzar

We return to the Outlands and mount Tavian's horse once more. "Metsi is even more mad than I heard," he says, half to himself.

I frown. "And you thought going to her was a good idea?"

"She wasn't always so. Once she was kind and wise and good. Seeing her people slaughtered must have changed her."

"What happened back there, when the room grew dark?"

He sighs. "You know of the four elements, yes? Riku, Wadu, Zyra, and Tauren. Most Fae tap into their power to cast spells. But there is another power. That of Darkness. That of the Midnight Star. It is life. It is death. It is the beginning and the end."

"Is that the power you use?"

He looks away, something lurking in his eyes. Shame, perhaps. "Long ago, before the Unraveling, I was a scholar of sorts. I studied at a library so great, there are none that even compare now. My colleagues and I developed a theory, a theory that the power of the Midnight Star can be accessed by others. Not only the chosen High Fae.

"It took years of research and experimentation, but finally we created a ritual. We spoke the incantations under a full moon, covered in the colors of night. And we saw it...the Darkness. But we could not control it. The power spread like a plague, killing all it touched. All but those who had called it forth.

"When I realized what was happening. I ran. I ran back home. To my family. My wife. And when I reached them. I saw their rotting bodies, covered in blackened flesh. I still remember my wife, reaching for me, pleading for me to save her. But I could do nothing."

He goes silent, and I can tell he will say no more.

"I'm sorry," I say, wrapping my arms around him in a hug.

"It was a long time ago," he says.

And then, we ride in silence.

I look to the fresh sky and watch the rising sun. The climate here, even the time of day, is so different from Avakiri. I try to lighten the mood. "So, since you decided not to sell me to the crazy Wild One, what next?"

He doesn't face me. Just looks at the snow, lost in thought. "Don't know. But there's a storm coming. We need shelter." I wonder how he knows. I see no signs. "We'll be there soon."

"There?"

He motions forward, and then I see it, in the distance.

A small village built from gray wood, surrounded by palisades. The houses little more than huts. When we ride in, a Fae woman with blue hair and dark gray robes greets us as she leans on her withered walking stick. "Tavian, so good to see you, my lad." She hugs him.

"And you, Madrid."

The woman, Madrid, turns to me. "And who is this—"

"That be Kayla Windhelm," says another Fae, walking up beside us. His hair is red, his short beard too, and he wears a leather vest made for fighting. "She's the dead king's bastard. Saw her once in Stonehill. Sorry girl, but we don't need yer kind here."

Madrid places a hand on her companion. "Now Durk, be calm. Remember, we welcome all in this village. As long as they swear to bring no harm."

Tavian side eyes me, and I nod. "I swear."

"So do I," he says.

"Wonderful," says Madrid, smiling. "Now, follow me. The two of you look like you haven't bathed in weeks."

She's not quite wrong. I reek.

Durk mumbles and curses under his breath, but lets us pass as we travel through the village. Children play in the snow, building figures from sticks and singing songs about the Primal One. Women wash clothing in barrels of water. Men patch together a broken rooftop.

A horse neighs. In the center of the town. Something is wrong.

A woman yells as a giant black mare almost crushes her with its hooves. "What's gotten into you, Mally?"

Mally, the mare, neighs again, still restless and wild.

I rush forward, then slow down, my hand forward. "Easy girl. Easy." I've done this before, when one of the horses pulling my cart got spooked, and it works now. Mally relaxes, letting me pet her head. "Good girl," I say. "What's wrong, huh?"

"And who would you be?" asks the woman who seems to own Mally.

I ignore her and examine the horse. "Her shoe is shot. Where's the blacksmith?"

"There is none," says Durk, catching up. "Died a few weeks past.

"Then where's the forge?"

"Why, you have some skill?"

"Maybe."

Tavian laughs. "So you know of Kayla Windhelm, but not her skill at the forge?"

Durk grunts, and says nothing.

"Here," I say, passing the reigns to Tavian. "Watch her while I make a new shoe." He nods, and I find the forge. A shadow of what I had in Stonehill, but good enough. It takes me a while to make the horseshoe and a while to shoe the horse. Once I'm done, Mally is returned to the stable, and Madrid thanks me.

"No need," I say. "Something needed mending, and I mended it. That's what I do."

"You have a kind heart," she says leading me into a wooden hut. There, in the center of a room, is a wooden bath. "I already heated the water. Take your time. And after, feel free to cool off in the lake outside."

I thank her and, after she leaves, I slip off my clothes and sink into the bath. By the Spirits, it feels good. I let the water relax and soothe my muscles, as I lean back my head and think of nothing but happiness. When the water begins to turn cold, I reluctantly leave the bath, then wrap myself in a white towel hanging on the well. I step outside the house, onto a porch over-looking the lake. I see Tavian there. And he's...

Well...

He's naked.

Standing on the opposite side of the water, his muscles rippling in the sun. He notices me looking and winks, then dives in the cold water. "Woo!" he yells, breaking the surface and flicking back his thick hair. "What's wrong, Princess? Water too cold?"

I roll my eyes. Then jump in after him, letting my towel fall off. The water is freezing, and sends a shock through my entire body. It fills me with a rush, and when I break the surface, I realize I am right in front of Tavian. Our bodies almost touching.

"The Princess is braver than I thought," he teases.

I smirk. "Oh, you don't scare me."

"I should, Princess. I should." He wraps an arm around me. Pulls me closer.

I lean forward, drawing my lips to his. And—

"Time for the feast!" someone yells. Durk. He stands on shore, holding up my towel. "Unless you're too good to eat with us, Princess?"

"I am not a princess!" I say, my eye almost popping out of their sockets from exasperation at having to remind everyone of this.

Durk shrugs and walks away.

Tavian sighs. "We should go. It would be disrespectful to be late."

I nod, the moment between us ending too soon.

Once I'm dressed, Tavian leads me to the giant bonfire in the center of the village. Dozens of Fae sit around the flames, while others play drums and a few dance to the music. We join Madrid and watch as she passes sweets out to the children. Once she has no more to give, she wanders off, away from the fire.

"Something wrong?" I ask Tavian.

He shrugs, his gaze fixed on the dancers, who twirl blue and green ribbons through the air, their bodies in sync with the tribal beat.

I touch Tavian on the shoulder. "I'll be back in a moment." Then I stand and look for Madrid, finding her near a gravestone.

"Are you okay?" I ask.

She nods, rubbing at her eyes. "Yes. I'm fine. Just honoring the dead in my own way."

I notice the tears in her eyes. "This person. They were important to you."

"Yes. Yes, he was. We grew apart at the end, but I still loved him."

"What happened?" I ask, hoping I'm not pressing too far, but also knowing that discussing loss can help with grief.

She sighs, leaning more on her cane than before. "He died. In the battle at Stonehill. I found his body there, on the battlefield, and I would not leave it behind to rot with the rest. So I carried him here. Paid for it too. A vampire tried to rob me, but I got him before he got me. Though, he did wound my leg." She taps her walking stick on the snow.

"I have some skill in healing. I could try to help, if you'd like?"

She chuckles. "Thank you, girl, but I have done all the healing one could on this leg. Perhaps it will get better with time, but I doubt it. Now, let us return to the feast. And honor the dead by enjoying what they fought for."

I follow her back to bonfire, and we sit together near Tavian.

"Here, let me see your palm," says Madrid, and I let her study my hand. "Your life has been short, for a Fae," she says, "but not devoid of hardship. Yet, there is much more to come." She closes her eyes, murmuring some incantation. She speaks softly, her voice low and hoarse. "I see a silver bird and a tiger, black. I see a serpent and no way back." She opens her eyes, and jolts backwards, as if startled from a dream.

"What does it mean?" I ask.

She glances at Tavian, then back at me. "I do not know. But you will see the signs."

Somehow, I feel she knows more than she says. So why not tell me? Is my future truly so grim?

I try to focus on something else. "So, how do you know Tavian?" I ask.

She smiles. "Oh, Tavian has been around a very long time. I'd be surprised if there's someone he *doesn't* know."

I look back at the sexy Fae, studying his hair and skin. He does not look like the ancient Fae I've seen. His hair isn't white, and his joints and muscles are full of power. But he did mention a time before the Unraveling. A time ages ago.

"Have you seen Metsi recently?" asks Tavian.

Madrid nods somberly. "She is not as she was. And I fear, after Oren's death, she has descended even further into madness."

"Oren?" The name sounds familiar. "The Fire Druid? He passed?"

Madrid looks away from the fire, to the darkness she had just visited. "Killed in battle." She doesn't offer more.

"So what brought you here?" asks Tavian. The question surprises me. I'd assumed this was Madrid's home.

Madrid glances at the children, playing and dancing by the fire. "Durk and I wanted to help those injured in the battle, and the families whose father and mothers and children never returned. This seemed like the place to start." She turns to me. "What of you, Kayla Windhelm? What brought you so far north?"

"I..." I can't muster the words. I can't tell her I came here to raid and pillage and murder her people. My people. No. We are still different, I tell myself. I am Shade. And they are Fae. We are not the same.

Tavian seems to notice my troubles and puts a hand on my shoulder. "It's not where we came from, or why, that matters," he says. "What matters is where we go from here."

Madrid nods. "Wise words, Lord Tavian."

"Lord?" I ask.

He glances at Madrid, then chuckles. "Only a nickname she likes to tease me with."

"Yes," Madrid says, looking down. "Yes. Only a nickname."

I study Tavian. This man who is so much more than he seems. "Who are you?" I ask.

For a moment, he says nothing. Then he looks at me, his green eyes deep and mesmerizing. "Kayla, I—"

An arrow streaks through the sky.

It hits one of the dancers in the chest, and they collapse in the snow. People scream. The children cry.

"Raiders," I call out. "Get everyone inside. Bar the doors. Grab anything that can be used as a weapon."

Madrid nods and stands, moving swiftly despite her walking staff. "Everyone, follow me! Come, children." She glances at Tavian, before moving on, and he nods. Why?

Arrows begin to rain from the sky, hitting a woman in the shoulder. One lands near my foot. Tavian and I duck behind a cart.

He grabs my arm. "Kayla. Follow them inside. Now. You need to trust me."

"No. I'm staying. I can fight."

"Trust me," he growls.

Something in his tone, in his eyes, sways me. "Fine. I'll hide." I touch his hand. "Be careful." He nods, and I run, dodging arrows until I reach the forge. My breath turns to smoke in the air. My limbs tremble with cold. Thunder roars above, lightning streaks the sky. The storm Tavian spoke of. I find an old rusty sword and hide behind a wall, searching for attackers. I see none yet, but they will come. I turn my gaze to Tavian.

He steps out from behind the cart, out into the snow and rain of arrows. Over the hill, a company of dozens descends. Vampires wielding torches and swords and spears. They howl like beasts and laugh like madmen.

Tavian does not waver. He unfastens his cloak. He pulls off his shirt. And then he changes.

He leaps forward, and midair his skin turns to fur, his hands to claws. When he lands, it is on top of a man, and he tears him in half, spraying the snow with blood. This is not what Tavian was before. He is not white. But black with silver stripes.

The tiger, black, echo Madrid's words.

He is larger than any natural beast and far more fierce. As he fights, smoke curls around him, covering the battlefield in darkness. The raiders who choose to attack him soon find themselves maimed or dead, and those who flee are caught quickly, their bodies turned to shreds.

This isn't a battle.

It's a massacre.

It's the reason Metsi wouldn't face Tavian. The reason she let us go.

This is the Darkness Tavian spoke of. The power of life and death.

Someone screams. Not one of the raiders. Closer. The nearby hut. Someone found their way inside. I clutch my sword and run forward, jumping into the building.

It can't be...

Salzar stands inside, his dagger at the throat of a little girl. He yells at Madrid in the corner. "Call off your dog, or I kill the child!"

"Please," pleads Madrid. "I can't control him. It is too late for that."

"Then the girl—"

"Let her go," I roar, raising my sword.

Salzar notices me for the first time, and his eyes go wide. "You survived?"

"Let her go!" I repeat.

Salzar laughs, licking his lips compulsively. "Or what? You strike at me, and I kill her."

He's right. There has to be some other way. I step forward, holding out my hand, an idea coming to mind. "Salzar let her go now, and you can leave. Now one will follow you."

He tilts his head, thinking.

I continue. "Your men are dead. This raid is over. Save yourself while you can."

He glances out the door, where Tavian slaughters all who remain.

"My men!" he roars. "I need them. They're mine. Mine." I see the madness in his eyes. This is a man who has just lost the power he so cherishes. The man who has nothing unless he takes it.

"Salzar, please..."

"No," he says. "You brought this upon her." And then he squeezes his blade into the girl's throat.

I think of Daison. I think of all that has been lost.

And I throw up my hand.

Silver flame blazes from my fingertips. Bright and immense. It hits Salzar and nothing else, lighting his clothing on fire. He falls back, letting the girl go, her throat only slightly injured. "How?" he screams, running outside. He falls into the snow, rolling, trying to put out the fire, but the flames only burn brighter. And then his screams no longer resemble words. They turn primal and full of pain.

I follow him outside, my steps light, the snow around me turning to steam. My movements are not my own. My words are not my own. I raise my sword. "You have been witnessed. And you have been judged. And you will never hurt a soul again."

Silver flame covers my blade.

And I swing down, cleaving Salzar's head from his body. It rolls in the snow, leaving no blood, the wound cauterized already.

Something stirs in the darkness.

I look up and see the black tiger before me. Its eyes so green. It stares at me for a moment, then turns and disappears into the forest.

Whatever compelled me begins to fade, and I drop my sword and turn around. The hut. It burns. But how? I only hit Salzar.

I look at my hands, trembling at what I have done. Then I take a deep breath, calming myself, and as I calm, so do the flames. They fade, until only wisps of smoke remain.

Madrid emerges from inside, the children at her heel. "You have returned," she says, reaching for me. "Riku. You have returned."

12

DARKNESS AND MOONLIGHT

Kayla Windhelm

"Reverse psychology. Works every time."

—Asher

My blood is boiling. I can't stop shaking. What the old woman said can't be true, can it? I can't be the Fire Druid. It's impossible.

I look around at the bodies strewn about. Everyone from Salzar's company is dead. I killed them. Tavian killed them. I don't even know who died by my hand and who by his. So much death. I attacked and killed my own kind to protect Fae I barely know. I killed men and women I'd fought beside. Men and women I'd raided with.

What have I become? I look down at my hands. They no longer glow with the silver flame of my new power, but I can feel it there, just under the surface. "I have to find Tavian. He...he was different this time. His tiger form was black, and...the things he did...I have never seen such things."

Madrid hobbles over to me on her walking stick. "That is the dark magic. The old magic. That of creation and destruction. He has no control in such a state. It's powerful. Dangerous. Unwieldy. He left to protect you, and that alone is remarkable."

"He went into the woods. I must find him. Help him." I need to be near Tavian right now, that's all I know. Nothing else makes sense. Nothing else matters. All other thoughts are jumbled in my mind. I run back to the cottage and grab our packs, then swing onto the horse. I pause before leaving. "Thank you for your hospitality. I am so sorry you were attacked. And for the fire I caused."

"It is because of you that we live at all," the old woman says. "You and Tavian saved this village. You are the Wild One. You are the Fire Druid. And you will always have a home in our tribe, if you need one."

A sob grows in the back of my throat, but I swallow it down. I can't let her words settle into me. I can't consider what they mean, that there are Fae who would accept me, who would treat me with equality and fairness, who would offer me a home and a life. I can't think such things. Not right now. Maybe not ever. I no longer know what I am, but I know what I must do.

I head in the direction I last saw him, where he entered the woods. There I pick up his tracks in the darkness and follow them as quickly as I can until I reach a grove surrounded by trees and a clear pool of water fed by a waterfall off the mountain.

The horse whinnies, and I slide off him and tie him to a tree, then make my way on foot.

And there he is. A giant black tiger. Bigger than anything nature would make, prowling through the grove. He looks restless. Angry. Black smokes twirls around him and lightning sparks in the darkness.

I move slowly, cautiously, with my hand out, like I'd do to calm a horse who was spooked. "Tavian? It's me, Kayla. It's over. The fighting is over. You need to come back to me now, okay?"

The tiger watches me with eyes I know so well, but I can't tell if he understands what I'm saying. I inch closer, holding my breath as I do.

And then he leaps into the air and lands on my chest. He growls, saliva dripping off his sharp teeth. His claws dig into my skin. I ignore the pain and try to remain calm. The fire magic in me is welling up, pushing out, but I can't let it. "I don't want to hurt you," I say through the pain. "I don't want to fight."

His nails dig deeper and I can't hold in the scream. Then his teeth are on me and I feel a bite in my shoulder. "Tavian!"

I don't know if it's my scream, or the taste of my blood, but something happens, and it's instant. He falls back, off of me, his eyes growing wide. And I can tell that he finally sees me. Really sees me.

It takes a moment, but the tiger shifts back into Tavian Gray.

I pull out my crystal and hold it over my shoulder, muttering a spell as I do. It's doesn't heal me completely, but it was a surprisingly shallow wound, and by the time Tavian has stood and walked over to me, I'm mostly recovered.

"Tavian..." my voice gives out as he takes me in his arms.

"I thought I'd done something awful," he says into my hair as he holds me too tightly.

"You saved them. And I'm not hurt. Not really. But you are. Let me see your wounds."

I run a hand over a cut, but he stops my hand with his. "They're scratches. Nothing more."

The air around us feels charged with something new. Something heady and thick and delicious.

When his lips land on mine, I'm already lost in the feeling of his touch, of his body pressed against me. Of his need. Of my need.

There are no thoughts. No considerations for the future, for what this means, for anything beyond our bodies coming together as one. And then we are lost, floating in a place where time doesn't exist.

Being with Tavian is like nothing I've ever experienced. It's more than physical. More than emotional. It's a coming together of two souls into one. Even my newly awakened magic latches onto his, joining into a swirl of power pulling our bodies closer. When we finally pull apart, satiated and exhausted, I'm filled with a loss unlike anything I've ever felt, and we cling to each other on a bed of grass, unwilling to break the moment with words.

I don't know how long we lay here like this, naked and wrapped up in each other, but it is the horse's neighing that pulls us out of our reverie.

Tavian kisses my head before speaking. "You saved me today, Princess."

"I'm not a princess," I mumble into his chest, my eyes still half closed.

"You are to me," he whispers, and another part of me melts into him.

"What do we do now?" I ask.

"I don't know," he says. "This—you—have thrown my plans in disarray. I can't very well bargain and barter a woman I'm falling in love with, can I?"

"Love. That's a powerful word." I choose my own words carefully, as my heart beats too hard in my chest.

He shifts so that we are looking each other in the eyes. "Am I wrong? Did you not feel what I feel?"

I sigh, because no, he's not wrong, and it scares the hell out of me.

He grins. "I thought so."

"That still doesn't answer my question. What now?"

"Now," he says as he brings my fingers to his lips to kiss. "Now, we go back to Stonehill and find out what happened to the Midnight Star and your brother."

13

REFORGED

*"I've got a sword and a very angry wolf. That will
have to be enough. Now I just need a plan."*
—Arianna Spero

In the great hall of the Pleasure Palace, seated on a
lounge by a fire, Es sips a mug of hot cocoa as Pete sits
next to her reading something he found in the library.
I tuck my feet under me and curl into the corner of
the lounge, thinking. Yami sleeps around my neck,
exhausted from the recent events. He has been mood-
ier of late, and I think he remembers the destruction
he caused. Soldiers managed to save some of the grove.
Three trees, they told me. The rest burned and died.

I haven't trained since then. I haven't done much
of anything.

A servant girl draped in silk comes by and hands
me a hot drink and a plate of candied fruits and breaded

meats. I thank her and set the food on the table next me, but I hold onto the drink. The warmth helps dispel the chill in my body, so I sip at it without tasting anything.

"You should eat, darlin'," Es says. "You look pale as a ghost."

To appease her I pick up a honey-glazed strawberry and take a bite, but that's all I can manage. "I'm not hungry."

"It wasn't your fault," she says. "And we're fine."

"People are hurt. Buildings ruined. The grove gone. And it was my fault. Varis warned me, but I didn't listen."

We're interrupted by a voice coming from the hall. "Where is she? Is she injured?"

I set my drink down and stand, a smile coming to my lips for the first time in awhile.

Fen runs to me and wraps me in his strong, warm arms. "We heard the news. A dragon laying ruin to the city? What happened?"

I quickly explain what I did and the harm I caused.

Then Dean walks in. "The people will rebuild. And the grove..." he turns away, and I see he is devastated by what I did. "We will plant more trees. It will take centuries, but eventually, the grove will be restored."

I reluctantly pull away from Fen and hug Dean, whispering in his ear. "I am so sorry. If I could change things, I would."

He smiles briefly, then leaves me to sit down and drink wine.

"What? No hug for me?"

That voice...

"Asher!"

He stands in the doorway, his arms spread out and a big grin on his face. I run forward and embrace my second favorite prince.

He smiles and pets Yami. "I see you've taken to setting the world on fire more literally these days?"

I scowl at him. "It's not funny. But yes."

"We've just come from Stonehill," Fen says. "It's worse than we could have imagined."

I find that hard to believe, until he describes what they saw.

Asher leans against the wall, studying his perfectly manicured nails. "I can't tell you how relieved we were to hear of Yami in full form. We're going to need him in the coming battle."

"That's not going to work," I say, my chest tightening. "I can't control the power."

"Then don't," Asher says. "Unleash him and let him win this war for us."

"The innocent will suffer," I whisper, ashamed. "Too many will die."

"There are no innocents in war," Asher says.

He's darker than usual, more anger behind his eyes. But I haven't seen him in nearly a month. Who knows what he endured.

Fen looks down at me, squeezing my shoulder. "I do not presume to know what it does to you to summon such power. But you didn't see what we saw. The torture. The suffering. The deaths. If there is a way to stop Levi from spreading his darkness to the rest of Inferna and beyond, we must take it."

I can see the pain in his eyes, at having witnessed what he did—at having to ask me to do something he knows causes me hurt—and part of me breaks. "I can't..." I step away from him and look at all of them. "I can't decide this right now. I must think on it."

I walk away before any of them can respond, my whole body alert to someone reaching to stop me. But none do. They allow me the time, and for that I am grateful.

The moons are still high when I exit the palace, and a gentle breeze carries the smell of fire and soot on the air. And worse, burning flesh. Tents have been erected in the palace square, and they are quickly filling with burn victims in need of treatment. My illusion should make me anonymous to anyone who would otherwise recognize the princess, but even then, how many people really could? With no technology, no televisions and photographs and smart phones capturing every moment and face on film, these people live in oblivion. They know of royalty, but don't know what they look like half the time. And if they were to see them at all it would be from a great distance, where they are but well-dressed specks on the horizon.

Still, the added precaution gives me boldness to enter one of the tents and offer my help. Just another person offering to give aide to those in need.

I work for several hours before a familiar voice interrupts my flow. "Diana?" asks Seri, repinning her hair. "I haven't seen you the last few days."

"I…I was feeling sick."

She touches my hand. "What happened…it wasn't your fault."

"It…" I pull away, shocked. "What do you mean?"

"I know who you are. Who you truly are."

I don't know what to make of this. "Let's walk." She nods and we take a break, leaving the healing tents and walking by the canals. The light breeze from the water calms my nerves.

"It wasn't hard," says Seri. "Your mannerisms. Speech patterns. The way you always wash your hands before working with the sick." She grins. "Once I knew, it was easy to see past the illusion with a simple spell."

And I didn't even realize she knew. I need to work on being more observant. "Keep it under wraps, please. I just want to help. I feel so bad."

"Everyone in the tents will be fine. Mild burns, but nothing serious. You do what you must to win this war. It's hell in the north for my people." Her face crumbles. "You have to stop him. Please. Promise me."

How has it come to this? That I must destroy to save? That I must choose who to sacrifice. And there's never a right choice.

Before I can say anything, Dean walks over to us, and Seri excuses herself to get back to her patients.

"Your presence is requested, Princess," Dean says with a bow and a wink. "At the war meeting. It is time to prepare for battle."

He offers his arm, so I take it and walk with him back to the Pleasure Palace, to the War Room. We come in at the middle of a discussion between Fen and Asher, and I get the distinct impression this room doesn't see a lot of use. Cobwebs dangle in the corners and the air is stale and damp despite the fire blazing in the corner.

"Can we engage a frontal assault?" Asher asks, adjusting the cufflinks on his sleeves.

Fen shakes his head. "Not until those within the city unlock the gates. I suggest we sneak in a few men, masquerading as traders, and support the rebels inside. Then, once the gate is breached, the rest can follow."

Dean nods. "Solid. So what's the timeline?"

"We strike in a week," Asher says. "That is when the rebels plan their attack from within." He points to Stonehill on the map and—

Something clacks against the wooden door behind me, and I get a shiver up my arms. I walk to the entrance, and when I open it, Seri is there, about to come in.

"Hello," she says, turning to the group. "I'm sorry, is this not a good time? I needed to speak to Prince Asher."

Asher shakes his hand. "Not a good time. Find me when this is over."

Seri nods. "Apologies. I'll speak with you later, then."

She closes the door as she leaves, but my arms still tingle. Something feels odd. Seri seemed uneasy. So I slip out quietly and follow her.

I stay far enough behind that she does not see or hear me down the long hallways, but close enough that I can see if she turns or changes directions. It's a delicate dance, but one that ultimately pays off. We exit the palace and head to the edges of the city, to the forest. What business does Seri have in the woods?

Between the trees, I must stay closer to keep sight of her, so I use an illusion to muffle my steps, making me near silent. Sometimes, I still lose track of her, and then I follow her footprints. Eventually, she comes upon a clearing and sits down on a stump. Near her, on a tree, sits a black owl, and I see its leg is tied to a branch. Seri pull something out of her bag. Pen and paper. And she begins to write.

Dread fills me. I know what's happening, but I don't want it to be true. Silently, illusion masking my steps, I walk up behind Seri and read the letter she writes.

They will attack Stonehill in a week. This is your chance to strike while they are distracted.

I've known for some time we had a spy amongst us.

And now I know that spy is Seri.

...

The Keeper turns, noticing me. Her voice is cold. "If you choose to have me killed, I understand."

I draw my sword, holding it up to her neck. "Why?"

"My family died in this war, and now my people are tortured in the north. The rule of the vampires must come to an end. The rule of the Fae must return."

She speaks so casually, while inside I spin with rage and sorrow. I pull back my sword, ready to strike.

"Go ahead," she says. "I would do the same in your place."

I feel something stir within me. The wind howls into the night. The shadows grow darker. The earth begins to tremble.

My sword glows a pale blue, and I hold it against Seri's throat, and when the blade touches her flesh, it burns—a fire so hot it's scorching.

Fire that killed so many. That killed Daison. Fire that burned into my body when Oren tortured me. Fire that burned the grove and the innocent.

How many more will die? How many more will suffer?

No. This will stop. Now.

I calm my mind, wiping away all thoughts of anger and vengeance, and the wind and earth grow still. My blade no longer glows. The Darkness recedes.

I let the sword fall from my hands and clash to the floor.

I'm not here to destroy. I'm here to bring peace.

"I will not kill you," I tell Seri, whose eyes widen in surprise. I don't even know if I can trust her. Or if she will betray me again. But I know I will no longer be the cause of pain. "Instead, you will help me. You will help me bring peace to all the people in these lands."

She nods, a tear sliding down her cheek. "I'm sorry…"

I clutch her shoulder. "Go back to the Healing Tents. Burn the letter. I will find you later. But right now, I have something I must do."

I walk back to the Crystal Garden. Back to the stone and the flame.

And I forge.

...

It takes a week, working night and day—sometimes with magic, and the aid of master armorsmiths and who live in this realm, to accomplish my task. On the last day, I take a drink of cool water and admire our work.

A set of armor, half black, half white. Like my sword. It shimmers. Like Yami.

An iridescent dragon is engraved on the chest. And the moonlight steel is built in folds like scales. Strong but light. A midnight cape flows behind, clasped to the shoulders.

I don the armor and go to see Fen. The look on his face is all the praise I need. Then I tell him my plan, and he agrees. It's time for a presenting of our own.

He dons his brown leather armor and thick fur cape, and then Dean leads us to the highest balcony in the Moonlight Garden. He lures his people to the palace with promises of free drink and food, and once hundreds have gathered, he speaks to the masses. "You have heard that Arianna Spero and Fenris Vane were killed by the Prince of Envy." He pauses for effect. "You heard wrong."

I drop our illusions.

Fen and I step forward.

And the people cheer.

...

After, there is the feast Dean promised. And when he promises, he delivers in spades. Wine and ale flow freely, as well as much stronger liquors that glow suspiciously. Nectar of the Elders Ones is the favorite, of course. I stay away in favor of wine and celebrate late into the night with my friends. I eat too much, drink too much. Because tomorrow...

It's time.

Time to march north and stop Levi.

Time to unleash the Midnight Star.

Fen and Baron escort me to my room, and we stand by my door looking deeply into each other's eyes.

I kiss him, and his body responds instantly, clutching at mine, returning my kisses—my passion. I am consumed by him and can't let him go. "Come in with me," I say, my eyes pleading with him to do what I ask. To join me. To complete what we've started so many times.

His body presses harder against mine, and then he pulls away, and I know his answer before he speaks it.

"You've had a lot to drink and we have travel tomorrow. You need rest."

Before I can object, he kisses me chastely on the forehead and walks back to his room, Baron whining at his heels as the wolf steals glances back at me and Yami.

I sigh and let myself into my room. "I guess that's that, my little dragon. He's a stubborn ass sometimes."

I fall asleep quickly, my dreams peaceful without potions for the first time in weeks. And I am heavy with exhaustion when something wakes me. It's the door to my room, opening. A figure slips in. I'm about to reach for my sword when he speaks from the shadows. "Ari, it's me."

"Fen!" I sit up as he walks over to my bed. "You came back? But I thought—"

"I changed my mind."

Those are the last words we speak the rest of the night.

He rushes forward, grabbing me in a fierce embrace, his breath heavy against my ear, his heart strong against my chest. His mouth explores mine with a hungry passion, and his hands tear away my sleeping gown. Our bodies come together. Gently, at first, then with a desire I can barely contain. We lose ourselves. To all that we are. To all that we have wished.

It becomes like a drug, being with him. Our magic finds each other's, the powers blending into a radiant warmth that fills us both and molds us together into one.

And when we finally finish, falling asleep in each other's arms, I look outside and see the sun begin to rise. And as night turns to day, I realize everything has changed, and I smile for what is to come.

14

THE BARGAIN
Kayla Windhelm

"They wouldn't dream of turning on you."

—Asher

It nearly breaks my heart to see what Stonehill has become when we arrive at the gates. Tavian uses an illusion to mask his Fae features, at my advice, as we walk through a gruesome display of torture and death. The roads are lined with wooden pikes sporting the heads of Fae and Shade. At first, the guards do not want to admit us into the city, because I am Shade. But when I explain who I am, they acquiesce.

Tavian is quiet, and I don't blame him. These are his people even more than mine. And what has been done to them is gruesome.

We pass a cart full of barrels and Tavian sniffs the air. "Powder. Explosives."

"Why?"

"Perhaps they are preparing for battle."

I nod, looking at what once was my forge. Now, men I don't recognize forge crude weapons there, preparing for war with the Fae. I hurry forward, eager to remove them from my line of vision.

In the center of town, on a wooden platform that has become the stage for the cruelest of deeds, a group of soldiers torture two slaves, as more of Levi's men look on and laugh. Tavian flexes, and I slip my hand around his arm. "We can't interfere," I say. "We can't fight them all."

"I know," he says through gritted teeth. "Doesn't mean I have to like it."

"Let's just find Fen and Ari and figure out what's going—" the words die in my throat as we approach Stonehill Castle. For there, on either side of the entrance, are two more pikes. With two more heads. Fires blaze in my hands and I feel my blood boil with rage and grief and shock.

"They're dead!" I turn to Tavian, my wrath pouring out of me as I misplace it onto him. "You said she was alive. You gave me hope."

He pulls me into his arms and though my flames singe his skin, he doesn't let go. I breathe in his scent, cling to his chest, and let the fire in me die as sobs tear through me. I hadn't realized how much I needed that hope until now. Until it was ripped away from me.

When I have myself under control I pull back to look at him. "I thought you would know if she were dead?"

"I would. I can't explain it, but this does not make sense. We need more information. All hope is not lost," he says, wiping a tear off my cheek.

"Dum spire spero," I whisper. "While I breathe, I hope. Ari always said that. She always had hope. Always believed things could improve."

"Do not yet speak of her in the past tense. We will discover the truth."

Something shifts in the air. I pull back from Tavian, and see that we are surrounded by men in red, their armor shining in the sun. Their weapons pointed at us.

Levi stands at their head. "Well, well. When I heard Kayla Windhelm had finally returned, I couldn't believe it. Had to see for myself. But here you are. Alive and well. Took your time answering my summons, didn't you?"

I clench my jaw, filling with rage. "You murdered Fenris and Ari."

"Now, now. It wasn't murder, but justice. Arianna was the Midnight Star. She was the reason for the Druids' return. And Fen was Fae all along. His wolf was the Spirit of the Earth."

I flinch. "That's not possible."

Levi smiles. "Oh, but it is. Our mother turned him when he was a babe, you see. I knew he was Fae from the beginning, but only recently did I discover he was Druid." He tilts his head at me. "Why the long face? With the Midnight Star gone, the Druids will soon return to slumber, and then we shall have peace once more."

I spit at his feet. "There can be no peace under your rule."

Levi rolls his eyes, then looks at Tavian. "And who might you be?"

"A traveler," he says. "I saved Kayla in the Outlands."

"And I assured him he would be well compensated," I add.

Levi nods. "You have my thanks. Kayla is a valued blacksmith." He motions to his men. "Now, I'm sure you will follow us quietly. It would be such a shame to upset the townsfolk."

I draw my sword. "We leave. Now."

Levi chuckles. "If you try, my men will beat you. They will cut into your friend and do far worse to you. I'll make sure my entire garrison gets a turn. Who knows, maybe I will even partake at the end."

I glance at Tavian. "We can't surrender."

He looks around, at the traders running their stores, at the wives drying their clothes, at children playing with stones. "I'm sorry," he says. "But I cannot fight here. I cannot harm these innocent people."

I remember last time he shifted, how he attacked without cause and reason. I remember how he almost killed me.

And I drop my sword.

Levi smirks and opens his hand, revealing a vial of purple liquid. "Now, would you be so kind as to drink this? It will help make things more manageable?

I grab the vile and swallow my share, then pass it to Tavian. His emerald eyes are the last things I see before my strength fades, and I fall into nothing.

15

VENGEANCE

*"They are strong, Ari. Powerful. We are the Fallen. The first
of our kind to come to this world. The original cursed. You
wouldn't stand a chance against them. Against any of us."*
—Fenris Vane

I say goodbye to Es and Pete, and then we march north.
Varis does not follow. "This is a fight between vampires.
It does not concern the Fae." I try to argue with him.
To convince him that defeating Levi is good for all, but
he does not listen. In truth, we've barely talked since
I unleashed the Darkness and burned down the grove.
And we barely talk now. "Goodbye Arianna. May we see
each other again." Then he leaves, flying off on Zyra
into the sunrise.

It takes a day to reach the outskirts of Stonehill,
and we set camp in the forest, making no fires in fear of
attracting attention. Our army is not great. Only a few

hundred. So we will wait for tomorrow, when the rebellion begins.

Fen and I share a tent, but we do not repeat lasts night's romantic interlude, nor do we speak of it. I think, perhaps, we both worry that to do so would be to break the happiness we have found. And so, we simply enjoy each other's company, joking and laughing, falling asleep side by side.

The next day, I am jolted awake. "Grab your gear," says Fen. "The rebellion started early."

I don my armor and grab Spero, then find my horse. Dean, Asher, Fen and I lead the front lines as we emerge from the forest and onto a hill overlooking the city. The sun has just begun to rise, casting everything in dark orange and leaving long shadows.

We wait.

We wait for the gate to open.

And when it does, we charge forward, shouting battle cries and screaming to the heavens. Our soldiers cut down everyone in their path. Blood and mud slashes through the air. Men and women scream in pain, clutching wounds and dismembered limbs. Buildings are set on fire. Horses lose their riders and flee in panic, trampling people to death. It is chaos. Everywhere. And I can only hope the innocent are safe, for I cannot tell. It all looks like madness and death.

Amidst the turmoil, Fen leads me and his brothers to the side of the castle, to a secret passage behind a waterfall few but him know of. He taps on a rock embedded in a stone wall, and a doorway opens. Quickly, we rush inside, and Fen closes the passage behind us. Dim torches light our way, as we run through cramped tunnels and over small stairs. When we reach a dead end, Fen taps another rock in the wall, and the way before us opens. I cast an illusion on us all, muffling our steps, and we creep into the castle.

I know this place.

The dungeons.

The Warden sits at a table, eating a loaf of bread, his hands still bloody from his nasty work of torture. He starts to turn, about to see us, but then Fen leaps forward, and in one movement takes off his head. "One of Levi's" he says, spitting on the dead corpse.

"We need to make haste," says Dean. "Before Levi realizes we are in the castle and tries to flee." I nod, and we move for the stairs. But something catches my eye.

A man in the corner, broken and bloodied, his back shredded into ribbons of flesh and skin.

Marco!

I run to his side and break the chains that bind him with my sword. "Fetch him some water. Now!"

Asher obliges, brining me a jug from the table, and I pour the cold water down Marco's throat.

He gulps down what he can, then turns away, signaling he is finished. His face is bruised and purple. Barely recognizable. When he looks at me, he smiles. His voice is barely a whisper. "Arianna...you came back..."

I nod, stroking his hair in soothing motions. "Yes. You're safe now."

"Levi...he...after I helped..."

"I know." Levi did this to him. Because he helped me escape. Tears well in my eyes for the man before me. For the pain he's endured. Levi must never cause such pain again. No matter what happens, today I capture the mad prince.

Marco tilts his head to the side. "There...friends..."

I follow his gaze to the back of the dungeon, where large steel cages stand covered in shadows. "Make sure he's comfortable," I say to Asher, and then I run to the Warden's corpse, grab the keys off his belt, and open the cell in the back.

Inside, I find a woman. Dirty and bloody. Curled into a small ball. Shaking and murmuring nonsense. I step closer to offer water. And then I see who she really is. "Kayla?"

Kayla scrambles back, her eyes wild and bloodshot. "No. No. No! Don't punish me again. Not again. I've been good. I swear I've been good."

I sit down, bringing myself to her level. "Kayla, it's me. Arianna."

She brushes her messy hair out of her eyes, squinting. "Arianna? Arianna!" She jumps forward, grabbing me and holding me tight, weeping against my chest. "I saw your head on a spike. You were dead. You were dead!"

I grab her shoulders and make her look at me. "It was only an illusion. I'm here. I'm alive. You're safe."

She nods, then looks away, to the cage. No. The cage beside hers. She reaches for the bars. "Tavian. Tavian!"

I don't know who she speaks of, but I understand what she means. I run outside and unlock the second cage. A man lies within, unmoving, his back bloody, his gut covered in recent wounds stitched back together. I check his pulse. "He's alive!"

Kayla falls to his side, clutching him dearly. "Oh, thank the Spirits. Tavian. Tavian, please wake up."

Someone grabs my shoulder from behind. Fen. "We must go. Before it's too late." He glances at Kalya. "I am glad you are safe, sister."

She looks back at him. "Go. Make Levi pay."

...

When we reach upstairs, it's chaos. The slaves have taken advantage of the rebellion and attack the guards using kitchen knives. Brooms. Anything they can grab. Some manage to kill a vampire and take their sword.

Baron joins the fray, tearing out the throat of a soldier. Viscously striking at anyone he deems an enemy.

Our party carves our way through the hallways, avoiding as much combat as possible. Sometimes soldiers rush to fight us, but then they see Fen, drenched in the blood of his enemies, Dean, with the thrill of battle in his eyes, and Asher, swift despite new wounds. They see me, clad in the colors of midnight, a dragon upon my shoulder. And then the soldiers flee.

A group of Fae block the path ahead. And I recognize Kara with her golden hair and Julian with her green eyes, the Fae girls who tended to my needs in Stonehill and later at Sky Castle. They fight off their attacker, a man soaked in blood, a sword in his hand. Before he can strike I rush forward.

And cut off his arm.

The girls scream. Then they see me. And their eyes fill with hope.

"Go," I say. "Find a room and bar the door. Don't come out until you hear no more battle." They nod and disappear down the hallway.

Something nudges at my feet.

I look down and see Kal, laying against the wall, clutching his belly.

"How bad is it?" I ask, already examining the wound.

He chuckles. "Nothing a Keeper can't handle. I'll be fine."

I can't tell if he's being honest, or just saying what I want to hear. Kal was one of my only friends when I arrived at Stonehill, one of the few who understood my struggle to help the Fae. I reach down and kiss his head. "May the Spirits bless you," I say, casting an incantation to heal. Then I stand and walk away. I have done all I can. No point in worrying now. I must focus. Levi awaits.

A few more steps, and we reach the entrance to the grand hall. A dozen elite guards protect the door, slaughtering all Fae who try to break in. Fen and Dean rush forward, engaging them in battle. But I have other plans. As the brothers fight, I dash through the opening they create and ram open the door. I seek the head. Cut it off and the body dies.

I jump into the throne room, and find myself away from the chaos, in a hall empty and quiet. Leaves cover the floor, fallen from the great tree that stands in the center of the room. Once, this was a place of happiness. A place of comfort and safety. Now, it is a barren field, rotten, corrupted. I move through the hall, sword raised. And then I see him. Sitting on the throne in gold and red robes. Running his pale fingers through his long white hair. He studies me, and then he laughs. "Oh, well played, Princess. Well played. You made it all the way here. But you have yet to win."

He stands, drawing his sword, a giant silver blade with a ruby in the pommel.

I glance back, searching to see if my allies have caught up with me. They haven't. The elite soldiers are keeping them at bay. I start to turn back to Levi.

And see his sword lunging for my throat.

I spin out of the way, then strike back. Our blades clash, and the ring of steel echoes in the empty hall. Levi pivots, then strikes for my legs. I parry and strike for his hands. Yami screeches, and Levi flinches in surprise. I see an opening. I strike.

And stab Levi in the heart.

He collapses, blood pouring from his lips, his eyes fading.

I tremble, unable to accept that this is over. The war with Levi is over. Stonehill is reclaimed. Tears of happiness well in my eyes, mixing joy with shock. I had heard Levi was a master swordsman, but it must have been a jest. A lie to scare his enemies. He was weak all along. As weak in body as he was in mind.

I look at the Prince of Envy one last time. And I watch him fall.

And then...

Then I see the blood begin to disappear.

I see his clothing fade away.

I see his face change.

No. It can't be.

The man at my feet isn't Levi. He's an imposter. A decoy. Masked by illusion. How could I have missed it?

I look around, shaking with dread. If this is a fake, then where's the real Levi?

I flinch at every shadow. Shake at every sound. And then I glance at the windows.

And outside, at the top of a snow-covered cliff, I see Levi.

His red cloak sways in the wind. His white hair falls over his dark eyes. He lifts a hand.

And the throne room explodes in fire.

...

I feel the force of the explosion first, pushing me back, throwing me against a wall, crushing my bones. The hall before me rips open, stone and wood splintering into oblivion. Next, comes the fire. It shines like the blazing sun, setting flame to the great tree, burning stone itself, and it makes it way forward. Forward. To me.

There is no time. Nothing I can do.

I glance at Yami once last time, and then I smile, facing my end. I will not fear the flames as I did before. I will fall into their warm embrace. I will see Daison once again.

I sigh, letting go of all my fear and hate. Forgiving all those who I had yet to forgive. I do not know how I do this in a blink of an eye, but I do.

I surrender myself to what comes next. The fire falls upon me.

And then he is there.

Fen.

He jumps in front of me, his face twisted in pain and effort. He throws up his arms, and a wall of stone rushes up from the ground. It blocks the fire. It blocks the end.

And finally, time seems to move at a normal pace.

I grab Fen as he falls to the ground, panting heavily and shaking. He used too much power to control the earth and summon the wall. He needs to rest. Without proper training, the act could still cause his death.

Dean and Asher run in behind me, Baron at their heels. "Get him to a healer," I say. And then I run.

I run past the wall of stone.

I run over the burned and shattered floor.

I run through the torn away window.

And I jump.

I fly through the air, Spero raised high. I come for justice. I come for Levi.

He sees me, and his eyes go wide. He dashes forward, jumping off the cliff, down below to the frozen lake. I fall after him, pulling back my hands to speed my decent. And then I feel Yami against me. He is bigger than before. Not as giant as when consumed by the Darkness. He is more my size. And I grip the spikes on his back and let him take me down and forward. Together, we glide over the frozen lake. Over Levi.

I leap off Yami.

Striking at Levi as I fall.

He dashes out of the way, and Spero pierces the ice. I rend my blade free and strike again. Levi parries, then retaliates with a series of attack so fast I barely avoid death. This is the real Levi. The sword master.

Yami swoops down, striking at Levi from behind, but he avoids the assault, and I need to dodge to evade the dragon myself. I regain my stance and lunge. But no matter what attack I try, Levi is always a step ahead. He fights both Yami and me at the same time. And he's winning.

There's a reason the vampires won the war, I think. Even the Midnight Star could not stand against them.

I spin forward, lashing out with my blade. But Levi sees a weakness in my technique. He slashes through my assault.

And cuts into my shoulder.

The pain sends me to my knees, makes me shake and scream.

Levi raises his sword. One final blow. He strikes.

And the ice between us shatters, throwing both of us back. A serpent, massive and wild, rushes up from the water, roaring into the sky. Wadu.

She's here.

I jump to my feet and run.

Wadu lunges forward, razor sharp teeth aimed to tear me to shreds. But Yami crashes into her head, clawing at her eyes. It's the distraction I need. I can flee. Wait for Dean and Asher to reach me. To help me.

But I forget.

Where Wadu is, Metsi isn't far behind.

She springs from the ice before me, blocking my path, her dark skin gleaming against the white of the snow and ice.

"You're mine now," she says.

And then Wadu breaks through the ice below me. Wrapping around me. Pulling me under.

My lungs fill with water as I thrash and fight and try not to scream.

But the water is so cold. And thinking so difficult.

So I close my eyes.

And let the ice pull me in.

...

My lungs burn as water pours out of my mouth. I choke. I gag. I try to move. Try to break free, but I am shackled.

Chained. My wrists and ankles immobilized. I peel my eyes open and see Metsi, the Water Druid, standing before me, using her magic to pull water from my lungs.

I inhale oxygen and try to clear my head. Try to remember what happened. The battle. Stonehill. Levi.

He fled. I chased him. Fought him. Stonehill was ours once more.

And then...

Metsi.

She knew where we were. Knew exactly when to attack. But how? Did Seri betray us after all? Was I a fool for trusting the Fae healer?

I look around, studying the building of green stone I find myself in. I see only one window. The room is dark. Guards block the doorway. I do not know where I am. Do not know how to escape or where to go if I do.

So I do the only thing I can. I calm my mind. And when my breath returns, I speak, though it hurts my throat and I am still light headed. "Where is Yami? What did you do with him?" I reach out to my dragon, trying to summon him, but I feel nothing.

"He is safe. Captured and caged until he can be wielded by one we can trust," she says.

"What do you want with me? To torture me like Oren did? Kill me?" I try to be brave through my fear, but this is not like the last time the Fae captured me. There is no illusion of respect. I am a prisoner. I am in danger.

"No," she says with a small smile, caressing my hair, and then my stomach. "I would never kill you. My magic would begin to fade. I need you alive. But... you have been far too much trouble. So I must keep you contained somewhere safe. Somewhere you can do no harm."

The torches flicker on the wall, and I realize I am in a dungeon once again.

Someone screams in agony.

"Keep the other prisoner quiet!" Metsi snaps.

"Apologies, Wild One. I think we went too far this time."

I stretch my neck to see who's speaking. It's another Fae standing over a man tied to a post. The man is naked and bleeds profusely as strips of his skin fall to the ground like shredded cheese. I don't even recognize him until he turns his face toward me.

Levi.

I turn back to Metsi. "Am I next?"

Metsi puts a hand over my stomach and smiles.

"I cannot risk it," she says. "After all, it wouldn't be good for the child you carry."

EPILOGUE
Asher

"A man walks out from the shadows. A man I have come to know over the last few weeks. A man I thought I could trust."
—Arianna Spero

The castle is ours. People parade through the streets, feasting and drinking, celebrating the return of Fenris Vane. They curse Levi's name and sing praises to the Prince of War.

But not everyone can be so joyous. Many fell in the battle, and the city fills with burials and funeral pyres, everyone honoring their dead in their own way.

Those who were injured are taken to the healing tents, and Seri works tirelessly to ease their pain and save their lives.

Kayla heals quickly, recovering her senses and strength after a few days. So does the new man. Tavian

Gray. He is unknown to me, and that is troubling. But so far, he causes no problems.

The Keeper Kal'Hallen survived, though must live with a giant scar across his belly now.

Fenris heals quickest of all. Whatever power he unleashed to save Arianna did not drain him for long. And he seems to have taken an interest in the Fae texts since then. Once, I saw him on a balcony, speaking to Varis about something. I suspect it was about unlocking more of his abilities.

A week after the battle, Fenris, Dean, and I meet in the War Room. It is not the first time and likely won't be the last. "We must find Arianna," says Fenris, motioning to maps of the Outlands. "We must send every warrior we can spare to look for her."

"Caution, brother," I say, adjusting my suit collar and finding no way to make it comfortable. "You forget, we never found Levi. Likely he escaped and is mustering an army with Niam to retake Stonehill. Zeb and Ace are likely to join them as well."

Fenris growls. "Do what you wish with your soldiers. But I go after Arianna."

Dean sighs, pulling off his shirt, though I cannot say why. "So do I," he says. "I will send my best men to search for her."

I shake my head at their foolishness. "Then I suppose I will be here, protecting the base of power we just sacrificed everything to reclaim."

"I suppose you will," says Fenris. Then he walks away, slamming the door behind him.

Dean shrugs, and we decide the meeting is over. I leave the warm room, passing the great hall on my way. Slaves toil with stone and wood, working to rebuild the ruined wall. It will take months of work, but I notice even vampires helping with the repairs. Perhaps they will speed the process.

Once I am in my chambers, I sit down on my bed, and pull of my suit. It is far too tight for my liking. I much prefer the feel of armor.

I put on a simple white shirt instead, and then I see her.

She materializes from mist in my window. Her skin is dark. Her blue tattoos shimmering in the moonlight. "Your plan worked," says Metsi. "Arianna and Levi are now under my power."

I grin and wink at her. "I knew you'd find a way to take advantage of the chaos."

"She is with child," says Metis.

This is news. "Good. Then we shall raise the next Midnight Star together."

"And the Fae shall be free once more."

"Yes…" I say, reclining in the soft bed. Too soft for my taste. "And all will be set right." I look back at the window, and see that Metsi is gone. Good. I dreaded a longer conversation. And besides, I have other important matters.

The night grows darker, and I leave my chambers, descending deep into the castle. I push a stone on a wall, and open a passage so ancient even Fenris doesn't know of it; he wasn't yet born during its making. Then I descend the spiral steps, deep into the bowels of the earth, until I reach a dark chamber, where torches cast wonderful shadows.

And there, in the center, a man sits on his knees, his arms stretched out and held up by chains.

There is the *real* Asher.

He looks up at me, his eyes sunken, his lip bloody. "You will not keep me here forever. I will escape. And when I do, father, I will end your life."

I laugh, dropping my illusion, and examine my own hands. Lucian's hands. It is good to be myself again, even if just for a while.

I step forward and take a tray of meat and cheeses from the floor and place it before Asher. "One day, my son, you will understand the reasons for what I do. And you will thank me."

He spits in my face.

I wipe away the phlegm and blood and turn to leave. One day, he will understand, and he will ask for forgiveness. The pieces are falling into place. And soon, the power of the Primal One, shall be mine.

TO BE CONTINUED

Call us Karpov Kinrade. We're the husband and wife team behind *Silver Flame*. And we want to say...Thank you for reading it. We worked hard on these characters and this world, and we're thrilled to share this story with so many readers. We hope you enjoyed *Silver Flame*, the third book in this fantasy series. Want to find out the moment the next book is available? Want to see a sneak peek of the next book cover and get teasers before launch? Sign up for the Karpov Kinrade/Vampire Girl newsletter and get all that and more at KarpovKinrade.com!

And visit our website for more great books to read. If you're looking for something to keep you engaged while you wait for the next *Vampire Girl* novel, check out *Court of Nightfall*. It's an epic adventure full of suspense, love, betrayal, friendship, and twists and turns that will leave you breathless. Keep reading for a look at *Court of Nightfall*, chapter 1.

USA TODAY BESTSELLING AUTHOR

KARPOV KINRADE

COURT OF
NIGHTFALL

NIGHTFALL CHRONICLES

PREFACE

Some say my story began when my parents were murdered. It did not.

Others say it began when I died. They are wrong.

I remember the pain.

The bullet of fire entered my body and moved through me, leaving a trail of burning agony in its wake.

I slumped over the crystal box that held the weapon we'd all fought to protect, my blood seeping out of me, staining the opaque quartz.

Red. Scarlet. Evie whispered the color of my own name into my ear as I slowly died.

My last vision was of that blood—still just grey to me—spreading into the cracks, into the intricate carvings that decorated the encasement. It almost seemed to glow, and I smiled and closed my eyes as the crystal shattered and darkness took me.

My story begins long before that—and if the historians take issue, I care not and neither should you. It's my story. I begin at the start.

With the test.

With the twins.

And what happened to them.

1

SHADES OF GREY

"Negative."

"Test me again."

The nurse shakes her head. "Sorry, Scarlett."

I slide off the table, rubbing under my shoulder where she took my blood. "The test is wrong."

She frowns. "Most kids would be grateful."

I walk to the door. "I'm not most kids."

The nurse escorts me to the waiting room, informs my parents of the results, and leaves. My parents sigh and exchange a look. My mom drops down to one knee and hugs me. "I know this isn't what you wanted, but—"

"The test is wrong," I say.

My dad stares at me for a moment. His voice is soft. "Why would you think that, Star?"

"I heal quick. I'm stronger than other girls my age." And I can just tell. It's my body. I can tell.

He bows his head.

My mom squeezes me tighter. "You're healthy. That doesn't make you Zenith."

They look tired, so I don't say any more. This day has been hard for everyone.

My mom sighs. "Why don't you go play outside while we fill out paperwork?"

I shrug and walk out the doors, passing posters of Zeniths stolen from their homes. A little girl with big eyes and a sad smile stares back at me from the eScreen in front of the office. She's out there somewhere. They all are. And it's no mystery who took them. It was Apex. He who runs the self-named group, The Apex, that traffics Zeniths for profit. But no one cares. So it will just keep happening. I understand why my parents are relieved. I just wish they understood why I'm not.

Kids squint at me from the playground, checking if I was tagged. When they don't see anything new on my ear they turn back to their play. One boy dives head first down the slide. It's red, with cracks in the thick plastic. I asked my dad the color once. I don't know what red looks like, but it's my favorite color. I turn away and run the dirt track around the school. Dust flies up around me. I build speed and jump, glancing at the gray sky, imagining I can fly. Not with an airplane, but with wings. I wish for them. But I don't tell anyone.

You don't dream of flying.

Not if you want to live.

...

There is war. You can hear it in the sobs of a mother weeping for her daughter. You can taste it in the rationed food and smell it on your tattered clothes. You can see it in the empty houses and roads and faces. You can feel it inside.

I'm a child, so people assume I know little of such things. But when you are young and free and happy, pain stands out all the more. I'm too little to fight, so I spend my days playing and planning. I plan to end the suffering.

"Why don't the Nephilim give up?" I ask, sitting on the swing, making patterns in the gravel with my foot. "They'll never conquer the world. It's a stupid plan."

"It's not about that," says Jax. He sits on the swing next to mine, his shirt dark and his pants darker. I can't see colors. I never have. But I imagine Jax is wearing blue. I hear it's a calm color. And I find Jax calming.

The sky is dark and cloudy. The rusty carousel we used to play on creaks in the wind. Two boys sit by a nearby anthill, poking at it with sticks as they laugh. So many of the children are gone.

Jax leans closer and lowers his voice. "One night, I heard my dad yelling at the eScreen. He said the Nephilim were fighting for their rights. He said all the news was a sham. I think he'd been drinking."

I cringe. My parents let me try wine last New Year's. The taste still disgusts me. But I noticed something about my parents that night. They answered all of my questions. "Sometimes, drunk people are more honest. Maybe your father's right. Maybe we should give the Nephilim rights."

He shakes his head, his hair falling in his eyes. "It's not so simple."

"No. But it can be." I finish a circle in the gravel. "One day, I'll leave the kingdom of Sky, and I'll train to be a Knight."

Jax sighs. "If we had the right families."

"I'll join a Domus first and work my way up the ranks, gain patronage, gain a patrician family. Then, I'll apply to be an Initiate. It's been done before."

Jax grins. "Then I'll join you. We'll be Jax the Courageous and Scarlett the Clever."

I giggle at my title. I only wish I understood my name better. Scarlett. I've tried to imagine the color, only to learn imagining a new color is impossible.

People tell me it's fiery and fierce.

I like that.

Jax looks over to the sand pit where a girl builds a castle. I've seen her around the playground and the park. We've spoken twice, both times about how to build proper fortifications. Her name's Brooke.

"Poor girl," says Jax, his eyes distant.

"What do you mean?" I ask. And then I see it.

The tag in her ear.

She tested Zenith.

The two boys notice the tag, too. The big one frowns and spits on the anthill. He nudges the small one, and they approach Brooke.

She doesn't notice them.

They kick her castle down.

"Hey!" she yells, standing, her hands balled in fists.

The big one shoves her back. "Get lost, Zenith scum," he says.

"Get lost, biter," says the small one.

They pick on her because she is different.

I've been different all my life. When people speak of colors, I speak of shades. It makes me no worse. They think this girl is weak and alone.

They are wrong.

I jump off my swing. I walk up behind them.

My parents tell me to approach things peacefully, but bullies aren't peaceful. They understand one thing. So I pick up a rock.

And throw it at the big one's head.

The collision with his skull is nearly silent. But the boy is not. He yells and collapses, grabbing at his bloody hair. His eyes are foggy.

The small one backs away.

The big one climbs to his knees. "Stupid Zenith lover. My big brother knows how to deal with you. He'll find you."

Jax walks up beside me. He's three years older and almost as big as the bully.

I palm another stone.

We say nothing.

The bullies exchange looks. Then the small one helps the big one up, and they walk away. "My brother will hear about you biters," yells the big one.

Fine. Let him tell others what I've done.

This world likes violence and winning.

And I'm good at both.

...

"Are you okay?" I ask.

The girl in front of us is tiny. My age, but shorter, more petite. She brushes a strand of hair off her face and shrugs. "Yeah. Thanks."

"Brooke! What happened?" Another girl runs up to us.

"Nothing. It's fine, Ella." Brooke turns to us. "I'm Brooke, this is my twin, Ella. Who are you?"

They look a lot alike, both dark haired with almond-shaped eyes and skin a few shades darker than my paleness, but where Brooke is unremarkable, someone who would blend into the crowd if not for how small she is, Ella would never blend in. She's got the face of a pixie, with big eyes and full lips and a dimple in her cheek. She's beautiful.

"I'm Scarlett. This is Jax."

We all awkwardly shake hands. They are both tagged. We aren't. If any of the teachers saw us they would separate us, but I don't care. I don't go to this school. I'm only here for the testing. They can take their segregation and discrimination and eat it.

"Do you want to play together?" I ask.

Brooke raises an eyebrow. "Really?"

Jax smiles. "Why not?"

We sit in the sand with them and begin building a castle. Brooke and Ella exchange a glance, then sit with us. Our hands dip into the cool sand and we pack it into shapes as our creation comes to life.

"Do you go to school here?" I ask, to break the silence.

Brooke nods. "Yes."

I smile. "We're homeschooled."

Brooke looks at up at us. "Are you brother and sister?"

I blush, but I don't know why. "No. But we might as well be."

"We've grown up together," Jax says with a grin. "I was there when Star was born."

We fall into silence after that, building our castle bigger and bigger. The twins occasionally exchange glances, and I wonder if they have a secret language like me and Jax. A way to communicate so others don't know.

I'm trying to add a tower to the castle when my sand collapses. "Again?"

Jax chuckles, tracing out a detailed window with a stick. "That's what happens when you don't plan out the foundation." We once competed in a wood carving competition. He built a palace with miniature knights. I built a house, though a lot of people mistook it for a rock.

Brooke grins and looks at Ella.

"Be careful," says Ella.

Brooke nods, then looks back at me. "Let me help."

She holds her hand over the castle, and the air buzzes. The sand comes together and floats. With care she moves her hand until the sand is packed into a tower.

"You're a Gravir," I say. "That's awesome."

Brooke smiles, but it slips from her face a moment later. "No one else would think so."

"They would, and they would be envious, and they would never admit it."

"Are you envious?" she asks.

I pause. "I try not to be."

Brooke bows her head, her eyes glistening.

I reach over and pat her hand. "There's nothing wrong with you. The problem is with them."

"How old are you?" Brooke asks me.

"I'm nine."

Brooke squints her eyes at me. "You don't sound like a normal nine-year-old."

Jax laughs. "She's not. I keep trying to figure out how she got so smart. I can only assume it's the great company she keeps." He nudges me playfully and I laugh with him, but inside I, too, wonder why I'm so different. I don't think like others, or respond like others my age, or even older. It's why I don't really have any friends other than Jax. The twins look at us strangely.

I don't know what more to say on the subject of my oddity, so I turn to Ella. "What can you do?" I ask, wanting to compliment her on her abilities as well.

Ella blinks a few times. "Notice my eyes?"

I squint. "What about them?"

Jax sighs. "Star's colorblind. She can't tell the difference."

"Oh," says Ella, playing with her hands sheepishly. "I can change the color of my eyes. I'm a dud."

I shake my head. "You may be listed as a dud in the system," I say, pointing to the building we came out of, "but that doesn't mean your abilities are useless. My mom is always trying to match her outfits to her eye color. You'll never have to worry about that."

After a moment, Ella smiles.

My parents emerge from the school, ready to go, but I ask if Jax and I can walk Brooke and Ella home instead. My mother glances at the tags on the girls' ears. "Where are your parents?" she asks.

"Home," says Brooke. "They knew we'd test positive."

My mom sighs, her lips in a tight line. My dad puts a hand on her shoulder. He looks at Jax and me. "Walk them home," he says.

We pass two people on the way. One sneers. The other takes one glance and imagines we don't exist. It takes five minutes to get to their house. On the porch, I ask if we can visit.

Ella turns stiff, but only for a second.

"Maybe," says Brooke. "I'll ask our mom. Thank you, for—"

There's a thud, like someone walking into a table, and a man in a loose tank top opens the door. His grey beard is uneven, and he smells like alcohol. He points at me with a beer bottle. "Who are you?"

"Scarlett. This is Jax."

"You bothering my kids?"

"No. We're friends."

He smirks like he doesn't believe me. "Brooke, Ella, come inside. You have chores to catch up on."

"Yes, Dad," says Brooke. The twins enter the house, and, with a swig of his beer, their dad slams the door shut in front of me. I sigh, hoping he treats his daughters with more manners than he treated me.

We walk down the porch, and I notice a mark below one of their windows. They must not have seen it yet, for they would have removed it. I clench my fists, wondering who painted the black A. Someone knows Zeniths live here.

Someone wants them gone.

...

On the way home, we pass a gated community, a Zenith-Free sign on the door. Old posters of a Knight in silver armor cover the light posts. The text underneath reads: *Zenith? Then we want you. Fight for the Orders.* A figure cloaked in black with a mask of white is spray painted on a wall. The words *Nox Aeterna* are written next to him in thick spiky text. The graffiti is of Nyx, leader of the Nephilim, the one they consider a saint, maybe even a god. The boy who painted it was captured and executed two days ago. I saw it on the news.

I stop and stare at the painting, surprised no one has removed it yet.

Jax looks at me. "I know what you're thinking," he says with a frown.

"What am I thinking?" I ask with a challenge in my voice.

"Dangerous thoughts."

"It's not dangerous to dream," I tell him.

"When those dreams involve flying with Nephilim it is."

I've never told Jax about my secret dreams to fly with the Nephilim, but he knows me too well. He always has. I scowl at him. "You don't know anything about it, Jaxton Lux."

He grins and nudges me. "You can't hide yourself from me, Scarlett Night. I see you."

I ignore him and keep walking. He just chuckles and catches up with me in long strides.

We pass the small church. The grass around it is dead. I attend, but only when it's mandatory. I respect the religion, the values, but the priest preaches more. He speaks of Fallen Angels and how they had children with man. How those children, Nephilim, are our enemy. And how if you are Zenith, then your ancestors bred with Nephilim, and your bloodline has sinned, and you are sinful, and you must repent every day of your life.

I do not believe people should be held accountable for the mistakes of others. Even if the Angels who fell were cruel and deadly, why does it make all their children so?

Every year, the priest reminds us that we used to be three estates: plebeian, patrician, and clergy. It was only plebeians, like me, who chose to mate with Angels. They created the sinful Zeniths. And now, we are four estates. It is why patricians rule, he says. Because they remained pure.

I focus back on the present as Jax and I turn the corner. A Streetbot, which looks like a large ball on wheels, hums and beeps irregularly. The robot strikes the curb over and over, stuck until its battery dies. Years ago, a maintenance crew would have fixed the issue in a few hours. Now, no one will come. I grab the Streetbot and turn it around, and it rolls down the road, on track once again.

Jax stands beside me, staring ahead. "It won't get any cleaning done. Its dusters are jammed. "

"I know. It just seemed wrong to leave it that way."

"What way?"

"Stuck in a life it wasn't meant for," I say softly.

He nods, and we watch the robot disappear into the sunset.

...

We arrive at a sprawling farmhouse with a chipped roof. Faded paint peels in the corners and the front porch creaks, but it's home, it's where I was born, and it fills me with a kind of peace.

A small tree grows in our front yard, shifting in the wind. I pat the dirt—freshly watered—and check the strength of its branches. They're strong.

My dad and I planted the tree a few months ago. He let me pick, and I picked a weeping willow. They remind me of the maidens in old tales.

It grows darker, and Jax and I walk inside. My mom and dad sit together on the couch, watching the eScreen. There is an image of a man in shackles. There is a crowd around him, throwing stones and food. They scream for blood. The man—

The eScreen turns black.

My dad holds the remote. He smiles. "How was the walk?"

"Long," I say. "What are you watching?"

"Boring grown-up stuff. You know how we are." He chuckles and stands. "Hey, how about you and I go flying?"

I know this a distraction, but it's a good one. I nod.

Jax faces my mom. "Anything I can help with?" he asks.

"There are some dishes left."

Without hesitation, he marches into the kitchen. I hear the tap water start. Jax always helps around the house, and he stays here most nights. His father doesn't seem to mind. He and Jax don't get along.

I follow my dad outside, to the small runway behind our house. He hands me a clipboard with the preflight checklist. "Want to help me out?"

I take it from him and focus on checking the engines and gas. My palm flattens against the cool steel of the plane and I close my eyes, imagining the flight, the feeling of weightlessness as the air currents propel me into the endless sky.

I work in a daze, and when I'm done, a large hand lands on my shoulder—strong, warm, comforting. I look up at my dad.

"Ready?"

I climb in next to him, my heart beating harder in my chest as my body prepares to surrender to the shift in gravity. My dad turns on the engine, and the seat rumbles beneath me. We drive down the strip.

And become airborne.

My stomach drops and my heart stammers. But as we drift higher, amongst the clouds, my breathing slows. Here, up in the sky, I am at ease.

I grin out the window and try to imagine what a blue horizon would look like. Though the sun is setting now.

There would be reds and oranges then. Not blue. It's hard to remember how things change in colors. For me it's only shifting shades of grey.

I watch our house fade into the distance. "When I grow up," I say. "I'm going to be the best pilot the world has ever seen."

My dad glances over at me, his smile briefly wilting. "You have lots of time to figure that stuff out, Star. No need to rush."

He doesn't understand, but he will someday. I know the course of my life. And nothing will change me.

...

That night, while Jax watches movies in the basement, my parents sit me down, and my mom hands me a cup of hot chocolate. It's her way of asking forgiveness for what's about to happen.

"What's wrong?" I ask.

My parents share a look and a frown.

"Nothing," my dad says. "Everything is fine. But we wanted to talk to you about your future."

I relax into the kitchen chair and smile. We've had similar talks before. They said I shouldn't go into a Teutonic Domus with my heart set on being a pilot. I said I'd consider their opinion.

They exchange that parental glance that's endearing and annoying at the same time. Their wordless communications that I envy.

My mom presses her lips together in a line. "So you want to be a pilot?"

I nod and sip the hot drink. "That's the plan."

"Star, there are requirements for getting into that program. For even getting a pilot's license. Physical requirements."

I look between them, confused. "I'm healthy. Strong. And when I'm older—"

"There's a vision test," my dad says.

My heart flutters in my chest. "I can see just fine."

"Star—"

"My vision is 20/20. Better, even."

"Star—"

"It doesn't matter that I can't see color."

My mom sighs and takes my hand. I know what she wants to say, and I don't want to hear it. She must know it, too, because she smiles. "Maybe they'll change the rules by the time you're older. But…" she raise a finger before I can interrupt, "But…you should have another plan."

I swallow the rock in my throat. I don't show emotion in my voice. "I'll consider your opinion."

They nod.

I leave my half-finished hot chocolate on the table. Then I stand and run upstairs and slam my door. I fall into my bed and weep.

...

My parents think they can control my path. They are wrong.

I grab my laptop. The airplane sticker on the cover is half torn. I tear off what remains. Then I search for the video my parents wouldn't let me see. It's not available publicly online yet, but that's not a problem. My mom got me hooked on computers as a kid. When I could barely walk, I was already learning to type. A year ago Jax declared me the world's best hacker.

I find the video and play it. A man, handcuffed, is escorted down a street by another man dressed in long robes. People gather around, gawking.

I hear someone twist the handle on my door, and I click the power button to shut down the video before they come in.

"What were you just watching?" my mom asks.

I shrug, playing it cool. "Just something I found online. It's—"

She sits down next to me on my bed. "Scarlett? Are you lying right now?"

I debate whether to keep lying, but my mom would know. She always knows. "Yes," I say, shoulders slumping.

She smiles gently. "Then let's try again. What were you just watching?"

"The news reel you wouldn't let me see. I hacked the news network."

I glance up at her to gauge her level of mad, but she's suppressing a grin. "Why?"

"Because you wouldn't let me watch it. Zeniths are being mistreated, and people need to do something. *I* need to do something."

"What do you intend to do?" she asks, still curious more than anything.

I think about it, glad I'm not in trouble—yet. "Well, I haven't settled on a plan. With some time, I could hack the Inquisition security system."

She shifts on the bed to look at me better. "If you do, they will find you."

"I could cover my tracks."

She tilts her head, a long curl coming undone from her clip and falling over her shoulder. "Some of them. But, Star, understand that other people have been at this for far longer than you. Whatever you can do right now, no matter how amazing, Inquisition security can do much better."

I fold my arms across my chest, knowing I probably look like a pouty kid but not caring. "But I have to do something."

She smiles again, her eyes crinkling. "You can keep practicing."

"Practicing doesn't change anything," I say, dropping my chin to my chest as feelings of impotence and frustration build in me.

My mom is still for a moment, her eyes distant, reflective, before she focuses on me again. "Come with me," she says. "I want to show you something." She stands and leaves the room, walking downstairs.

I hurry to follow. "What?"

"The video I didn't let you watch," she says over her shoulder.

The eScreen in our living room covers nearly the entire wall in a grey reflective material. With it we can access networks or play videos sent via satellite signal from an eGlass. My parents both own one. I have one on my Christmas list.

My mom clicks her eGlass and a video appears. A man is tied to a beam on a wooden platform surrounded by hay. People circle him, throwing food, stones, rotten vegetables, calling him names and sneering.

Another man dressed in a cloak walks forward holding a torch, speaking to the crowd, but the people are too loud to hear the Inquisitor's words.

"That man on trial was a hacker," my mom says. "He wiped multiple Inquisition bank accounts. They found him a day later."

I feel a small surge of pride for what he did. "He must have really messed them up."

My mom sits on the couch, and I join her as she asks, "Do you think those accounts mattered?"

"I imagine they would. Money's important, right? But..." I think about it more and realize..."The Inquisition isn't hurting for money, are they? They can always get more."

My mom nods.

"Well," I say, "at least he showed people they could fight back."

"Did he?" my mom asks. "Or did he simply become another example of the Inquisition's power?"

I look back up at the video just as the Inquisitor sets the torch to the haystack. As the hacker begins to burn, his cries mixing with the cheers of the crowd, my mom shuts off the video and sets the display to a serene mountain scene.

She turns to me and reaches for my hand, squeezing. "My Star, one day, when you're older, you'll make a difference. A *real* difference. But you need to be ready. Hone your skills. And..." she ruffles my hair, "try to avoid stupid mistakes." She stands and walks toward the kitchen, and I slump in the couch, depressed.

All of my practicing was for nothing. I don't want to end up like that guy in the video. "I guess I'll stop hacking then," I announce to the world in all my despondent pre-teen angst.

My mom turns back, a mischievous grin forming on her face. "I didn't say to stop," she says, winking. "I just said to be careful."

ABOUT THE AUTHORS

Karpov Kinrade is the pen name for the husband and wife writing duo of USA TODAY bestselling, award-winning authors Lux Kinrade and Dmytry Karpov.

Together, they write fantasy and science fiction.

Look for more from Karpov Kinrade in *Vampire Girl*, *The Nightfall Chronicles*, *The Forbidden Trilogy* and *The Shattered Islands*.

They live with three little girls who think they're ninja princesses with super powers and who are also showing a propensity for telling tall tales and using the written word to weave stories of wonder and magic.

Find them at www.KarpovKinrade.com

On Twitter @KarpovKinrade

On Facebook /KarpovKinrade

And subscribe to their newsletter for special deals and up-to-date notice of new launches. www.ReadKK.com.

~~~~~

If you enjoyed this book, consider supporting the author by leaving a review wherever you purchased this book. Thank you.

Made in the USA
Lexington, KY
27 October 2017